THE PATIENT HUSBAND

The Viscount Astor prided himself on his under-standing of his young wife. After all, Arabella was innocent and country-bred. It would take time to teach her the ways of the world.

Therefore he was not annoyed when Arabella became upset on learning that he was keeping a mistress. Instead he quietly and clearly explained the differences between *that* kind of love and the duties of the marriage bed.

How could so level-headed a girl deny his logic? How could so obedient a wife defy his authority?

How could she, indeed . . . ?

MARY BALOGH, who won *The Romantic Times* Award for Best New Regency Writer in 1985, has since become one of the genre's most popular and best-selling authors. She also won the Walden Books Award for Best-selling Short Historical in 1986, for *The First Snowdrop*.

The Obedient Bride

Mary Balogh

A SIGNET BOOK

SIGNET
Published by the Penguin Group
Penguin Books USA Inc., 375 Hudson Street,
New York, New York 10014, U.S.A.
Penguin Books Ltd, 27 Wrights Lane,
London W8 5TZ, England
Penguin Books Australia Ltd, Ringwood,
Victoria, Australia
Penguin Books Canada Ltd, 10 Alcorn Avenue,
Toronto, Ontario, Canada M4V 3B2
Penguin Books (N.Z.) Ltd, 182–190 Wairau Road,
Auckland 10, New Zealand

Penguin Books Ltd, Registered Offices:
Harmondsworth, Middlesex, England

First published by Signet, an imprint of Dutton Signet,
a division of Penguin Books USA Inc.

First Printing, May, 1989
11 10 9 8 7 6 5 4 3

 REGISTERED TRADEMARK—MARCA REGISTRADA

Printed in the United States of America

1

VISCOUNT Astor yawned widely enough to hear his jaws crack and lifted one booted leg to join the other on the plush velvet upholstery of the carriage seat opposite him. He wriggled his shoulders against the cushions at his back in a futile attempt to ease aching muscles and find a comfortable position. It really was almost pointless, he reflected, spending a king's ransom on a handsome, luxuriously padded, and well-sprung traveling carriage when the only place on which to demonstrate its superiority was English roads. Under such conditions springs were about as much use as wings would be.

He was regretting for perhaps the dozenth time in the past three days his decision to travel in the coach with his valet and his baggage instead of bringing his curricle. At least with the curricle he would have had fresh air and the mental and physical activity of propelling himself along the road. Perhaps too he would be capable of seeing and avoiding more potholes than his coachman seemed able to do.

But then, he thought, yawning hugely again and crossing his boots at the ankles, he could not have foreseen that the late-February weather would be quite so gloriously springlike. The sun was shining down from a flawless sky; the trees were beginning to bud; he could glimpse snowdrops and primroses in the hedgerows; and he could imagine the freshness of the air and the singing of the birds, though the dust of the road and the noise of the horses and carriage wheels blotted them from his senses.

Oh, for the chance to ride astride a horse or to be seated in his curricle, ribbons in hand! The sight of his valet's head flopping from side to side on his chest and

the faint whistling sound of his snoring were beginning
to grate on Lord Astor's nerves. He had tried clearing
his throat loudly a few minutes before, but that had succeeded only in causing Henry to jump, rumble in his
throat, smack his lips, and resume the head lolling and
the gentle snoring.

Lord Astor examined his Hessian boots glumly,
twisting his feet from side to side in order to do so.
There should be some consolation in the fact that he
would be reaching his destination within the next couple
of hours. But under the circumstances, he thought that,
given the choice, he might prefer two more days on the
road, even if they were to involve two more nights at unspeakable inns like the one of the night before.

Four females. He was to face four female strangers.
And they were strangers even though they were
connected by some distant relationship. Only that fact
accounted for his present newly acquired title and
wealth. He was the closest male relative of the lately
deceased Viscount Astor. It was rather a shame, the new
Astor thought uncharitably, that he was not also the
only relative of the dead viscount. The man was sur-
vived by a wife and three daughters. And he was on his
way to pay his respects to them and to view his new
home and estate.

It was a deuced embarrassment, actually. He had
known he was the heir, of course. How could he not,
when he had lived a life of relative poverty, especially in
the six years since he had come down from university
and settled to an expensive life in London? But he had
never been in communication with his cousin—a term
he used for want of a better one. The connection was
actually quite distant. His father had quarreled with the
late viscount about fifteen years before and had never
seen him after. And he himself had had no occasion to
renew the acquaintance after the death of his father
almost four years before.

So he found himself in this predicament, Lord Astor
thought, putting his feet back on the floor of the

carriage and looking impatiently through the window for he knew not what sign of nearness to his destination. He was on his way to visit four females whose home was now his, whose whole security had been cut from under their feet by the untimely demise of his predecessor. The solicitor who had brought him the news of his good fortune had told him that the late viscount had made no provision whatsoever for the future of his family, an almost unbelievable oversight in view of the fact that its members were entirely female.

And what had he done: the new Viscount Astor, basking in the glory of his new importance, bursting with euphoric feelings of goodwill to the world? He had offered to marry one of the daughters, that was what he had done. Sight unseen! He had learned that their ages were twenty, eighteen, and fifteen. And that was all he had learned. He did not know their names, their dispositions, their appearances. He had not even specified which one he wished to be his bride. He had left that decision to their mother.

He was on his way, then, mainly to meet his future bride. And his offer for her had been quite formally and officially made. He could not back out now even if he found all three girls to be as ugly and uncouth as his nightmares were beginning to depict them.

It had been a rash offer. It was true that his acquisition of the title had made him feel the necessity of also acquiring some respectability. What was more respectable than the presence of a wife in one's home and perhaps a child or two in one's nursery? And really he was not too fussy about what female would be found to fit the role. He spent little enough of his time at home. A wife would not upset his habits to any great degree. Provided she was a lady of the proper breeding and provided she conducted herself with the proper decorum, she would suit his purposes admirably.

But even though he felt he would be relatively easy to please, it had perhaps been rash of him to offer for any one of three females he had never seen and about whom he had not even heard any report. He could become the laughingstock if the sister selected were unusually ugly or if her manners were noticeably awkward or worse.

Lord Astor shrugged and cleared his throat loudly once more. The whistling of Henry's snores had progressed from gentle to piercing and were setting his lordship's fingers to clenching and unclenching. There was really no point now in teasing his mind with all the horrors his rash offer might have in store for him. There was nothing whatsoever he could do about the matter. Except perhaps to leave his bride in her childhood home with her mother and sisters when he returned to London for the Season.

He would have to wait and see what she was like. It might be amusing to introduce her to society if she were at least passable. And it might be personally gratifying to have a female constantly on hand for his own pleasure. Not that he would expect much of a country-bred wench, of course. His tastes ran far more to mature and experienced courtesans. Like Ginny, for example—who liked to be called Virginia and who became furious enough to throw things when he laughed at her preference and pointed out all the inappropriateness of the name. Ginny was his resident mistress and had made something of an art of her trade.

No, really, he must not expect too much in the way of sexual satisfaction from his new wife, even if she turned out to be pretty. It would be unfair to do so. And as for companionship—Lord Astor shrugged again—he had never looked to any female for that. He had friends enough in his various clubs, and activities enough to make of his home little more than a place in which to sleep at night—or for what remained of the nights after he had left Ginny or a late card game or drinking session.

He must not allow himself to become too apprehensive of the ordeal that faced him within the next few hours. A wife was really going to be a fairly unimportant adjunct to his life.

Lord Astor yawned once more, glared balefully at the unconscious figure of his snoring valet, wriggled downward in his seat, and allowed his eyelids to droop and his thoughts to slide into oblivion.

The Honorable Miss Frances Wilson was in tears. Again, her sister Arabella thought, watching from her place in the window seat and marveling as she always did that Frances succeeded only in looking more beautiful when she cried. Perhaps that was why she did not make more of an effort to overcome her sensibilities. Now, when Arabella cried, which was a rare-enough occurrence, her tears left a red and swollen face in their wake. And her younger sister Jemima was no better. She always wailed loudly when she wept, so that an unsympathetic Papa had once told her that she sounded like a cow in pain.

But Frances, the oldest sister, the beauty of the family, could weep and be beautiful. Not that she needed to weep in order to accomplish that result, of course. She was slim and shapely, with big expressive blue eyes, a creamy complexion, and masses of silky blond hair. And dark eyelashes that could fan her cheeks when they were lowered, as they frequently were when some gentleman was by.

Frances. The beauty. Her parents' favorite. And her sisters' favorite too. One could not *not* love Frances. She was all gentle and weeping sensibility. She was not even weeping for herself at the moment. She was crying for Arabella. And not for the first time. Surely every day for the past two weeks she had wept for the great sacrifice, as Arabella's decision had come to be known.

Arabella was touched to be so appreciated, and perhaps a little proud of herself too. But in all honesty she could not see herself as a great heroine. She had no particular objection to marrying Lord Astor—strange to think of another man than Papa with that title. It was true that the new viscount must be close to Papa in age, as far as Mama could remember from her last encounter with him many years before. But that did not matter. Arabella had always been fond of Papa. And she had never been fond of any of the horrid boys who had pulled her braids as a girl and refused to let her climb trees with them and who now expected her to dance with them at assemblies and simper at their awkward compliments. If she must marry, she would as soon marry an older man.

"Frances, my love, do not take on so," Lady Astor said, hovering at the shoulder of her eldest daughter, vinaigrette in hand. "Remember that there are compensations for Bella's sacrifice. Lord Astor—oh, your poor dear papa, my love—may be an older man, but he will be steady, you may depend upon it. And Bella will be the new Lady Astor and mistress of Parkland. She will be set for life. And a viscountess at eighteen, my love." The mother had turned her attention to Arabella. "Really, there is scarce any sacrifice at all."

Arabella drew breath to agree quite sensibly with her mother. But Frances sobbed so affectingly that she closed her mouth again.

"But to be married to an old man when she has seen nothing whatsoever of life. To sacrifice her youth and all her hopes for our sake, Mama. Dear, dear Bella! How very much I love you. And how guilty you make me feel that you have taken off my shoulders the burden of making the sacrifice myself."

"It really would have been foolish for you to do so, Frances," Arabella said, swinging her legs against the wall behind them, as her feet did not quite reach the floor. "You have other prospects. And Theodore would be brokenhearted if you were borne away by our cousin. And besides, as I have told you and Mama a thousand times, I really do not mind. His lordship must be a reasonably kind man, for he has offered for one of us when he has not even met us, just so that we will not be destitute."

"He will surely allow us to continue living here after you are married, Bella," her mother said. "And you shall persuade him, my love, to take Frances with you to London so that she may be presented to society. It is only right for one of such rare beauty to be seen in the capital.''

Truth to tell, this often-mentioned idea was the one part of the plan that Arabella disapproved of. She had released Frances from the necessity of marrying the viscount mainly so that her sister could marry Theodore. Sir Theodore Perrot, she had to accustom herself to calling him now. They had called him Theodore—sometimes even Theo—all their lives, but it seemed that there was proprieties to be observed now that they were all grown up.

Frances and Theodore—Sir Theodore—had always planned to marry, and Arabella was only too glad to make it possible for them to do so. Theodore, stocky, blond, and ruddy-cheeked, was so thoroughly solid and dependable that Frances would be safe with him. And she would need keeping safe. Frances would never cope with life if she did not have someone to carry her through it. Arabella did not like the thought of Frances being borne off to London with her and the viscount in order to be viewed by other, less-steady gentlemen. One of them might just run off with her, and then where would her poor sister be for the rest of her life?

Arabella was wearing her best day dress. She looked down at the light sprigged muslin with its wide blue sash and thought again that it was quite inappropriate for February. It might be springlike outside, but it was hardly the time of year for muslin. She was thankful that the sun shone so strongly through the window that she felt almost too hot despite the thinness of the fabric. At least it was pleasant not to be wearing black. Mama had announced that they would leave off their mourning for the new Lord Astor even though poor Papa had been gone for only eight months.

Arabella wished as she had for the past two years that she had not stopped growing when she was still such an unimpressive height. She was perhaps a little too plump

too, though she supposed it was rather unfair to herself
to make comparisons between her own shape and
Frances'. Mama was always careful to assure her that
she was not plump, but merely well-rounded and short
of stature. And she could not yet compare herself to
Jemima, who was still as thin and shapeless as a rake
and who frequently and loudly bewailed the fact that
she would never be any different. But Jemima was already taller than she. And her hair was too thick,
Arabella thought. It was quite a becoming shade of dark
brown, as Mama kept pointing out soothingly, but it
was very difficult to make it hold any style.

Arabella had no great craving to be a beauty. One in a
family was blessing enough, she had concluded with
great good sense more than a year before. And since she
had not started to consider suitors and marriage until
the viscount's startling letter had arrived more than two
weeks before, she had had no particular desire to be
attractive to gentlemen. She had no great wish to be so
even now. After all, the viscount was an older man who
would not care for such things as a girl's looks. He was
marrying her out of kindness only. And she had no
desire to attract his admiration. She would marry him
because it was necessary to do so and because she would
thereby be released from the nasty chore of finding herself a husband within the next few years.

But she did wish that she looked less childish. She was
eighteen years old, fully a woman. And yet she looked
like a child, younger even than Jemima, she sometimes
thought in despair. She was small and plump—her
mother's protestations to the contrary never convinced
her—and her round face accentuated by her thick hair
did nothing to reveal to a stranger that she was a woman
of mature years already. To a man of close to Papa's
age she was going to look like a veritable babe.

Arabella sighed. Perhaps she should have been more
insistent when Mama had recommended the blue sash
that she not wear it. It really did make her look as if she
had just stepped out of the nursery.

"There, my love," Lady Astor was saying to Frances, patting her shoulder, "you are showing great fortitude, as I knew you would. Put your handkerchief away; your eyes are quite dry again. His lordship will be here at any moment, and it would not do at all for him to see you cry, even though it is Bella he is to marry. He will think that you and Bella have quarreled over him, and that would not give him a favorable impression of our family."

"Dear Bella," Frances said, her voice quavering and her eyes looking suspiciously bright again. "His lordship will see immediately how dearly we all love you. He must see that we have not sacrificed you but that you have sacrificed yourself entirely of your own free will. Oh, I do hope he is not quite bald or white-haired or toothless."

"Gracious, my love!" her mother exclaimed. "Papa was none of those things. Papa was quite a handsome figure of a man to his dying day." She removed her own handkerchief from her pocket and dabbed at her eyes. "Bella, my love, I think it would be as well to remember not to swing your legs like that when his lordship arrives. It does not look quite ladylike."

"Yes, Mama," Arabella said, holding her legs still immediately. "Perhaps I should carry the stool over here to rest my feet on. Else I shall surely forget."

The door to the sitting room opened with a sudden crash and a tall, thin young girl in muslin and wide pink sash remarkably like Arabella's rushed into the room, auburn ringlets bouncing against the sides of her head. "Mama, he is come," she said. "In a strange carriage. Two men. I think one is a servant. They are in the hallway even now. I came down from the schoolroom as you said I might even though Miss Roberts said I should wait until I was summoned. But if I had done that, Mama, you might have forgotten and I would not have seen his lordship meet Bella. He did not look a very old man from upstairs. He does not stoop."

"Gracious, child!" her mother said. "The man is not

old. Merely Papa's age or close to it. Straighten your sash and sit down quietly. Quietly, mind! Young ladies still in the schoolroom are to be seen and not heard, remember. And don't forget your curtsy in your eagerness to stare when his lordship is announced. Frances, my love, you are not about to cry again, are you? And, Bella, dear, don't swing your legs. Jemima, before you sit down, carry the stool across to Bella, if you please."

Viscount Astor felt almost instant relief after he had been announced and had made his entry into the drawing room of Parkland Manor. For one thing, Lady Astor displayed perfectly civilized manners as she crossed the room to greet him, hand extended, and curtsied as she welcomed him to his new home. And the three younger females behind her appeared suitably well-bred. Each had risen to her feet and was curtsying low to him.

His relief was mainly attributable, though, to the fact that he had seen his future bride during one sweeping glance around the room before focusing his attention on his hostess. And to say that he was relieved was perhaps an understatement. She was a beauty of the first order, with exquisite features and delicate blond coloring and a figure to satisfy even the most exacting male's dreams.

Her two sisters were much younger and quite unremarkable. The report he had had of their ages must have erred.

"But there must be some mistake, my lord," Lady Astor was saying. She was looking somewhat bewildered. "You cannot possibly be my late husband's cousin whom I met many years ago. Why, you must have been in leading strings at the time."

He bowed. "You must be referring to my father, ma'am," he said. "It is sometimes confusing to share the same name as one's father. My mother insisted on naming me Geoffrey after him. You were not informed, it seems, of the fact that my father passed away four years ago."

"How distressing your loss must have been for you," she said, clasping her hands against her bosom. "But of course I remember that your poor dear papa had a son. And you are now Lord Astor, sir. I am delighted to make your acquaintance and only sorry for the ancient quarrel that has kept our families apart for so many years. My girls are as eager as I to renew the family acquaintance. May I present my daughters to you, my lord?"

Lord Astor assured her that he would be honored. He bowed in turn to Miss Frances Wilson, Miss Arabella, and Miss Jemima. And finally he took a seat close to the beauty of the family. He was not disappointed at his closer scrutiny of her face and figure. She had beautiful, trusting blue eyes—when he glimpsed them. Most of the time she kept them modestly lowered. But even so there was a great deal to admire. Her dark eyelashes were thick and long and fanned her blushing cheeks most becomingly.

She did not speak a great deal. But who would demand conversation from a female who had so much to offer the eye instead? As he sipped his tea, Lord Astor could picture to himself already the sensation she would create when he presented her to society as his wife. He could imagine the pleasure he would derive from taking her to a fashionable modiste and decking her out in the latest styles and fabrics.

Lord Astor conversed almost exclusively with his hostess. She tried to include one of the younger girls in the conversation—the tiny one with the masses of dark hair who sat on the window seat swinging her legs whenever she spoke—but the viscount did not give the girl a great deal of his attention. Or the other one, in fact—the thin auburn-haired one who stared mutely at him throughout tea. He did wonder briefly, as he had several times during the past few weeks, whether he would be expected to take his wife's mother and sisters back to London with him. But he suspected now that it would be unnecessary to do so. The two younger girls must be too young to make their come-outs yet.

He found, though, as he continued the conversation with Lady Astor, that he no longer cared greatly what good manners would compel him to do on the matter. So vast was his relief to find that after all he was to have a lovely and refined bride that he would have been prepared to drag along to London a dozen sisters if it had been necessary.

Lady Astor rose to her feet eventually and offered to escort him to his room—the master bedchamber, she was hasty to assure him—where he might wish to change from his traveling clothes before dinner.

He bowed to the beauty and her sisters and followed his hostess from the room, well-satisfied with his first hour at Parkland Manor. For the remainder of the day, he decided, he would confine his conversation to polite topics. Time enough tomorrow to have private talk with Lady Astor concerning his coming nuptials and the future of herself and her two remaining daughters.

2

ARABELLA was sitting on the lawn north of the stables, playing with George, her collie. He was not allowed in the house because he gave Frances the sneezes. But he certainly did not suffer from lack of human love. Arabella spent every spare moment out-of-doors, and George could usually be seen loping along in her wake or dashing on ahead of her. Today, though, she was sitting, scratching his ears, ignoring his frequent invitations to get up and romp. She did not want to be seen from the house.

She had left Frances crying in her mother's sitting room. Her sister had been unwilling or unable to say a word but had merely wilted gracefully onto a sofa and buried her face in her lace handkerchief. Mama, who had summoned Arabella to inform her that Lord Astor had requested a private audience later in the morning, suggested that perhaps Arabella should leave again. Perhaps Frances would speak to her mama alone.

But Arabella knew what had upset Frances. She was weeping even more bitterly than she had during the previous two weeks, knowing that the sacrifice Arabella had so cheerfully agreed to make had now turned into a bitter sacrifice indeed. Frances had guessed that the prospect of wedding the viscount was far more daunting to her sister now than it had been before, and her tender heart had set her to crying again.

Arabella had felt almost like crying herself since the afternoon before, except that she would not really know how to go about deriving any comfort from sobs and tears. From her limited experience with both, she would only make herself feel worse. Sobs caused a sore chest, tears a blocked nose. And both, of course, caused shiny red blotches on face and neck. No, she would not cry. And she would not complain or otherwise show her mother and sisters how insupportable her fate had now become. She could not burden them further with the knowledge that she now wished it were Frances who had been chosen as Viscount Astor's bride.

How could she possibly marry Lord Astor? He was not at all the comfortable older man of her expectations. He was young—surely no more than ten years her senior at the most. And—worse—he was a handsome man. He was not tall, not very much above average height, in fact. But he was slim and graceful and had a manly, good-looking face and shining dark hair. Quite the sort of man who would turn female heads even in a large assembly of gentlemen.

And worst of all—oh, far worse than his youth or his good looks—he was a confident, experienced man of the world. At least, he had given every indication of being both during the afternoon and evening of the day before. He had conversed with Mama on a wide variety of topics and had told them a good deal about London and the Continent. And there was an air about him—Arabella could not put it into words exactly. There was something about him that suggested knowledge of the world and experience with its workings.

There was that way he had of looking at Frances, for example, as if he knew and appreciated her even from so slight an acquaintance and was confident that she must return his regard. And there was the way he had of not looking at herself. She did not even exist for him. She had very clearly been dismissed as an uninteresting child of no account. Although she had spoken ten times as much as Frances the day before, she would swear that he had not taken note of a word she had said or afforded her more than an occasional glance.

She was finding it very difficult to support the prospect of marrying Lord Astor. She would never be able to lose her awareness of her own dreadful shortcomings with him. She would always be uncomfortably aware of how young she looked, how small and plump, how round and childish of face. She would always be aware of the dullness of her conversation and the narrowness of her experience with life.

Oh, dear, Arabella thought, rubbing George's stomach with such energy that he waved his paws in the air in perfect ecstasy, she could never be comfortable with Lord Astor! And all she had ever asked of this marriage was that she feel at ease and that she be able to make her husband comfortable. Everything would have been all right with an older man. She need not have been conscious of herself with an older man.

But with this viscount! She would forever feel inferior. And she would forever feel uncomfortable in the knowledge that he must constantly look at her with distaste at worst, indifference at best. She would want to impress this man, and in her wildest dreams Arabella knew that there was nothing on this earth she could possibly do to draw his admiration.

Oh, how she wished that it were Frances who was to marry him. Frances was at least as beautiful as he was handsome. It was true that she had no more experience with life than Arabella, but with Frances that did not matter. Indeed, her very innocence gave her charm. A marriage between Lord Astor and Frances would be such an equal match. They would suit. They would be happy. He would be proud of Frances. Arabella had seen the day before that he already admired her sister.

And Arabella had a dreadful suspicion that Lord Astor had thought that Frances was his chosen bride. She had assumed that Mama had communicated her choice to him, but perhaps she had not. Perhaps the viscount had come to Parkland not knowing which sister was to be his bride. And if that were so, it was the most natural thing in the world that he would have thought Frances was the one. How dreadfully disappointed he would be when he discovered the truth this morning. In fact, perhaps he would renege on his promise and leave alone for London immediately.

What a dreadful humiliation that would be! Worse
even than having to marry the man.

Arabella became suddenly and paralyzingly aware
that the viscount, clad with suffocating handsomeness
in green superfine coat, buff pantaloons, and white-
topped Hessians, was striding toward the stables from
the direction of the house. Perhaps he was leaving already. Or perhaps he had come in search of her, having
learned the dreadful truth.

She ducked down, trying to make herself invisible
even as George scrambled to his feet, barking furiously,
and rushed toward the stranger. She might as well have
waved a large red flag above her head, Arabella thought
ruefully as she got to her feet with as much nonchalance
as a wildly beating heart would allow, brushed at her
skirt, and walked toward him, a smile of welcome on
her face.

Her second guess had been the correct one, she
thought with a sinking heart; he was on his way to talk
to her. He turned immediately in her direction, and
without any hesitation. Arabella stood still and waited.
And smiled.

Lady Astor had been successful in persuading her
eldest daughter to express her grief in words. It was not
quite as Arabella thought, though.

"Mama, oh, Mama," Frances said, sniffing against
her handkerchief and dabbing at her eyes with it, "why
did no one think to inform us of the demise of his lordship? No, he was not his lordship, was he? Papa was
still alive when he died. He was Papa's heir, yet no one
told us of his death."

"It was on account of that quarrel, doubtless," her
mother said. "So foolish it all was, to be sure. I cannot
even rightly recall what it was all about, though I do
remember that Papa was entirely in the right of it. But it
was remiss and indeed spiteful of the family not to
inform us of the passing of Papa's heir. I do not wonder

that the news coming suddenly as it did has shocked your sensibilities, my love.''

"Oh, Mama, if I had only known!" Frances wailed, wringing her hands affectingly. "He is so young and handsome and fashionable. And amiable.''

"Indeed, his lordship is a pleasant surprise," Lady Astor said. "A very agreeable young man indeed. He has not once made me feel that I am merely a guest in his home.''

"Don't you see, Mama?" Frances' voice had become tragic. "There would have been no need for Bella's sacrifice if I had just known. I might have taken the burden upon myself.''

"Indeed, my love," her mother said with a sigh, "you would make a far lovelier viscountess than Bella. And I am sure his lordship would prefer to have you. He has had eyes for no one but you since his arrival yesterday afternoon.''

Frances pressed her handkerchief to her eyes again.

"Of course," her mother said, brightening, "I have not spoken to his lordship yet. He does not know which of you is to honor him with her hand. I am sure that Bella would have no objection to a change in plan. Shall I talk to her, my love, and suggest that you marry Lord Astor after all?''

Frances looked up, tears sparkling on her lashes, her eyes a deeper blue than usual. "Oh, Mama," she said, "that you should be the one so to tempt me. No, I could not do it. Dear Bella has made the sacrifice so cheerfully for all our sakes, and I was only too ready to allow her to do so when I imagined that his lordship was an old man. Now she is being rewarded for her selflessness. She is to have a young and handsome husband. She deserves her good fortune, Mama, for she is an angel. I am happy for her. I truly am.''

She proceeded to prove her point by dissolving into tears yet again.

Lady Astor rose to her feet and patted her daughter reassuringly on the shoulder. "I think I have two angels for daughters," she said. "You have a generous heart, my love. Many is the sister who would be jealous of Bella under the circumstances. But you are right. She deserves this reward. His lordship will be fortunate indeed to acquire such a sweet bride."

She patted Frances on the shoulder again and announced that it was time to join his lordship in the morning room to make the nuptial arrangements.

Lord Astor did not want to be on his way to find Miss Arabella Wilson. Not by any means—she was the small dark-haired one, he gathered. But he supposed there was no point at all in delaying the moment. Sooner or later he must go through the formality of making the girl an offer. It might as well be sooner, since there was no earthly way he could get himself out of the predicament.

Just the day before, he had been prepared for disaster. He had talked himself into expecting that his bride might be ugly or awkward or vulgar. He had even persuaded himself of the possibility that she might be all three. It was cruel of fate to have buoyed up his spirits as it had done from the moment of his arrival until just half an hour before.

It had not even entered his head since the previous afternoon that perhaps his chosen bride was not the beautiful Frances. Indeed, he had not dreamed that either of the other two girls was old enough to be considered. He had not taken a good look at either, but his distinct impression had been that both were mere children. Yet it seemed that the solicitor had not erred in the one detail he had given about the three daughters of his predecessor. Miss Arabella Wilson was eighteen years old.

Old enough to be his bride.

It had been a cruel blow, when he had renewed his offer to Lady Astor a little earlier, to be told that, yes, she was sensible of the great honor he was doing her family and that her second daughter would be happy to receive his addresses. He feared that his jaw might have dropped at first, so unexpected had her words been. Her second daughter? He could not even recall at that precise moment exactly which of the two sisters that was not Frances was the elder.

But what could he do or say? He had bowed and said all that was appropriate to the occasion. And Lady Astor had released him, assuring him that she understood that he would wish to acquaint himself better with Arabella and settle the matter with her before discussing details of the nuptials.

He had bowed and asked where he might find Miss Arabella.

She had told him that the girl was probably outside where she usually was. She was possibly with her dog in the vicinity of the stables.

And so she was, Lord Astor found with some relief. He might have lost his nerve entirely if he had had to hunt for her. He saw her as soon as he turned his head in the direction of the black-and-white collie that was bounding toward him, barking enthusiastically. She was sitting on the grass, but she rose hastily to her feet and began to walk toward him. Clearly she was expecting him.

Lord Astor changed direction and smiled as he approached her.

"Good morning, Miss Arabella," he said, bowing and coming to stand a few feet in front of her. "That is a fine dog. He is yours?"

"Yes, my lord," she said, turning to pat the dog on the neck as it put its paws on her waist and panted upward into her face. "No, George, we may not go walking now. You will just have to wait. And do get down. I am not at all sure that your paws are clean."

She was indeed tiny. She must reach scarcely to his shoulder, even though he was not himself a tall man. It must have been her height that had misled him into thinking her a child. She had the shape of a woman. On the other hand, she had the eager and flushed face of a child.

"Perhaps you would care to stroll with me," he said with a bow, "and thereby give, ah, George his exercise. Is he meant to bear any resemblance to any royal gentleman, by the way?"

She laughed. "It is just that Papa had all the other dogs named King and Rex and Prince and Duke and such," she said. "There did not seem to be anything very regal left by the time poor George came along."

"Shall we?" he said, indicating the lawn to the west, which appeared to lead down to a pasture.

She fell into step beside him. Her plain blue woolen dress and shawl made her look somewhat older than whatever it was she had worn the day before. Her hair was dressed in a plain chignon, but one heavy lock had come loose and hung down her back. It was a quite unbecoming style anyway, Lord Astor thought, making a mental comparison between it and Ginny's riotous curls.

And Miss Arabella Wilson was not pretty.

"I have had the honor of talking with your mother this morning," he said, clasping his hands behind his back. "She has given me her permission to pay my addresses to you."

"Oh," she said, and blushed. She looked up into his eyes for a brief moment. "I am most dreadfully sorry. I mean, I am sure that you offered so that we would not be destitute and so that we would not feel ourselves beholden to you for charity. And I am sure that you would vastly prefer it to be Frances, for she is the acknowledged beauty of the family. And I am not beautiful at all. But Frances is to marry Theodore, you see—Sir Theodore Perrot, that is—and so it was decided that I should be the one to accept your so generous offer."

Lord Astor was lost for words. The girl prattled like a

twelve-year-old. And did she not know that there were pretenses to be upheld? One did not openly admit that one was making a marriage of pure convenience.

"I offered because the daughters of the former viscount seemed eminently eligible," he said carefully. "And indeed, I would consider it a deep honor if you will accept me. I did not specify, you know, which of you I would offer for, for I had not met any of you until yesterday and I thought your mother would be able to make the most sensible choice. I am quite satisfied with the decision she has made. I will be happy if you will accept me, Miss Arabella."

"Oh, I will accept you, of course," she said. "No, George, I will not throw sticks for you today. Run along, and pray do not be trying to trip me with every step I take. I am sure Mama assured you of that, my lord. And it really is most civil of you to say that I am to your liking when I am sure you cannot be vastly pleased. I shall try to make you comfortable, my lord."

"I am quite certain you will succeed," he said. "And I shall try to make sure that you do not regret your choice, ma'am. I shall suggest to your mother that we be wed here as soon as the banns can be read. Will that suit you?"

"Oh, so soon?" she asked, looking up at him with a blush.

They had reached a stile leading into the pasture. Lord Astor had intended to turn back or to lean on the fence for a few minutes. But Arabella climbed over the stile without hesitation and without giving him a chance to assist her. And she showed a quite indecorous expanse of ankle and petticoat in the process. The viscount hid a smile and climbed over after her.

"Is it too soon?" he asked, hope grabbing at him for a brief moment. "Would you like some time to accustom yourself to our betrothal, perhaps?"

"Oh, no," she said, smiling briefly in his direction. "I suppose we might as well get this over with. Mama will be pleased that you wish the wedding to be here. She was afraid that you would wish it to take place in London.''

''Do you have a dread of London?'' he asked. ''Would you prefer to live here after our marriage? You are very young to be taken from your mother and all that is familiar to you.''

''That is for you to decide, my lord,'' she said. ''If you say that we are to live here, then of course I shall not complain. But if you wish to return to London, I shall not try to dissuade you. I shall go wherever you wish. I shall know my duty, as you will see.''

''Then London it will be,'' he said with a smile. ''You will have a chance to be a part of the Season. You will enjoy it, I believe. Your dog should be taught some manners, ma'am. I marvel he does not bowl you right off your feet when he jumps up at you like that.''

She looked up at him with a smile. ''Oh, but he does sometimes when he takes me by surprise,'' she said. ''I do not mind. I love him, you see.''

She stooped down so that the dog's paws rested on her shoulders, and wrapped her arms around him. He licked at her face until she laughed and pushed his head away.

Her upper lip curved upward slightly, away from her teeth and her lower lip. He did not know what caused it to do so, as her upper teeth did not noticeably protrude. But it was a somewhat attractive feature.

It was still hard to believe that she was eighteen years old, he thought, standing silently as she hugged her dog and resisted its desire to pant into her face. She was far more like a small and unruly and slightly disheveled child. And she had a childishly candid tongue.

She was to be his wife, his life's companion. His bed-fellow. He again made the swift mental comparison with Ginny and the other females who frequented his bed. It was quite ludicrous—almost embarrassing, in fact—to contemplate doing any of the things with this child that he was in the habit of doing with his nighttime companions. But then, he supposed that the whole point of keeping a mistress when one had a wife was that one's senses might be satisfied. He could not honestly imagine any of the married gentlemen of his acquaintance enjoying their wives as they did their mistresses.

Miss Arabella Wilson was not ugly. She was not uncouth, though her manners were not quite what one would expect of a young lady of the *ton*. He could have done a great deal worse. If he blanked from his mind the image of the lovely Miss Frances Wilson as she had appeared the day before, he could still feel relieved that his bride was not a great deal more of an antidote than she was. He could contemplate the thought of marriage with her without any real cringing or repugnance.

She would try to make him comfortable, she had said a few minutes before. Well, and perhaps she would succeed, too. There would be some satisfaction, while he continued his life where he had left it off a few days before, in knowing that a wife who knew her duty and who wished to make him comfortable was ensuring the respectability of his name and his home.

Lord Astor was not entirely displeased with his morning's work.

Arabella was not feeling nearly so complacent. She buried her face against George's neck, talked to him, and played with him in order to hide her dreadful discomfort.

There she was, in the middle of the pasture at Parkland, in company with a very handsome young gentleman who looked for all the world as if he must have stepped off a street in London. And she had just accepted his marriage proposal. She had had no idea how to go about doing so, and no idea how to proceed with the conversation now that it was all settled.

It was only now perhaps that she realized fully how very secluded a life they had all led during her youth. They had never been anywhere farther than five miles from home or met anyone except the inhabitants of that area and the occasional visitor. She really had no idea how to converse with as grand a gentleman as Lord Astor, or what to converse about. And she had no idea how she would go on when they went to London. What would she do there, and how should she behave? The prospect was suddenly quite terrifying.

She had assured Lord Astor that she would know her duty. Would she? Beyond obeying him, what would her duty be? And she had told him that she would try to make him comfortable. How did one go about making such a grand gentleman comfortable?

If only he were at least fifty years old and white-haired or bald!

If only he were not quite so handsome.

And if only he did not stand there in the pasture so poised and elegant and so disapproving of poor George's affectionate nature.

Oh, she should not have made the sacrifice, Arabella thought, stooping finally and picking up a stick for George to run and fetch. She was being punished for the sin of pride. For she had felt proud of the fact that she was willing to sacrifice her own future for Frances' sake. One should be thoroughly humble and selfless when making a sacrifice, else it was none. She was being punished, all right.

"Shall we return to the house for luncheon, my lord?" she asked abruptly, thankful for her conversational inspiration.

He bowed and offered her his arm. Arabella stared at it, blushed, linked her own through it, and blushed even more deeply.

Oh, dear God, she wished he were not so handsome!

3

LORD Astor made arrangements for the banns to be read at the village church the next Sunday and the two following weeks. The wedding was set for one month from his arrival at Parkland Manor. Country living had never been greatly to his liking, but he succeeded in keeping himself quite well-occupied in the interim. He spent time with his bailiff both in his office and out on the estate. He had no intention of living at Parkland a great deal and no intention of displacing his future mother-in-law and her daughters from their home. But it was as well to be familiar with his new property, he decided.

In addition, he found himself much in demand in local society. Almost every member of the gentry for miles around called at Parkland within two weeks of his arrival, and as often as not issued an invitation to tea or dinner or to an evening of cards. When there were no visitors and no invitations to be honored and no estate business to be attended to, then he walked or rode out with two or more of the ladies of the house. There was much beauty to be seen in the surrounding countryside, decked as it was in all its fresh spring splendor.

But almost never was he alone with his future bride. He was not sure if it just happened that way or if she actively organized it so. He realized that Arabella was a very innocent and inexperienced young lady and lived in a secluded country area where everyone's business was frequently everyone else's. It would not do to be alone with her often or for any length of time. Besides, he had no great wish to be alone with her. He did not imagine he would find that they had much in common with each other, and he would doubtless find her interests tedious.

There would be time enough to condition himself to her conversation after they were married.

On the other hand, he had expected that there would be moments when they would be thrown together even when in company. When they were out walking, he had expected to have her on his arm. When sitting in the drawing room at Parkland or in someone else's, it was to be expected that much of the time he would sit next to his betrothed. As it happened, he far more frequently had Frances on his arm during walks, or even her mother. Arabella usually ran on ahead with her dog and the excuse that she had spotted some primroses that must be picked. And she habitually seated herself as far away from him as possible in the drawing room and struck up an animated conversation with whoever was closest to her. Never with him.

Lord Astor could not help suspecting that his betrothed deliberately avoided his company. Why it should be so, he was unsure. He had not found females to be in the habit of avoiding him, even before he came into his present title and fortune. Quite the contrary, in fact. It must be that Arabella had either an aversion to him or a great shyness of his person. She was certainly not generally shy—she was something of a prattler with almost everyone else of both genders. Then, of course, she was familiar with everyone but him.

Was she afraid of him? Lord Astor found the idea somewhat novel. But he supposed it possible. Her experience of life was very limited, the extent of her acquaintances necessarily small. The presence of a fashionable stranger in her home—a stranger who was her betrothed, moreover—was quite possibly bewildering.

He did wonder how she would cope with the removal to London, especially as she would be arriving there at the start of the Season. How would she be able to meet all the members of the *beau monde* who would be there in force, and how converse with them and behave as a married lady of her station would be expected to behave? He would consider it a great annoyance to have to cope with an abnormally shy wife. He would be compelled either to escort her everywhere and stay close to her side or to neglect her and leave her to amuse herself at home.

It was in an attempt to deal with the problem that Lord Astor approached Arabella's mother to suggest that her eldest daughter accompany her sister to London after the wedding. He had at first been reluctant to make the suggestion. He had no strong desire to have the beautiful older sister in his home as a constant reminder of his disappointment in finding that she was not his chosen bride. He did not wish to have always before his vision the contrast between his plain wife and her lovelier sister.

But he had changed his mind. He did not expect to spend much of his time at home anyway, once he had conveyed his wife back to town. And together the sisters would be able to entertain each other. He would have less need to spend his time with his wife. Besides, after a week or more spent at Parkland Manor, Lord Astor was finding Frances a trifle less attractive than he had at first thought her. She was beautiful, yes. But he was frequently called upon to talk with her during a walk or at table or in the drawing room. And he found her conversation trivial and sentimental. Her tendency to dissolve into tears at the slightest hint of a tender topic began to irritate him.

Lord Astor had not had a great deal to do with ladies. He had conversed with them at assemblies and at balls, of course, but never for long enough to become bored by any shallowness their beauty might hide. With his mistresses he was not much concerned with conversation at all. It mattered little to him if they were silly or shallow or suffered from excessive sensibility, provided they satisfied him in more essential ways.

Indeed, he would have been congratulating himself on not having to marry Frances after all if he did not suspect that Arabella would prove to be an even less interesting bride. And at least the elder sister would have been lovelier to look upon.

By the time the month drew to its end, Lord Astor was feeling resigned to his lot, as he had expected to do. He had not found the time quite as tedious as he had expected, but he would be glad to be back in town, back in his familiar haunts with his familiar companions. He would, of course, be forced to make some effort to introduce his wife to the *ton*, but on the whole that would not be too onerous a task. He usually frequented quite a number of *ton* events anyway. And she would have her sister to keep her company during the daytime and after the first half-hour of evening entertainments. On the whole, he felt, his normal way of life would not be seriously disrupted by his marriage. And Lord Astor was quite well-pleased with his normal way of life.

Arabella was feeling less resigned than her betrothed as the day of her marriage drew closer. She had had little enough courage when Lord Astor first arrived and made her his offer. That little drained away drop by drop as the days passed. News of her betrothal traveled fast, as did all news of even lesser import in the region of Parkland. And the news brought with it every last one of their acquaintances, eager to wish her well, even more eager to be presented to the new Viscount Astor.

And Arabella became more and more aware as the days passed of how superior her betrothed was in both appearance and manners to even the most splendid of her neighbors. There had been the time not so long before when she had blushed every time she was forced to be in company with Mr. Thomas Carr. Yet Mr. Carr looked quite ordinary when he stood talking with the viscount outside church on the first Sunday. And Theodore had always appeared to be a fine figure of a man. Now he appeared just a little too solid in build and just a little too ruddy of complexion.

The viscount conversed with ease with everyone. He

did not appear uncomfortable with the rector's talk of books as Mr. Carr always did, or avoid talking with the gentlemen farmers about crops as the rector did, or feel it beneath his dignity to converse with the ladies as several of the other gentlemen did.

And he clearly favored Frances. Arabella had known he would. She had fully expected it. And she deliberately arranged it so that he would have Frances or Mama to talk with instead of her whenever they were out walking or when they did not have visitors. She would not draw attention to her plain and childish person, and she would not force him to listen to her unpolished conversation. She was not in any way his match. He must find her dull. He must regret terribly having to marry her when Frances might have been his bride.

Arabella was not at all cheered by the favorable impression made on the neighborhood by her betrothed. She did not bask in the glory of her position as his intended bride. She merely felt a dreadful embarrassment. The contrast in their appearance and manners was glaringly noticeable, she believed. Everyone must think that it was a poor match—for him.

How he must wish that it were Frances he was to marry! The two of them looked so very handsome together, so very well-matched. Arabella was not at all sure that she had been right after all to insist upon releasing Frances from the obligation of making the marriage. She had done so convinced that Frances loved Theodore and wished to marry him. She had not wanted to see true love thwarted.

But as Mama had hoped, Lord Astor had asked her to allow Frances to come to London with them after their marriage. Not only had Mama agreed, but Frances had wept for a whole hour after being told of the invitation. And her tears had not been ones of grief, Arabella had discovered, but tears of joy. Frances wanted above all else to have a Season in London. That was understandable, Arabella conceded, but what about Theodore? Would Frances be content to return in the summer and marry him in due course?

But her uneasiness aside, Arabella admitted, she was more delighted and relieved than she could say to know that she would have her sister with her when she left for London with her new husband the day after their wedding. The thought of being alone with him, or having the burden of making agreeable conversation with him resting entirely on her own shoulders, terrified her. When he had only her to look at and only her to talk with, he would realize with full force just how very inadequate she was. Frances would help. He liked Frances, and Frances was beautiful to look at.

Arabella wished desperately that they were to leave for London on the wedding day. But it was not so. After a wedding breakfast at Parkland, Mama, Frances, and Jemima were to leave to spend a night with Mrs. Harvey, Mama's bosom friend. Lord Astor was to be left to occupy his home alone with his bride.

Arabella felt sick whenever she recalled this detail. Consequently she did not think of it a great deal. And inevitably the prospect rarely left her consciousness.

Arabella rode to church in the carriage with her mother, Frances, and Jemima. She could not grasp the reality of the fact that it was her wedding day even though all four of them wore new dresses and bonnets, and Frances was trying in vain to hold back her tears. Her own gown was the grandest she had ever owned. It was white with a wide pink velvet sash at the high waist and pink rosebuds embroidered around each of the three deep frills at the hem and around the single frills on the short puffed sleeves.

Arabella did not know quite why she did not look pretty in the dress. Though she had guessed at the reason earlier when she had looked at herself in the full-length looking glass in Mama's dressing room. She was too small to do justice to any gown. And this one definitely made her look less than slender. It did seem a little unfair. A bride had a right to look lovely on her wedding day.

The old stone church in the village was almost full. And it was not even Sunday. All those people looking back over their shoulders when she stepped into the porchway with Mama and the girls were there to see her. And the new master of Parkland, of course.

That was when Arabella started to feel sick. And cold. And wobbly at the knees. She had never been more thankful for Mama's steady arm and loving smile. She was aware of a figure standing close to the altar, a splendid and handsome figure who was about to unite himself with her, and she blanched. And smiled. And succeeded somehow in setting one foot ahead of the other, without either wobbling out of control or breaking into a panicked gallop, until he took her hand.

Lord Astor smiled at her. That was the only clear memory she had afterward of her wedding—that and her fervent wish that he was sixty and bald and toothless. And Frances' tender sniveling from somewhere close by.

Somehow afterward Arabella was scarcely aware of her husband. Frances wept and Mama talked all through the carriage ride home—Jemima had been taken up by someone else. And once they were home, the guests began to arrive, and there were ladies kissing her cheek and gentlemen kissing her hand and friends and neighbors wishing her well and telling her experiences of their own in London and giving advice on how she might best go on there.

And she chattered incessantly to everyone, it seemed, except to her husband. Whenever her eyes lighted on him and she thought of their new relationship, her knees threatened to wobble again and her stomach tried to stand on its head, and she smiled harder and chattered faster.

Frances, meanwhile, who had finally stopped both crying and making little runs at her sister to give her one

more hug, wandered into the garden after the wedding
breakfast, as did several other guests, Theodore at her
side.

"The last month has passed quickly," he said.
"Tomorrow you will be on your way, Fran. You must
be excited."

"I would give anything in the world not to be going,"
she said, her eyes on the ground ahead of her.

"What?" he said. "Have you changed your mind so
soon? A few weeks ago you were ecstatic."

"But then I was not one day away from having to
take my leave of Mama and Jemima," she said. "A
dear mother and a dear sister. And of you, Theo."

"But it will not be forever," he said, lifting one limp
hand from her side and drawing it through his arm.
"Just a couple of months, Fran. And it will be the
experience of a lifetime. The *beau monde* and the
Season."

"Perhaps," she said, her head drooping lower, "you
will be glad to be rid of me, Theo."

"Frances!" His voice had sharpened considerably.
"You know that it nonsense. We would have been
married two years ago if I had not been in the army.
And we would have wed last summer if your father had
not had the misfortune to pass away. You know it is the
dearest wish of my heart to marry you. But I think that
for all that we have been wise to have no formal
betrothal. You are very lovely and you have seen
nothing of the world. It will be good for you to have
these months in London and to be free."

"I do not want to be free, Theo," she wailed. "I just
want to be with you. Dear Theo. I shall not know how
to go on without you. And Mama."

"Don't cry," he said firmly, patting her hand.
"People will think we are quarreling."

Frances lowered the handkerchief that had been
creeping up to her eyes.

"I might even surprise you and appear suddenly in
London myself," he said. "And you will probably be

enjoying yourself so much that you will wish I had stayed at home.''

"Theo!'' she cried, raising large blue eyes to his. "Oh, how could I ever, ever be sorry to see you? I wish I were not going. But for Bella's sake I must. She is so very young and so very sweet and innocent. His lordship is kindness itself, but I am sure Bella will be glad to have me with her.''

"That is good,'' Theodore said. "You look after your sister, Fran.'' He raised her hand to his lips and kissed it lingeringly. "No, you must not cry. We will be together again before you know it.''

But her large blue eyes grew even bluer before his gaze as tears gathered in them and spilled over.

"Dear Theo,'' she said, her voice quavering. "How am I to leave you?''

Lord Astor was lying in his bed in the master bedchamber at Parkland Manor, his hands linked behind his head, staring up at the darkened canopy above him. He wished he could be back in London at a snap of the fingers. He did not much relish the prospect of a three-day journey. However, it was good to know that tomorrow he would be on his way.

And he supposed that he must accustom himself to stop thinking in the singular number. Tomorrow *they* would be on their way. He and his wife and his sister-in-law. It still seemed unreal. The whole day seemed unreal: the drive to church in the morning and the marriage ceremony; the wedding breakfast afterward and the afternoon spent conversing with the guests and receiving their congratulations and good wishes; dinner and an hour spent in the drawing room alone with his wife, trying to draw her into conversation; the early retirement.

Although he had decided many weeks before that he would marry one of the daughters of the late viscount, and although he had spent a month on his new estate, getting acquainted with his bride, growing accustomed to the idea that he was to be a married man, it was still difficult now to grasp the fact that it was all accomplished.

He was married to Arabella. She was his wife. The Viscountess Astor.

He did not think he was sorry. He needed to be married. He would need a family. It was as well to do the thing this way: acquire a wife and settle the problem of the family of his predecessor at the same time.

Even the consummation of their marriage had not been the disaster he had feared. The girl had avoided him so much since their betrothal that he had half-expected to have to deal with tears at best or hysterics and the vapors at worst when he went in to her. He had felt when he had left his own room earlier to go to hers as a soldier must feel when going into battle. He had not known how he would acquit himself. Would he force himself upon her? Or would he leave her alone until after their journey?

As it turned out, there had been no decision to make. She had been lying in her bed, her hands spread on the covers. She had watched him come into the room and cross to the bed, saying nothing after calling to him to come in when he had knocked on her door. If she had been frightened, only the wideness of her eyes and her somewhat heightened color had betrayed her.

He had flicked her cheek with one finger. "Are you afraid of me, Arabella?" he had asked.

Whenever she did speak to him, she rarely said what he expected. "A little, my lord," she had admitted.

"You have no need to be," he had said with a little smile. "I do not plan to be a wife-beater."

"You will have no reason to be," she had said, her expression perfectly serious. "I will be a dutiful and obedient wife, my lord."

"Will you?" he had said, reaching down and drawing back the blankets that covered her. She had not flinched. He almost forgot to snuff the two candles that stood on the table beside her. He normally preferred to make love with light around him, but he did not wish to make the consummation of his marriage an unnecessarily embarrassing ordeal for Arabella.

He had been somewhat touched by her quietness. If she meant to be as obedient throughout their marriage as she had been in the performance of her first duty as his wife, he supposed he must consider himself a fortunate man.

She had said nothing and had given no indication of discomfort or shock or pain. She had not resisted him in any way. She had lain apparently relaxed while he raised her nightgown, lowered himself on top of her, and eased her legs apart. And he had felt her take a slow and deep breath before he had mounted her. She had made no sign as he did so, even though he had felt the breaking of her virginity. And she had lain quiet and still until he was finished with her. It had taken rather longer than he would have wished. He was not used to proceeding immediately to the final stage of lovemaking without all the pleasurable stages that usually went before when one dealt with a mistress rather than a wife.

It was only as he had been withdrawing from her that a whimper had escaped her. It had been quickly stifled, and he had not remarked on it. He guessed that she had been feeling far more than her calm manner had indicated. He had not wished her to feel that she had failed. He had sat on the edge of her bed and touched her cheek again before getting to his feet. His eyes had become accustomed to the darkness, but he could not see her expression.

"I am afraid I hurt you," he had said. "But I believe you will find your duty less painful after tonight."

"That is what Mama said," she had replied. "But it was not your fault, my lord. It is always that way for a bride on her wedding night, Mama says."

He had smiled in the darkness. "Well, your duty is done for tonight," he had said. "Good night, Arabella."

"Good night, my lord," she had said.

Lord Astor found that he was smiling now at the canopy over his bed. She spoke just like a child, seeming not to choose her words with the diplomacy one expected of an adult.

It was a relief at least to know that he was not going to have trouble with Arabella. She was going to be obedient and dutiful, she had told him. And she had proceeded with unexpected docility to prove she meant what she said.

Strange! There had been something almost erotic about the stillness of her small body, her silent surrender, her total lack of involvement in what he had been doing to her body. He tried to imagine Ginny lying and behaving so, but he repressed the thought before it had a chance to develop in his mind. It would not be fair to make comparisons. Not tonight. Not when he had just left his wife's bed. She was probably still suffering from shock and pain.

• 4 •

THE dowager Viscountess Astor and her two unmarried daughters returned early to Parkland the next morning so that the travelers might be on their way. Arabella met them at the outer door, which a footman held open. Her husband came behind her, having moved from the breakfast parlor at a far more sedate pace than his wife when they heard the carriage.

"Mama!" Arabella cried, rushing into her mother's arms as if they had been apart for a month.

"There, there, my love," her mother said, patting her daughter on the back. "Let me look at you. Lady Astor! Whoever would have thought that one day you would have my title, my love? How pretty you look this morning."

Arabella doubted the truth of that remark. She knew that she must look more childish than usual with her cheeks flushed.

"Welcome back to your home, ma'am," Lord Astor said, coming up behind Arabella and extending a hand to his mother-in-law. "We will be on our way as soon as we can."

Frances was sobbing into her handkerchief. "Bella," she said. "Oh, dear Bella, how happy I am for you. Such a handsome husband! Even more handsome than Theodore, I do declare. I am so glad for you. I know you will be wonderfully happy."

"Are you very sad to be leaving Theodore?" Arabella asked, her face sympathetic. "It must be dreadful for you, Frances."

"I do not know why you say that, Bella," Frances said, dabbing at her moist eyes and putting her handkerchief away. "Sir Theodore is merely a neighbor and friend."

"Bella. Oh, Bella." Jemima was bouncing on the spot, waiting for some of her older sister's attention. "You will send me a present from London? You will not forget, Bella?"

"I will not allow her to do so," Lord Astor said, having finished his conversation with his mother-in-law. "Is there anything in particular you would like, Jemima?"

Half an hour more passed before Lord Astor's traveling carriage was finally on its way, a coach from the Parkland stables following behind with the baggage and his lordship's valet. The dowager viscountess had had a private word with both daughters and a hug for each.

"I can see from the harmony between you and his lordship that you did your duty last night as I instructed you," she said to a blushing Arabella. "You will continue to do so, Bella? It will not be near so fearsome from now on. Oh, my love. So young and a married lady already. It seems no more than a couple of years ago that you were a babe in arms."

Both Frances and her mother shed tears at the parting, but Arabella fought hers. The last thing she wanted was to have to face Lord Astor in his carriage with a shiny red nose, blotched cheeks, and bloodshot eyes.

Arabella was glad they were on their way. There was a certain anxiety, of course, about knowing that she was at the beginning of a three-day journey that would take her far from home, far from all the familiar people and places she had known in her life. She felt some misgiving too in knowing that at the end of that journey lay London and the Season and the *ton*.

But even so, given the circumstances, she was glad the journey had begun. The farewell from Mama and Jemima had been heart-wrenching. She had never been away from them for even so much as a night before last night. There had, of course, been some consolation in knowing that she was at least to take Frances with her. And perhaps it had helped her somewhat in the parting from her mother to be forced to spend the first half-hour of the journey consoling a weeping older sister. However, the worst was over. Arabella did not think she could endure too many such partings.

But perhaps her main reason for being glad she was on her way was knowing that her wedding day was safely behind her, that her new life was inevitable, and that it was as well to begin that new life without delay. In truth, she faced London and the Season with excitement as well as anxiety. She had always dreamed about seeing all the members of fashionable society of whom she was one by birth. And it would be wonderful to attend a real ball, to watch a play at a real theater, to see the queen, perhaps. If only the poor king were not indisposed!

Arabella was glad that the journey was to last for three days. For three days she would not have to undergo the embarrassment of being alone with her husband. He talked to Frances after she finally recovered from her grief, and answered her eager questions about the latest style in bonnets in town. Frances always knew what was appropriate conversation for a lady, though she had had no more exposure to fashionable living than Arabella. Why could she never think of anything to say to him?

The evening before had been pure agony. The day had not been so bad, as they had been surrounded by friends and family. And even when she had stood next to Lord Astor at the altar she had known what to say. There were certain prescribed responses, and she had had no difficulty at all in making them. But at dinner and during the evening they had been alone. And she had become almost paralyzingly aware again of what a poor excuse for a bride to such a handsome gentleman she was. How dreadful it was to know that he must be looking at her undergrown, plain, and childish person, knowing that she was his wife.

She had found herself horribly tongue-tied. She had been able to think of no fascinating topic on which to converse, though she had searched and searched her mind while she chewed each mouthful of food far longer than was necessary. Yet during the few moments when she had forgotten herself, she had suddenly discovered that she was gabbling on about George and his exploits or about Emily, her horse. She had even asked him about the health of the poor king, when she knew she should have maintained a polite silence on the topic. Who wished to admit that the King of England—poor dear gentleman—was mad? She should have asked about the Prince Regent or Princess Charlotte. But she had not thought of them.

It would be a great relief to have Frances staying with her in London. Perhaps her husband would not notice her plainness and her dullness so much while he had Frances to look at and converse with. Though of course he would also be able to see them together and be reminded of the contrast between them. How he must wish that Frances was his wife and she his sister-in-law.

Arabella was hoping quite fervently that she would not have to perform her marriage duty until they reached London. They had not brought a maid with them. Surely, then, Frances would not be expected to occupy an inn room alone for three nights. She would certainly have fits of the vapors and the hysterics at the prospect of some desperate villain breaking in upon her in the dark of the night. Besides, it would not be at all proper. It stood to reason that Arabella would share her room and Lord Astor stay alone.

Arabella hoped so. She even crossed her fingers on both hands and pressed them hard into her lap for a moment to induce the fates to be kind to her. It was not that she was undutiful. She was Lord Astor's wife now, and she planned to spend the rest of her life obeying him, doing all within her power to make him comfortable. But she needed the three days to recover from the night before.

She was so dreadfully sore. Mama had not warned her of that, and Arabella had not been able to muster the courage that morning to ask if it was a natural result of a wedding night. She had expected to feel pain only at the actual moment of the consummation.

She certainly had felt pain then, but it had not ended there. Arabella had not been unduly shocked by the marriage act. She had grown up surrounded by animals, and at quite a young age she had concluded that what applied to them probably applied somewhat equally to humans. But she had not expected quite such a deep invasion of her person. And she had not expected that it would hurt quite so much. She had thought, as she lay quiet and submissive beneath the weight of her husband's body, that his movements would never stop. Each stroke had seemed to rub her raw.

She had concentrated all her thoughts on doing her duty like a good and obedient wife. By some superhuman power she had resisted the impulse to push at his shoulders and to cry out to him to stop, to please be finished quickly. She had let sound escape her only once. He had stopped finally and blessedly, and she had been vastly relieved. But when he had begun to withdraw, she had thought for a moment that it was all going to start again, and she had been unable to quell that sound of protest. She had been horrified. She had fully expected that he would express deep displeasure with her. But he had said nothing.

She was still sore. Arabella stole a glance at the dismayingly handsome profile of her husband as he discussed parasols with Frances. She would perform her duty again tonight if she must. After all, it was something to which she had to accustom herself. But please, dear God, she thought, let it wait until London. She could still feel the raw hurt along every inch of her he had used the night before.

Arabella set one hand loosely on top of the other in her lap and watched her husband and her sister as if she

were a child who must not interrupt adult conversation.
If only she were taller, she thought, and thinner. If only
she could converse interestingly about bonnets and
parasols. If only she could weep and look pretty. If only
she could look pretty even without weeping!

It seemed strange to have ladies in residence at the
house on Upper Grosvenor Street. Lord Astor, used to
burying his head in the morning paper at breakfast
while partaking of his usual kidneys and toast and
coffee, was somewhat taken aback to find his wife
already seated at the table when he came downstairs the
morning after their arrival in town. He had always
assumed that ladies kept to their beds until noon.
Though why he should have thought so of Arabella, he
did not know, since she had usually been outside riding
or walking with her dog at Parkland whenever he came
downstairs.

He bade her good morning, helped himself to breakfast at the sideboard, and sat down at the head of the
table. He glanced regretfully at his paper, folded as
usual beside his fork. He left it where it was. He wished
Arabella were easier to talk to.

"I had thought to take you shopping this morning,"
he said. "Both you and your sister will need completely
new wardrobes for the Season. However, on second
thought, perhaps it would be advisable to have a lady of
some taste to help advise you. I plan to call on Lady
Berry, my aunt, this morning. Perhaps she will have
time to accompany you to a modiste this afternoon or
tomorrow morning. Will that suit you?"

"If you wish it, my lord," she said, looking up at him
brightly. "I know I am no beauty and I know I am
ridiculously small for a lady. But I wish to do credit to
you when I appear in public."

He smiled. "Very few people are raving beauties,
Arabella," he said. "Most of us have to make the best
of the assets we have. You are not an antidote and I do
not wish to hear you repeatedly belittling yourself."

Lord Astor sighed and looked up at the heavy gray sky. It was a decidedly chilly day for the beginning of April. But the weather perfectly matched the type of day that he was expecting to have. The whole of the morning was going to be taken up with talking to his aunt and seeing if Monsieur Pierre—London born and bred despite the impressive name, he would wager—could call on Arabella and do something with her hair.

That would not have been so bad if he could at least have looked forward to an afternoon to himself. He was impatient to see Ginny after five weeks away from her. But he would have to be at home to present his wife and her sister to his aunt. Doubtless Aunt Hermione would wish to meet Arabella without delay. And it was probable that they would make a trip to Bond Street to have Arabella and Frances fitted out for new wardrobes. He could quite easily avoid that excursion, of course, but he had definite tastes in feminine apparel, and he would wish to approve Arabella's colors and styles. She would have to choose both with extreme care to suit her very small stature.

And he must not forget to send a groom on his way to Parkland to arrange to bring her horse and her dog to London. During their long journey, he had begun to realize how very important they were to her happiness. And if he were soon to get his own life back to its contented normality, then he must see to it that his wife too was as happy as he could possibly make her.

Perhaps he would be able to call the evening his own, he thought hopefully for one moment. But of course, good manners would dictate that he take dinner at home with his wife and their guest on their first day back. And if he was to visit his wife's bed with any regularity, he must not be in the habit of staying from home too late at night. It would be unfair to expect her to arouse herself at all hours of the night in order to be at his service.

Lord Astor lifted the knocker on his aunt's door with the head of his cane and allowed it to rattle back against the metal plate. He hoped that his life would quieten

close not only to the park but also to the Grosvenor
Gate leading into it.''

"Oh," she said. "Grass and trees and the chance to
walk and run?"

"Yes to the first three," he said. "But perhaps before
you run, Arabella, you had better look around you carefully to make sure that there is no audience."

"Yes," she said, and blushed deeply before starting
the muffin on its travels again. "I would not wish to do
anything that might prove an embarrassment, my
lord."

Yes, it was very strange to have ladies in his keeping,
Lord Astor thought as he left the house an hour later
and set out on foot the short distance to his aunt's house
on Grosvenor Square. He was finding Arabella just a
trifle amusing, but amusing very much as a child would
be. It was hard to see her as a mature woman. She had
sat quietly through the three days of their journey,
saying hardly a word except on the rare occasions when
she forgot herself and burst into speech.

This morning at the breakfast table, in fact, was the
first time he had been alone with her since their wedding
day. The first time he had been alone to converse with
her, that was. He had, of course, visited her on their
wedding night and again the night before. But one did
not visit one's wife's bed in order to converse.

He found her amusing now. But for how long? He
had not expected to have to share his breakfast table
with her. He supposed that soon he must show her that
it was his normal practice to read his paper at breakfast.
Surely he would tire of her silences and her bursts of
speech before many days had passed. Even so, he
preferred her speech habits to those of her sister. He had
wished for his horse or his curricle on the return journey
even more than he had when traveling into the country.
Miss Frances Wilson's conversation was even more
trying than Henry's snoring had been. She was very
beautiful, but rather tiresome. Thank heaven that she
had not been his chosen bride!

Lord Astor sighed and looked up at the heavy gray sky. It was a decidedly chilly day for the beginning of April. But the weather perfectly matched the type of day that he was expecting to have. The whole of the morning was going to be taken up with talking to his aunt and seeing if Monsieur Pierre—London born and bred despite the impressive name, he would wager—could call on Arabella and do something with her hair.

That would not have been so bad if he could at least have looked forward to an afternoon to himself. He was impatient to see Ginny after five weeks away from her. But he would have to be at home to present his wife and her sister to his aunt. Doubtless Aunt Hermione would wish to meet Arabella without delay. And it was probable that they would make a trip to Bond Street to have Arabella and Frances fitted out for new wardrobes. He could quite easily avoid that excursion, of course, but he had definite tastes in feminine apparel, and he would wish to approve Arabella's colors and styles. She would have to choose both with extreme care to suit her very small stature.

And he must not forget to send a groom on his way to Parkland to arrange to bring her horse and her dog to London. During their long journey, he had begun to realize how very important they were to her happiness. And if he were soon to get his own life back to its contented normality, then he must see to it that his wife too was as happy as he could possibly make her.

Perhaps he would be able to call the evening his own, he thought hopefully for one moment. But of course, good manners would dictate that he take dinner at home with his wife and their guest on their first day back. And if he was to visit his wife's bed with any regularity, he must not be in the habit of staying from home too late at night. It would be unfair to expect her to arouse herself at all hours of the night in order to be at his service.

Lord Astor lifted the knocker on his aunt's door with the head of his cane and allowed it to rattle back against the metal plate. He hoped that his life would quieten down again soon. He hoped that this marriage business would not after all disturb the hitherto satisfying pattern of his days.

Arabella was standing very still even though she was aching in every limb and muscle and was fit to scream with boredom. Mama and Miss Carter, the seamstress from the village, had never taken longer than a few minutes to measure her for a dress and to decide upon a fabric and a pattern. She could not quite understand why Madame Pichot needed to measure and remeasure every last inch of her body. It was quite decidedly tiresome.

She might have reassured herself that once the business was over with, then Madame would be able to use the same measurements for the rest of her life. But that was not true. Arabella was planning to lose weight. By the time she needed winter clothes, all these measurements—except those relating to her height, alas—would be inaccurate.

Frances was enjoying herself enormously. She had positively buzzed with animation all the time they had been in Madame's parlor looking at fashion plates and examining endless bolts of cloth carried in by tireless assistants. With the help of Lady Berry she had finally decided on a dazzling array of new garments and had gone happily off to the workroom to be measured.

But then, of course, Frances had good reason to be delighted. She would look beautiful in a potato bag. She looked lovely in Miss Carter's unfashionable frocks. It went without saying that she would be quite breathtaking in all the new clothes that Lady Berry had assured her would be quite essential for a young lady making her come-out.

Arabella herself had not been in the charge of Lady Berry. Lord Astor had decided to accompany them to the modiste's, though Arabella had been quite dismayed when he had said so. She had expected that perhaps he would stay outside in the carriage or would hover somewhere just inside the door. But no—he had come right into the parlor, seated himself beside her, and proceeded to tell her exactly what clothes she needed and how they should be designed and what color they should be and what fabrics would best suit her figure. No, he had not told her. He had told Madame Pichot while she had sat, a silent and obedient child in their midst.

She must not be seen in any heavy fabric, it seemed. Not velvet and not brocade. Her gowns were to be adorned with the minimum of frills and flounces. And there were to be no wide sashes. Stripes could be allowed to go downward, apparently, but not across. As well as white and pastel shades, she was permitted to wear bright greens and yellows, but definitely not reds or dark blues. These colors were much too heavy, for some reason. Her sleeves were not to be too puffy.

Madame had agreed with all of Lord Astor's suggestions and had even added some of her own. In fact, the two of them had had a most comfortable coze about her, the silent third. She had wanted to suggest to him quietly, when Madame turned her attention to Lady Berry and Frances at one point, that perhaps he would be wasting his money to outfit her so lavishly. She could never look more than barely presentable anyway. She was far too small and plump. But he had forbidden her that morning to belittle herself, so she had kept her lips closed and folded her hands in her lap.

He wanted her to have all these new clothes. All of us have to make the best of the assets we have, he had said at breakfast, though it was easy for him to talk when he had nothing but assets. He wanted to make the best of her. And if that was what he wanted, Arabella thought, standing still while Madame busied herself with a measuring tape at the back of her waist, then she would stand here for five hours if necessary so that the dressmaker could get the measurements right. She could not be beautiful for him, but she could at least allow him to do his best for her.

He had approved with a nod all the plans for Frances

that his aunt had described, though he was paying for
all of those clothes too. Obviously Frances did not need
to be dressed with such care. He would realize that she
would look lovely in any fabric, color, or design. How
he must have wished that he could have changed places
with Lady Berry and allowed her to worry about Arabella. He would not have had to worry about her if
Frances were his bride and she a mere sister-in-law.

Arabella sighed. But she cheered up almost immediately as she caught sight of herself in a looking
glass across the room. She really did like her hair. In
fact, she loved it. She did not look nearly so top-heavy
any longer with all the heavy masses shorn away. She
had felt a little sick and not a little panic-stricken that
morning when she had heard Monsieur Pierre's scissors
chop through the thick locks. Perhaps his lordship had
taken her at her word and ordered the man to cut it all
off.

But Monsieur had stopped short of doing quite that.
He had left a short covering all over her head, and
longer tendrils to adorn her neck and temples. And he
had done something with her hair to make it curl all
over her head. It felt as if there was almost no hair
there, but she loved it.

Frances had shrieked, remembered how Papa had
always loved long hair on his girls, wept for five
minutes, and then hugged her and assured her that it
was quite delightful and that dear Bella looked
positively pretty.

Arabella thought she agreed, but she had been almost
sick with apprehension as luncheon time approached.
What if his lordship laughed or disapproved? She
supposed she looked even more of a child now with her
hair short and curly. And there was Frances with her
long, very feminine blond locks!

He had looked at her for a long time before saying
anything while she stood mutely in the hallway where
she had had the misfortune to be as he stepped through
the door.

"I knew it would do wonders," he had said. "Do you like it, Arabella?"

"If you do, my lord," she had said, blushing and not knowing what she was expected to say. It did not occur to her that perhaps he expected a simple yes or no.

"Then you like it," he had said, handing his hat and cane to a footman and unbuttoning his greatcoat. "It makes you look very pretty."

"Oh, I am not pretty," she had said one moment before her hand flew to her mouth. "I beg your pardon, my lord. I thank you for the compliment."

And he had asked her that morning to call him Geoffrey, she had thought. But oh, she could not. It seemed far too presumptuous, far too familiar to call him by his given name. Her tongue would tie itself in knots if she tried to call him that to his face, though the name had come out of her mouth quite articulately when she had tried it in her dressing room. She would rather call him nothing at all than have to face the embarrassment of calling him Geoffrey out loud.

"Oh, Bella, is not all this unimaginably wonderful?" Frances said now, hugging her sister as she was finally released from the tyranny of the measuring tape. "And Lady Berry has specifically asked that one evening gown each be delivered two days from now so that we may attend her soiree. If only Mama and Jemima could somehow share in our joy."

Her eyes were suspiciously bright.

"We will go home and write them each a long letter," Arabella said briskly. "That way they can feel that they are somehow with us here. And it will be much better than merely crying because we miss them and wish they were here."

She wished she had not added that last sentence. Two tears glistened in Frances' lower lashes for a moment and trickled prettily down her cheeks. But she smiled and linked her arm through her sister's as they turned to reenter the parlor, where Lady Berry and Lord Astor were in conversation together.

"Ah, a task well-accomplished," Lady Berry said.
"You are both going to look quite splendid in my
drawing room two evenings hence. Arabella, my dear,
Geoffrey is going to spoil us all and take us for ices
before we go home. Miss Wilson, are you very tired, my
dear? I know that all this business of fittings can be
quite tedious."

Lord Astor waited while his wife put on her bonnet,
then offered his arm to escort her to the carriage.

"Will they order me out of the shop if I merely sit
with you and do not have an ice?" she asked him
anxiously as he handed her into the carriage.

He laughed. "Order Lady Astor from the shop?" he
said. "Not unless they wish to close their doors
tomorrow, Arabella. Do you not like ices?"

"Not greatly," she lied, wishing that she would not
have to watch the other three eat theirs. "Will you be
offended, my lord?"

"But, Bella," Frances began until she caught sight of
her sister's pleading face. Frances had been told about
the dieting scheme, though she had cried and protested
that she would suffer dreadfully if she had to watch her
sister starve herself to death. And anyway, where had
Arabella got the ridiculous notion that she was fat?

5

THE following afternoon, Lord Astor was lying on his back in his favorite position, his hands clasped behind his head, his feet crossed at the ankles. He was feeling sleepy and contented. Ginny's hand was slowly circling his naked chest. Her tangled curls and her warm breath were tickling his side. He wriggled his toes and sighed. It seemed an age since these visits to his mistress had been a regular afternoon or nighttime occurrence. It was nearly six weeks.

"I had almost forgotten how good you are, Ginny," he said, lowering one hand to fondle the back of her neck for a moment. "You have quite worn me out."

She raised her head and smiled in that slow, sensual manner that usually succeeded in making his temperature rise. "I take it that the bride is not thoroughly satisfactory if you have come back to me so soon, Geoffrey," she said. "And so very full of energy! I am only thankful that the bruises I am bound to carry around with me for the next several days are in places where they will not be seen in public."

"I would apologize," he said, grinning and returning his hand to the back of his head. "But we both know that you like it rough, don't we, Ginny?"

She pouted. "Sometimes I think you have no respect for me at all, Geoffrey," she said. "I have sung at the homes of no fewer than three titled persons since you have been away, you know, not to mention other establishments quite as respectable. And everywhere I have been treated with marked respect and praised for my voice. And I have been called Virginia and even Miss Cox. Sir Harvey Hamilton called me Miss Cox. Why will not you?"

"Call you Miss Cox?" he said. "Will you please remove your clothes now, Miss Cox? Will you please come to bed now, Miss Cox? Come on now, Ginny. Those people have not seen you as I have—at least, I hope for your sake they have not. And which would you prefer to have—respect or pleasure?"

She ran her finger over his lips and tapped them sharply. "I would like both," she said.

"Go to sleep, Gin," he said, turning his head and shaking off her finger. "Three times has quite tired me. I am not in the mood for conversation."

"Of course you have to perform for someone else at night too now," she said, wriggling closer to his warm, relaxed body. "You have to save yourself. Poor Geoffrey."

"Enough of that," he said. "I will have my wife left right out of any conversation between you and me, Ginny. Now, go to sleep, there's a good girl."

She seemed to obey him. At least she fell silent and motionless beside him. Lord Astor continued to stare upward. He did not think he wanted to sleep even though he felt drowsy. It was pleasant to have a few minutes in which just to relax. He must go home soon in order to be in time to bathe Ginny's perfume from his skin before getting ready for dinner. But not just yet.

It had been a pleasant day. Arabella had been at the breakfast table again, but she had seen his paper beside his fork and had suggested that he read it if he wished. She had seemed to relax once he did so. She had resumed her eating and finished her muffin as she had not the morning before. She was not very fond of butter, she had explained when he had lowered his paper briefly to ask why she ate it dry.

Aunt Hermione had been coming to take Arabella and Frances shopping again. There were all sorts of trappings like bonnets, slippers, fans, and ribbons to be examined and bought. He had not felt it necessary to accompany them this time, as he trusted his aunt to help his wife make suitable purchases. He had spent the morning at White's in delicious isolation in the reading room for a whole hour and then in company with a group of acquaintances who had come straight from Jackson's boxing saloon. He had promised to meet them there the following morning.

He had even eaten at White's and reveled in the sensible male conversation—all about interesting topics like horses and hunting and politics. No one so much as mentioned a bonnet or a parasol.

His wife and her sister had been invited back to Grosvenor Square for luncheon. Doubtless they would remain there for at least part of the afternoon. And so finally he had had the luxury of a whole free afternoon in which to visit Ginny. And an extremely satisfying afternoon it had been, too. He had not realized quite how much pent-up energy he had been waiting to unleash until he had found himself quite unsatiated after one lengthy and energetic performance on the bed with her, and then another. They had both sweated their way through the third, and lain tangled together, exhausted, for several minutes before finding the energy to move themselves into the positions they now occupied.

An extremely satisfying afternoon.

He did not want to think of Arabella. She belonged to a different world. It was not that he did not respect her. She was his wife. He intended to see that she had every material comfort he was capable of giving her. He intended to see that she became well-established in society. He would escort her everywhere it was necessary for her to appear. And he intended to see to her happiness whenever he could, as in this business with her dog and horse, for example.

But he could not be faithful to her. No one of any sense would expect him to be so. It was true that scarcely a week before, he had made a promise at the altar to keep himself only for her. But everyone knew that the wedding service was just a quaint ceremony. No one took the words quite literally. He was doing no harm to Arabella by keeping a mistress and spending such afternoons as this with her. Indeed, he would go home refreshed and with new patience to spend an evening with his wife and her sister.

He did not want to think about Arabella. He glanced down at Ginny's tangled fair curls and thought of his wife's dark curly locks. She really did look almost pretty with her hair cut short. She looked like a little pixie. How absurdly anxious she had been when awaiting his verdict in the hallway the morning before. Had she expected that he would rant and rave and demand that she have the severed hair stuck back on again? Lord Astor grinned. Her eyes had been enormous and very dark with apprehension. And that upper lip of hers had curved upward, showing the very white teeth beneath.

He would not think of her, Lord Astor decided. He closed his eyes. He would sleep for a few minutes. She was so very small. He felt large and virile when he covered her on her bed. In fact, the night before, he had raised himself on his forearms while he took her. He was afraid of squashing her, of suffocating her. He had wondered if he hurt her. She always lay so still and compliant beneath him that it was impossible to tell. He had looked down at her once to find that her eyes were open and looking off to one side. Her face had been calm, as far as he had been able to see in the darkness.

It would not seem quite fair to go to her tonight and violate that innocent little body with his own, which had taken its wanton pleasure with Ginny all afternoon.

Lord Astor opened his eyes again. He really did not want to be having these thoughts. He wanted to relax and savor his sexual satisfaction. He wanted to sleep.

He was not going to develop a conscience, was he? How damnably tiresome that would be. He would buy Arabella a string of pearls tomorrow. He had planned to do so anyway for her first ball. Why not for her first appearance in public at his aunt's soiree? He would buy the most costly string he could find.

Lord Astor yawned and dozed for a few minutes.

* * *

Arabella was finding it hard to concentrate on the Crown Jewels. They were very beautiful and obviously quite priceless, and normally she would have been paralyzed with wonder. But his lordship had said they were to see the royal menagerie, which was also housed in the Tower of London, and Arabella was all impatience to go there.

Indeed, seeing the animals had been their main reason for coming. His lordship had told her at breakfast that George and Emily might be expected in about a week's time, but that in the meantime she might enjoy seeing some different animals. There was even an elephant in the menagerie, apparently. Arabella could not imagine an animal that was reputedly so large.

Frances had exclaimed with delight when Arabella had told her late in the morning that they were to go to the Tower of London when his lordship returned home after luncheon. He had gone to a boxing saloon for the morning. Arabella wished she could see him box. She would wager that he would pummel into the ground any opponent he cared to challenge.

Frances had not been interested in the menagerie. She had wanted to see the Crown Jewels. So here they were, Arabella thought as she stood quietly at her husband's side, her arm tucked within his, while Frances sighed in ecstasy over every diamond and pearl in Mary of Modena's crown, with its purple velvet and ermine cap and its solid gold band.

"Just imagine being queen and actually wearing that," she said wistfully.

"Saint Edward's crown is very much grander," Lord Astor said, "as you will see when we come to it. It apparently weighs all of seven pounds."

"Gracious!" Arabella said. "It is amazing that the king's neck does not slide right down into his chest when it is upon his head."

Lord Astor laughed down at her. "It is no wonder that kings are reputed to sit on their thrones all day, is it?'' he said. ''It must take two muscular courtiers merely to raise them to their feet.''

They both laughed merrily while Frances moved on to gaze upon the ampulla and spoon.

''Do you suppose the king will ever regain his health?'' Arabella asked suddenly, sobering and gazing earnestly into her husband's eyes. ''Do you hear anything of his recovery, my lord?''

''I am afraid not much hope is held out, Arabella,'' he said, smiling gently down at her. ''The king is very sick.'' He touched her gloved hand lightly with his fingertips.

''Poor King George!'' she said. ''I wish he could know that his subjects still love him and admire him and wish him to recover. Do you think he knows, my lord?''

''I am quite sure he does,'' he said, and he curled his fingers under hers for a moment and squeezed them.

She flushed deeply suddenly and looked jerkily away from him. ''Let us see this crown,'' she said. ''The one the king wore at his coronation.''

Another twenty minutes passed before they finally moved on to the menagerie. Even Arabella stood spellbound before the grand crown and told herself in awe that she was within a foot of the crown that the king himself had once worn on his head. And then on the way out of the apartments that housed the jewels, Lord Astor was accosted by a tall, thin young man with carrot-red hair, pale eyebrows, and a boyish, lopsided grin. Arabella liked him immediately. He was not at all handsome or grand.

''Astor!'' he said. ''What an unexpected place in which to meet you. I thought you were in the country.'' His eyes slid curiously to Arabella and Frances.

''I returned three days ago,'' Lord Astor said. ''How d'ye do, Farraday? May I present my wife, Lady Astor, and her sister, Miss Wilson? Lord Farraday, an old university friend of mine.''

Arabella beamed at him while Frances curtsied. Here

was a man with whom she was sure she could feel perfectly comfortable. She hoped they would see more of him.

"How do you do, my lord?" she said. "Have you come to see the jewels too? They really are a splendid sight. The king's coronation crown weighs seven pounds, you know. His lordship has brought us here because we are new to London and want to see absolutely everything. At least, my sister wanted to see the jewels, so we came here first. I want to see the menagerie, and that is where we are going now. There is an elephant there. Have you ever seen it? Perhaps you would like to come with us?"

Lord Farraday bowed to her and grinned. "I would like nothing better, ma'am," he said. "But I have lost my mother and my grandmother somewhere around here. My mother will surely rip up at me if I take another half-hour to visit the animals. Will you be at Lady Berry's tonight, Astor?"

"Most certainly," the viscount said. "You can imagine how agog my aunt is to show off my wife to all her guests, Farraday."

"I shall see you there," the baron said. Then, turning to the ladies and smiling, "I shall do myself the honor of paying my respects to you again tonight, ma'am, Miss Wilson."

Arabella smiled, but her eyes had lost some of their sparkle. Lady Berry was eager to "show her off" to her guests? She was to be the center of attraction at tonight's soiree? She would be introduced as Lord Astor's wife. Everyone present there would see what a very unfortunate choice of bride he had felt obliged to make. They would see Frances at her side and wonder why she was not the new Lady Astor. And Arabella had not even had time to lose more than a few ounces of weight!

It was perhaps fortunate for her that Lord Farraday moved on in search of his female relatives and her own party turned in the direction of the menagerie. Her spirits rose immediately. Even Frances seemed eager to see the elephant.

They stood gazing at it a few minutes later. Arabella was speechless. It was huge. But there was far more than its size to stupefy the viewer. It legs were like tree trunks. And its skin was wrinkled and leathery. It looked a thousand years old. Its eyes were small and seemed almost human in its mammoth body.

"Well, what do you think?" Lord Astor asked after a while.

"I cannot imagine living in a country where such creatures run wild or where they are ridden down the streets," Frances said. "I would be extremely frightened to venture outdoors, my lord."

"Is there only one elephant?" Arabella asked.

"Did you expect a whole herd?" Lord Astor grinned down at her.

"But it has no company," she said. "It is all alone, my lord. And in a bare cage."

"The expense of having two and housing them in a larger area would probably be prohibitive," he pointed out to her.

"But he looks so lonely," she said. "Look at his eyes, my lord."

"I am very glad it is locked safely away in its cage," Frances said with a shudder.

"There used to be many different kinds of animals here," Lord Astor explained. "Unfortunately, now there are only the elephant and a grizzly bear, apart from various birds. Shall we look at the bear?"

Arabella was glad to move away from the quiet, patient, sad-looking elephant. But the poor bear looked even worse, she found. Its fur looked moth-eaten and dusty. It was pacing its cage with a slow, rolling gait.

"The bear is a far more deadly creature than it appears to be," Lord Astor explained to them. "One blow from one of those paws would doubtless kill any one of us."

Frances took a step backward. "I do hope the bars are strong," she said.

"You are quite safe, Frances," he assured her. "Would you feel better if you were to take my other arm?"

Frances hastily availed herself of the offer. Arabella felt herself unaccustomedly close to tears. She hated it! She could have howled with pity for the two poor animals, so far away from where they belonged, so irrevocably cut off from all communication with animals of their kind, so utterly devoid of activity or exercise or love.

"What do you think of it, Arabella?" Lord Astor asked.

"It is very nice, my lord," she said politely.

He looked down at her lowered head and smiled fleetingly.

"Oh, how I wish Mama and Jemima could have been with us this afternoon," Frances said half an hour later when they were all in the carriage on their way back to Upper Grosvenor Street. "How they would have loved the Crown Jewels. And the dangerous splendor of the animals."

Arabella sat beside her husband, her hands in her lap. "Thank you, my lord," she said. "It was kind of you to take us. I am very grateful."

Lord Astor looked thoughtfully down at the top of his wife's bonnet while his sister-in-law gazed eagerly from the carriage window. He reached across finally, lifted one of Arabella's hands from her lap, and drew it through his arm. He kept his hand over hers.

Arabella did not look up or try to withdraw her hand.

Lady Berry was an attractive and fashionable lady in her early forties. She loved to entertain and to be the focus of attention. There was a Lord Berry, an earl in fact, but people tended to forget the fact. He lived in his wife's shadow, seemingly content to finance her whims and to keep himself quietly out of sight. On the night of his wife's soiree, he spent the evening in his library with a bottle of port and two particular friends who enjoyed social pleasures about as much as he did.

Lady Berry was in her element, having a new niece to introduce to the *ton*. And if the niece was not a remarkably pretty girl, she was fortunate to have brought along with her a quite extraordinarily lovely sister, who was bound to have all the unmarried young bucks swarming around her in no time. The two of them would take quite nicely. There was a certain fresh charm about Geoffrey's bride that would set her off from the majority of the young girls who had begun to descend on London in large numbers.

And so Arabella found herself being conducted around the drawing room in Grosvenor Square on the arm of her husband's aunt, Frances beside her, being presented to a bewildering number of elegant people. She did not feel nearly as shy as she had feared. Lord Astor had been left behind almost in the doorway, and she did not feel quite as plain and inadequate without his splendid person at her side.

And he really did look quite dauntingly magnificent tonight, dressed to match her ice-blue silk gown—in dark blue velvet coat, paler blue silk waistcoat, and silver silk knee breeches. Arabella had quailed when she had joined him in the drawing room at home, despite the fact that she had been twirling before her looking glass a few minutes before, feeling quite delightfully pretty in her new gown and with her new newly acquired short curls. And she was inordinately proud of her new pearls, which his lordship had brought to her room one hour before and clasped about her neck himself. A present from her husband! He must not be entirely displeased with her if he had bought her such a costly and lovely gift. And surely she must have lost at least one pound of weight.

Frances, of course, looked breathtaking in her pale apricot satin gown with its netted tunic. And her blond hair was dressed in shining ringlets. Arabella looked eagerly at all the people to whom they were presented, especially at the young men, to see if her sister was properly appreciated. And she was not disappointed. Frances' blushes and shy, downcast glances were creating a decided stir. Frances would have a splendid Season before going home to Theodore in the summer.

Strangely, Arabella felt no inadequacy at all when in the presence of her far lovelier sister. She was always too busy feeling proud of Frances. And so her manner quickly became relaxed and unselfconscious. She smiled about her with the greatest goodwill and talked to everyone without first stopping to consider whether she had anything of interest to say. And Lady Berry was proved right. It seemed that the new viscountess and her sister would take very well.

Arabella was delighted to see Lord Farraday again. And she was not mistaken in her first impression of him. He was remarkably amiable. She felt quite as comfortable after a few minutes of conversing with him as she did with Theodore at home.

"Did you find your mother and grandmother this afternoon?" she asked him.

"Yes, I did," he said cheerfully. "And I was entirely to blame for losing them, of course. I got caught up in examining some old armor, they wandered off chattering nineteen to the dozen without even noticing I was not with them, got themselves lost, and I was to blame."

Arabella laughed.

"I have a family of nothing but females," he said. "Three sisters. All older than I. All tyrants. All expect me to be at their beck and call, and all complain that I am underfoot when I am." He grinned.

"I have a mother and two sisters," Arabella said, "but then, of course, I can see things from their point of view, being female myself. If I had had a brother, I think I would have made much of him."

"I shall have to present you to my female relatives,"

he said, still grinning. "They are all expecting me to marry. When I do, I shall probably produce five daughters. And love them too."

"Ah, Farraday," a somewhat languid voice said. "How are you, my good fellow? I have not set eyes on you for a veritable age. This is understandable, of course, since I have been rusticating. I do not believe I have had the pleasure."

Arabella found herself being regarded by a tall gentleman, his handsome face somewhat marred by a cynical twist of the lip. He was fingering a quizzing glass.

"How d'ye do, Hubbard?" Lord Farraday said. "I have been wondering when we would see you again. Ma'am, may I present Mr. Hubbard, another university friend of Astor's and mine? Lady Astor, Hubbard."

Mr. Hubbard sketched an elegant bow and raised one eyebrow. "Astor's bride?" he said. "I did not know he had tied the knot. I am pleased to make your acquaintance, ma'am."

He did not sound remarkably pleased, Arabella thought. She curtsied and smiled. "You are my husband's friend too?" she asked. "I am pleased to meet you, sir. And you have recently come from the country? Is it not lovely at this time of the year? I am truly glad I was there during March to see all the spring flowers. Have you seen his lordship since returning? He is over by the door. I am sure he would be delighted to talk with you."

"I shall stroll that way," he said, turning and walking away without another word.

Arabella looked at Lord Farraday.

"A sad case," he said. "Mrs. Hubbard left him a year ago, taking their son with her. He has not been able to recover from the blow, though he pretends."

"Oh, poor man," Arabella said, turning to look at the retreating figure of Mr. Hubbard. "How could anyone do anything so cruel? Oh, the poor man."

"He will not thank you for saying so," Lord Farraday said.

Lord Astor had been invited to join a table for cards in one of the salons. He would normally not have hesitated, as card playing had been one of his favorite pastimes for years. He had never been in the habit of playing very deep, as until recently he had had no great fortune to lose. And he had discovered since he did that his playing had lost some of its charm. Other men expected him to bet more rashly now that he had the money with which to do so, and yet at the same time he became aware of some of the responsibilities of owning a large fortune and having an equally large number of persons dependent upon him for their very life.

A card salon at a respectable soiree, of course, was not the sort of place in which whole fortunes were likely to change hands. It was not the fear of loss or—worse—the fear of losing all rational common sense that had made him hesitate. Rather, he felt obliged to stay in the drawing room for at least half an hour to make sure that Arabella was well-established and did not need his arm to cling to. She could be such a shy little thing. He had feared for her first appearance in polite society.

"Later," he had told the acquaintance who had asked him to play cards. "I shall play the next hand."

And he watched Arabella, who was glowing with excitement or fright or some emotion that had helped her through the ordeal of being promenaded around the room by Aunt Hermione and was now aiding her in conversing with various guests. Her mouth appeared to be moving almost constantly and at a rapid rate.

He was pleased. If only she could acquire a circle of friends and acquaintances and enough courage to face new people wherever she went, then he would be released from this sense of responsibility for her that had plagued him for three days. He could begin to live his own life again, confident that he was not cruelly neglecting a lonely and cowering wife at home.

The day before had been quite satisfactory, of course, except that he had felt obliged to sit at home all evening, having busied himself about his own pleasures all day. And then he had felt sorry he had done so because Arabella had said hardly a dozen words all evening and he had been left to make himself agreeable to Frances. And despite the early night they had all had, he had not gone to Arabella. He had wanted to, strangely enough, and had even prepared himself to go. He had twice had his hand on the knob of the door that led from his dressing room into hers. But he had not gone. He had tired himself out with Ginny that afternoon, he had told himself.

Today had been somewhat tiresome. He had spent a pleasant-enough morning at Jackson's with a large &°group of friends and had lunched with several of them   at White's. They had tried to persuade him to go to the races with them in the afternoon, but he had promised on pure impulse at breakfast to take Arabella to the Tower to see the royal menagerie. And of course he had been teased. Life sentences and leg shackles had been the main topic of loud conversation and laughter for all of five minutes before he had left White's. And then there had been the obligation to appear at tonight's entertainment. He supposed that he would be there even if he had not married Arabella, but he would by now be comfortable and conscience-free in the card salon.

"Astor!" a voice said as a hand clamped down on his shoulder. "I have not seen you for a veritable age. I had no idea you had taken on a life sentence, old chap. My commiserations."

"How are you, Hubbard?" Lord Astor asked. "Did I see you talking to my wife a moment ago?"

"Farraday presented me," Mr. Hubbard said. "She seems like a fetching little thing, I must confess."

"Thank you," Lord Astor said dryly. "I am a fortunate man, I believe."

"She is young," his friend said, raising his quizzing

glass to his eye and looking through it at Arabella, who was now conversing with two ladies as well as with Lord Farraday. "Straight from the cradle, Astor? Wise of you, old boy. You would do well to train her to obedience before she develops a mind of her own."

Lord Astor looked steadily at his friend and curbed the sharp retort he had been about to utter. "Arabella seems to be doing well enough here," he said. "Shall we play a hand of cards, Hubbard?"

6

LATER that night Lord Astor sat down on the edge of his wife's bed before snuffing the candles.

"You have had a busy day, Arabella," he said. "Did you enjoy the soiree?"

"Yes, I did, my lord," she said. "Your aunt was obliging enough to present me to a large number of interesting people. And Frances too. And a few of them have promised to send us invitations."

"Of course," he said. "You are Lady Astor. You will find yourself much in demand for a wide array of entertainments." He touched her cheek with one knuckle. "You did not like the menagerie, did you?"

She watched him, her eyes guarded. "It was very kind of you to take us, my lord," she said. "You know how much I miss George and Emily and you thought of a way to cheer me up. I am grateful."

"But it was not a good way, as it happened, was it?" he said. "You think it cruel to confine animals so?"

"I am just silly," she said. "You were very kind."

He smiled. "You may express your own feelings and opinions, you know, Arabella," he said. "I will not be offended if you occasionally disagree with me. And on this occasion, I am not even sure that you do. I saw those poor creatures through your eyes this afternoon, and you are quite right."

She looked earnestly up into his eyes. "I had a horrifying mental image of a country where dogs are strange," she said, "and I pictured George in such a country, confined in a little cage so that people could come and stare and marvel. And I could not bear the thought, my lord. I think I will have nightmares."

"George will be here with you soon," he said. "You

said that he was not allowed in the house at Parkland because of your sister? Perhaps we will allow him to inhabit the kitchen area of this house as that mangy little cat does who adopted us off the street about a year ago. Would that please you?"

Her face lit up. "Oh, yes," she said. "How kind you are, my lord."

"My name is Geoffrey," he said.

She flushed. "Yes, my . . . Yes," she said.

"Are you very tired, Arabella?" he asked. "Would you prefer that I said good night and returned to my own rooms?"

Her flush deepened. "If that is what you wish, my lord," she said.

He smiled fleetingly.

"I want to make you comfortable," she said. "It is my duty to make you comfortable."

He touched the backs of his fingers to her hot cheek and rose to remove his dressing gown and snuff the candles.

"Very well," he said. "I shall let you make me comfortable, Arabella."

One week later, Arabella was walking in Hyde Park, her face turned up to the early-morning sun, her mood entirely happy. She had George's leather lead wound around her hand. George himself was running across the grass, snuffling at the roots of trees, trying to find something familiar about this new territory. Arabella had let him run loose once they were safely through the Grosvenor Gate into the park. She herself kept to the footpath, as the grass was still wet from almost a week of rain.

George had arrived the day before while she was out paying afternoon calls with Lady Berry and Frances. Both he and Emily. His lordship had come out into the hallway with George as soon as she arrived home, and George had gone into an ecstasy of jumping and barking and tail-wagging and bottom-wriggling. She had not behaved with much greater dignity, she feared. She had gone down on her knees in full sight of two liveried footmen and hugged him. He had behaved like a perfect gentleman until she came on the scene, his lordship had complained when he could be heard above the din of reunion. But he had not been angry.

Even Frances had been pleased and had totally forgotten to sneeze. Arabella had decided to go out to the stables to welcome Emily before taking off her bonnet and pelisse. His lordship had gone with her after producing a leather lead with which to confine George, a contraption her dog had not liked at all. Arabella would have preferred to go alone, but truth to tell, she had been so happy and so grateful to her husband that she did not feel nearly as shy of him as she usually did.

And now she was out in the park with George, on a beautiful April morning. She could pretend she was in the country if she wished, all was so quiet and smelled so fresh. She felt like running with sheer joy, but she remembered that she was a married lady now and in London and that her husband had warned her against doing anything so improper.

She would heed his warning. Especially when he had been so kind to her. She was still terribly shy of him and still felt quite overshadowed by his splendor. But she had learned during the two weeks of their marriage to respect and even like her husband. He took her and Frances about much more than she had expected. And he had bought her those lovely pearls just the day after she thought perhaps she had displeased him because he had not come to her at night. And flowers the day after she had thought so for the same reason again. And he had taken her to see the menagerie because he had thought it would please her.

Arabella was not feeling nearly so unhappy with her marriage as she had expected when she had first realized the mistake they had made about the identity of the new Lord Astor, though she still wished that she were just a little prettier and he just a little less handsome. She was heartened, though, by the fact that she had definitely lost weight.

He had not hurt her since their wedding night. She had been very relieved to discover that fact on the night of their return to London. She very much wanted to be a good wife. Now she could be so without the danger that she would gasp with pain at an unguarded moment. It was not even unpleasant to perform her main marriage duty, she had found. She always lay still and relaxed for him, and thought about how fortunate she was to have a kind husband. And one who felt good. Yes, she had been surprised to find that, after all, the marriage act was not an unpleasant experience for a wife. At least, for her it was not.

She did not think his lordship could find her a very exciting partner. But she did hope that she made him comfortable. He had teased her about it that one night. After telling her that she might make him comfortable, he had got into her bed beside her and given her the chance to do just that. Then afterward he had rolled to her side on the bed and propped himself up on his elbow.

"Thank you, Arabella," he had said. "You have made me very comfortable indeed." And he had laid one finger lightly along the length of her nose.

Her cheeks had still been burning after he had returned to his own room, and even now she had not decided what the laughter in his voice had meant. Had he been laughing at her? Laughing at the idea that she could do anything to make him feel good? But she did not think so. He was a kind man.

"Why, it *is* Lady Astor!" a voice called cheerfully. "Good morning, ma'am. How do you do?"

Arabella had been aware of two horses approaching at a canter, but she had not looked toward them or their riders. She looked up now to see Lord Farraday and another gentleman whom she did not know. She lifted her hand and smiled gaily.

"Good morning, my lord," she called. "Is it not a

beautiful day? You see? My dog arrived from the country yesterday. His lordship was kind enough to send for him."

"So you told me a few evenings ago at the Pendletons'," Lord Farraday said. "I am glad he has come at last, ma'am. That black-and-white collie? He looks a bundle of energy."

"Will you present me, Clive?" Lord Farraday's companion asked.

Arabella was soon curtsying to Sir John Charlton, a slim, blond, good-looking young man, and feeling uncomfortable. She was glad that they did not stop for a lengthy conversation. She waved them on their way a minute later and called to George to begin the walk home for breakfast. Why could she never relax and be herself when confronted with handsome gentlemen?

Arabella and Frances were attending their first ball at the home of the Marquess of Ravenscourt. It was a come-out ball for his daughter, Lady Harriet Meeker. They had come early with Lady Berry, who had insisted that since they were new to the *ton* it was only right that they make an appearance soon enough to be seen and presented to some eligible persons.

Lady Berry had taken her job as chaperone quite seriously, Arabella thought. Not that she really needed a chaperone, of course, being a married lady. But Lady Berry had pointed out, and his lordship had agreed, that since she was a very young married lady and new to the *ton*, and since she had an unmarried sister with her equally new to society, it would be as well for them to be accompanied by an older lady.

They had been promenaded around the ballroom, greeting several acquaintances made during the previous week and a half, being presented to many people they had not met before. The cards of both began to fill with the names of prospective partners.

Arabella was gratified. His lordship had taken himself off somewhere as soon as they had reached the end

of the receiving line, after telling her that he would
return to lead her into the opening set of country dances
and writing his name in Frances' card for a quadrille
later in the evening. Arabella had expected that her
sister would be much in demand as a partner. A glance
around the ballroom as it began to fill showed her that
there was not another lady to match Frances in beauty.
But she had not expected to dance a great deal herself.
Who would wish to dance with a small, round-faced,
plump girl who was also married?

But Lord Farraday and Sir John Charlton had signed
her card, and then several gentlemen to whom she had
been presented for the first time that evening, and then
Mr. Hubbard, who reminded her that she had talked to
him at Lady Berry's soiree the week before. Not that she
had needed reminding. She had been affected by his sad
story. Indeed, before the orchestra began to make
promising noises that suggested the dancing was about
to begin, Arabella found that her card was full, except
for the spaces next to the two waltzes. She had no idea
how that dance was performed.

"Oh, Bella," Frances said beside her, "is your card
full too? I can scarce believe this is really happening. Is
not Sir John Charlton very handsome? How fortunate it
is that you were presented to him just this morning. Had
you not been, perhaps he would not have liked to seek
out our acquaintance tonight."

"Yes," Arabella said. "He is a little like Theodore in
coloring, is he not?"

"Oh, only slightly. And in coloring only," her sister
said, frowning slightly. "But Theodore is not nearly so
fashionable or so elegant, Bella. I think there is really
very little likeness." She turned to talk to a young lady
beside her with whom she had struck up a friendship in
the past week.

Arabella wished Frances had not reminded her of her
presentation to Sir John Charlton. She did not want to
think about that morning. Or the afternoon, for that
matter.

She had been so happy. There had been the walk with George in the morning, and there was to be a ride on Emily in the afternoon. His lordship was to accompany her into the park. And of course there was this ball—her first—to look forward to in the evening. There had seemed to be not a cloud in her sky. Until she had been summoned into the library after luncheon, that was.

"You took George for a walk in the park this morning, Arabella?" Lord Astor had said. He had been gone from the breakfast room by the time she had returned home.

For once she had forgotten her shyness with him. "Yes," she had said, smiling fully up at him. "It was so lovely, my lord. The grass was wet and glistening in the sunlight, and the sky was blue again. I could imagine myself in the country. You should have been there too."

"I wish I had been, Arabella," he had said, but he had not responded to her smile. "You met Farraday and Sir John Charlton?"

"Did Lord Farraday tell you?" she had asked. "He was obliging enough to stop to talk for a minute, and Sir John asked to be presented to me."

"Farraday should know better than to have put you in such an awkward position," Lord Astor had said.

Arabella's smile had faltered at last. "Is Sir John not a desirable acquaintance?" she had asked.

"I know of nothing against him," he had said. "Why did you not take a maid with you, Arabella?"

She had felt her color rise as she stared back at him. "I was merely going to the park," she had said at last.

"Merely the park," he had said. He had been standing before the fireplace, his hands clasped behind his back, his legs apart. He had looked very large and formidable to Arabella. "Do you not realize that Hyde Park is the gathering place of all the most fashionable people in London, Arabella?"

"It was very early." Her voice had been defensive, her eyes wary.

"It is very improper, Arabella," he had said, "for a

lady to appear in any public place unaccompanied. It is even more improper to converse with two gentlemen, one of them unknown to you, while you are doing so. Did you not know that?''

"Yes," she had said. "I did know, my lord. But I did not realize that it was such a strict rule. The park is so close and the hour was very early."

"I do not know Charlton," Lord Astor had said. "We must hope that he is a man of some discretion. But he asked to be presented, you say? I am disappointed in Farraday. He should have ridden past and pretended not to see you. However, I think he can be trusted not to make anything of the story. The situation is not serious, Arabella. But I will expect you to be more discreet in future. If your sister or I am not available to accompany you where you wish to go, then you must take a maid."

"I have failed you." Arabella's voice had dwindled almost to a whisper.

"That is undoubtedly an exaggeration," he had said, smiling for the first time. "I am merely concerned for your reputation, Arabella. I would not want you to be known as fast when you are not at all so in reality."

"I am sorry, my lord." She had stood mute and miserable before him, feeling the full force of her failure to behave as a well-bred and experienced lady of the *ton* should behave.

He had put a hand beneath her chin and kept it there for a moment. "We will not make a major issue of it," he had said. "You need not look as if you expect me to beat you at any moment, Arabella. Will you be ready to ride in about two hours' time after I have taken care of some business here?"

But the joy had gone out of her day. She had ridden Emily later and mingled with the crowds of riders, strollers, and carriage passengers who had come out to take the air after a week of wet weather. Her husband had been at her side, conversing with her, greeting acquaintances. But she had felt dull and unattractive and inadequate to the life she was expected to lead. She had looked about her with some apprehension, expecting to see everywhere fingers pointing her way, dreading that her indiscretion might have caused a great scandal. And she had felt an unreasonable resentment against the handsome man at her side who had taken her from an environment that was familiar to her and now expected her to behave with perfect decorum in his world.

"Arabella." Lord Astor's hand on hers awoke Arabella from her unhappy reverie. "Shall we join the set?"

She smiled and placed her hand on his sleeve.

"And what is your first impression of your first ball?" he asked as he led her forward.

"That everyone is remarkably civil and even friendly," Arabella replied.

"But of course," he said. "Did you think that the new Lady Astor would be left in a corner unnoticed?"

She thought for a moment as they joined a set and waited for the music to begin. "Yes," she said at last, "I believe I did."

He laughed. "I do not think I have ever known anyone with your modesty," he said. "You look remarkably pretty, Arabella, in your yellow silk."

"Perhaps people have taken notice of me," she said, looking up earnestly into his face, "because I have had Frances standing next to me all the time. She looks very lovely, does she not, my lord? I think she is lovelier than any other lady here. I am not being partial, am I? Do you not agree with me?"

"If any other lady asked me that question, Arabella," Lord Astor said, "I would know quite certainly that she was fishing for a compliment. But you are perfectly serious, are you not? Yes, Frances looks beautiful, and I can see that she will take very well. But for all that, there is one lady I would prefer to look at."

The music began before Arabella could do more than glance up at him with wide, startled eyes. They were soon caught up in the intricate and energetic steps of a country dance.

* * *

Frances had danced with five gentlemen before her brother-in-law came to claim her hand for the quadrille. Two of them were titled. She was flushed with triumph. She had been told for several years, of course, that she was beautiful, and she had come to believe it, though she was not unduly vain. But none of her admirers at home—not even Theodore—had paid her such polished and courtly compliments as the gentlemen with whom she had danced. She had certainly been right to come to London.

Viscount Shenley complimented her on the dancing master she had never had, and Mr. Kershaw complimented himself on having the loveliest lady in the room as a dancing partner.

But Frances was most smitten by her third partner, Sir John Charlton, to whom Bella had had the good fortune to be presented that morning. He looked rather as Theodore would appear if one could remake him to perfection—tall and slim, with thick blond hair and aquiline features. He was impeccably dressed.

"You are Lady Astor's sister?" he asked as they began to dance. "How very fortunate that Lord Astor has recently made her his bride. You might not have come to town else, and I might not have had the honor of making your acquaintance and dancing with you this evening."

Frances blushed. He had a way of looking at her along the length of his nose that was very impressive.

"Bella has been fortunate, sir," she said. "She has married well. But she deserves her good fortune. She is very dear to her family."

"And she is fortunate to have such a loyal and very lovely sister, I am sure," he said.

Frances blushed again. "Thank you, sir," she said.

"Do not thank me, Miss Wilson," he said. "I did not make you lovely."

He did not ever smile, Frances noticed. He looked very distinguished.

"I have only recently arrived in town too," he said. "I have been visiting my elderly uncle, the Earl of Haig. I am his heir, you know. He is fond of me and was unwilling to see me leave. But at this precise moment, I am glad I did." He regarded her steadily.

Frances looked at him, confused, and noted in some disappointment that the set was drawing to an end. But the next was to be danced with her brother-in-law, who was surely the best-looking of all the gentlemen in the ballroom, with the possible exception of Sir John. She could still look at Lord Astor and feel a pang of envy of Bella. But she always loyally quelled the feeling and rejoiced in her younger sister's good fortune.

"Perhaps I might do myself the honor of calling on you one afternoon?" Sir John said as he escorted her from the floor.

Frances smiled at him.

Arabella too was pleased with her partners. Even the first set she had enjoyed. It was, of course, her very first dance at her very first ball. And she danced it with the most handsome gentleman in the room—she had seen several female eyes turn his way. And he was her husband. She forgot about her inadequacy. She was wearing one of her new gowns, and her maid had curled her hair prettily, and she had lost three pounds of weight, she was sure. Best of all, she did not have to converse with his lordship while dancing with him, so did not have to face the ordeal of feeling tongue-tied.

She danced with Lord Farraday and relaxed to his easy manner and humorous stories about his sisters. She laughed when he told her he had lost his mother and grandmother again on Bond Street that morning. And she danced too with Sir John Charlton. That was perhaps the only set she did not fully enjoy. She felt uncomfortable with him. Was it just because he was undeniably good-looking? she asked herself. But she thought not. He was not nearly so handsome as his lordship.

"You have recently married, ma'am?" he asked. "Is it to your marriage that we owe the pleasure of your presence in town?"

"My husband has brought me here, sir," she said. "I go wherever he chooses to go, of course."

"Then I owe Lord Astor a debt of gratitude," he said, "for bringing such a lovely lady to participate in the activities of the Season."

Arabella noted with some misgiving that he did not smile or name Frances. He was looking full at her.

"I am fortunate to be here myself," he said, "since I have just left the house of my aged uncle, the Earl of Haig. I am his heir, you know. He is fond of me and hated to see me leave. But I am very glad now that I did."

"I hope you left him in good health," Arabella said politely.

She was glad when the dance came to an end.

7

LORD Astor had returned Frances to his aunt's side after the quadrille, spent a few minutes talking to a group of acquaintances, and was now standing watching the dancers. He had spent some time in the card room earlier, but he had not played. He had stood and watched. And he had wandered back into the ballroom and not danced, except the first set with his wife and the previous one with his sister-in-law. He was bored.

No, not bored exactly. Restless. He was not particularly enjoying his marriage. It was not nearly what he had expected. He had planned it with great nonchalance, expecting that once the business of the wedding and settling his wife in his home was done, he would be able to carry on with his life as it had been for the previous six years. The only difference would be that there would be a wife to dine with occasionally and bed at night, and children in his nursery eventually.

His marriage was not developing at all like that. He watched Arabella gloomily as she danced the steps of the Roger de Coverley with a gangly youth who looked as if he had never seen a dancing master in his life. Arabella was smiling dazzlingly up into his long, pale face, and succeeding in dancing gracefully despite his clumsiness.

She appeared to be doing well enough at the ball. Indeed, when he had asked her at the end of the opening set to write his name in her card next to the supper dance, she had told him first that that dance was taken, and then that there were no dances left for him to have. Except the waltzes that she was unable to do, of course.

It had been the perfect excuse for him. He should
have been able to take hmself off to the card room and
become involved in playing for the rest of the evening.
He should have been able to enjoy himself without
either a concern for his wife or a thought to his married
state for several blissful hours.

But he had found himself unable to do so. What if
one of her partners failed to claim his dance? She would
be left partnerless, feeling like a wallflower at her first
ball. He could not allow such a thing to happen to Arabella. And what if there were some gossip about her indiscretion of the morning? He must be there to turn it
off carelessly, mentioning the fact that her ladyship had
sent her maid home ahead of her from the park for
some reason.

It was quite absurd, of course. Not only was Arabella
clearly enjoying herself, but she was also well-supplied
with company. When he had returned her sister to Aunt
Hermione a few minutes before, Arabella had been
there too, but she had been deep in animated conversation with a group of two ladies and three gentlemen,
two of them men he did not know himself. He only
hoped that she had been properly presented to them. He
was pleasantly surprised by the ease with which she
seemed to fit into the society around her.

Really, Lord Astor thought, looking critically at his
wife as she continued to smile and talk to the gangly
youth, she did look good. His compliment to her earlier
had been largely designed to set her at her ease, but
there was truth in it too. If he were seeing her for the
first time tonight, he might even call her pretty. The
simple design and pale shade of her yellow silk gown
showed off the pleasing feminine curves of her tiny
body. Her short hair became her and looked pretty with
yellow ribbon threaded through the curls. He had dis-
suaded her from buying plumes, which she had thought
would give her some needed height and which even his
aunt had thought would make her look more dis-

tinguished. Although the majority of ladies at the ball
wore them, they would have looked ludicrous on Arabella.

Lord Astor caught the eye of an elderly matron who
sat nearby with another lady of his acquaintance. He
inclined his head and strolled over to exchange civilities
with them. A few minutes passed before he turned away
again, his ears having been assailed with congratulations
on his recent marriage and compliments on the looks
and vivacity of his wife.

It was not just this evening that he was having difficulty forgetting his marriage and his responsibilities,
he thought, singling out Arabella from the dancing
throngs again. It seemed to happen constantly. He
could enjoy his clubs, his visits to Tattersall's, the occasional attendance at the races, his frequent mornings at
Jackson's. But he found himself often hesitating over
joining his friends at any activity that would keep him
from home for any long period of time. There had been
the boxing mill, for example, that would have taken him
from home for one night. There was no reason
whatsoever why he should not have gone, since Arabella
had her sister for company, and anyway, the two of
them had been invited to join a theater party that
evening that did not include him. But he had not gone.

He was annoyed with himself. Worst of all was the
fact that he was beginning not to enjoy his afternoons
with Ginny as much as he had used to do. He had been
remarkably contented with her for a year, although
there had been other females too on occasion, and he
was certainly the envy of many men of his acquaintance.
She was beautiful and very desirable to the eye, in
addition to being a cut above the average kept mistress.
Ginny was a singer much in demand at private parties.

He tried to put his wife from his mind whenever he
crossed the threshold of Ginny's lavish establishment,
which he had provided for her. Certainly he needed her.
No robust male could be expected to satisfy his appetites
with the restrained and respectable beddings that were

all he would allow himself with his wife. And Ginny was enough to make any man forget even his own name when she was aroused to passion—a state that was not difficult to induce in her.

Why was it, then, that the last time he had been with her he had caught himself at the most energetic and usually most mindless moment of his performance wondering if Arabella were as attached to the scuffed leather saddle she used as she was to the horse beneath it, or if she would like a new one. And after his second effort with Ginny, in which he had succeeded a little better in blanking his mind to his wife, he had lain awake when he had wanted to sleep, picturing in his mind that upward-curving lip of Arabella's and the white, even teeth beneath it, and wondering idly if there would be any pleasure in kissing her mouth. He had never done so.

The set was ending. Both Lord Astor and his wife seemed to be surprised when the gangly youth escorted her to him rather than to Lady Berry and Frances, who were a little way off.

Lord Astor clasped his hands behind him. "You dance very well, Arabella," he said. "Are you enjoying yourself?"

"Thank you, my lord," she said. "Yes, I am. I expected that everyone here would be very grand and would dance divinely. But really, some people are quite ordinary. Poor Mr. Browning was very apologetic when he led me into the last set. In fact, he suggested that we sit out because he claims to have two left feet. But that is silly, as I told him. In a room that is so crowded, no one is going to single him out to notice that he does not dance quite as well as some of the other gentlemen. And he did not once step on my feet as he was afraid of doing. And I am no expert myself, as I was willing to tell him."

Lord Astor was amused. He enjoyed his wife's occasional bursts of speech in his presence. She was usually so quiet with him. He waited for the now-familiar blush and return to silence.

"The next set is a waltz," he said. "Would you care to stroll with me out on the balcony, Arabella?"

"Oh," she said, her head to one side. "I have promised to sit with Mr. Lincoln because he cannot dance at all. There is something wrong with his leg, though I do not know what. He limps."

"He had an illness as a child," Lord Astor said. "It has left him permanently lame."

"Poor man," she said. "Though he seems quite cheerful. With some people a handicap is not a thing to be pitied, is it? Some people rise above it. But I am sorry, my lord, about the walk. Do you mind?"

"Not at all," he said with a bow. "I was merely concerned that you not be alone during the waltz. Frances, I see, is in company with several other young ladies who are not yet allowed to waltz."

Arabella's face brightened as she looked at her sister. "Frances is a great success, is she not?" she said. "But then, I knew she would be. She is so lovely. She has always been the beauty of the family, you know. I am very proud of her. You must wish . . ." She smiled quickly up at him, and the expected blush and look of confusion came at last.

"I wish you had learned to waltz or that I had known earlier and could have taught you," he said, "so that I might take you away from Mr. Lincoln, Arabella." He took her gloved hand and laid it on the brocaded sleeve of his evening coat. "Do you see him? I shall take you to him."

Arabella was trying to write a letter to her mother before Frances joined her in the morning room the next day. It was not easy to do when there was all the excitement of the previous evening to convey in writing. She had enjoyed herself enormously and really had not had a spare moment in which to dwell upon the fact that she must look very much plainer and plumper and more childish than all the other ladies. She had danced every set she was able, and had had company for each of the waltzes. Lady Berry had even presented her to Lady Jersey, one of the patronesses of Almack's, and that lady had condescended to incline her head to her and congratulate her on her recent marriage to Lord Astor.

How was she to write it all down on paper, so that Mama and Jemima might almost see the ballroom and all the splendor of its occupants? How would she convey all the triumph she and Frances had felt at being so noticed by ladies and gentlemen alike? How could she describe just how very beautiful Frances had looked?

When the subject of her thoughts entered the room, Arabella put her quill pen down with care and gave up even the attempt to write. Frances had agreed the day before that they would both write to Mama this morning, but she had that dreamy look in her eyes that Arabella knew of old. There would be no writing for either of them for a while.

"How can you possibly be up early every morning even after such a late night, Bella?" Frances asked, yawning delicately behind her hand.

"I cannot waste the best part of the day," Arabella said. "I had to take George for a walk." She flushed. "His lordship came with me this morning."

"Dear Bella." Frances' eyes had their familiar brightness, a look that was usually a prelude to tears. "I never fail to marvel and to thank heaven for your sake that his lordship turned out to be the son of the man we expected. He is very attentive, is he not? I am so pleased for you. I cannot think of anyone who deserves happiness more than you. I shall never forget the sacrifice you made for me."

"Well, it turned out to be no sacrifice after all, did it not?" Arabella said briskly, noting that Frances was pulling a handkerchief out of her pocket. She recalled the discomfort she had felt earlier that morning, knowing that his lordship had accompanied her to the park only to give her respectability when he would doubtless have preferred to be at the breakfast table with his daily paper. And he had called George bad-mannered and had insisted on taking the lead in his own hand just because the poor dog could not get to the park fast enough and was threatening to pull her arm from its socket.

"You were a great success last night," she said in an attempt to divert Frances' mind from its sad contemplation of the sacrifice. "I declare, if there had been twice as many sets as there were, there would still have been gentlemen clamoring to dance with you."

Frances dabbed at her eyes and put her handkerchief away. "I do think it tiresome that I cannot waltz, though, Bella," she said. "I am twenty years old, after all."

"Lady Berry has promised to try to get us vouchers for Almack's," Arabella said. "And I was presented to Lady Jersey last night. Perhaps soon you will be granted permission. Until then you may not waltz, so there is no point in lamenting the fact. His lordship has said that in the meantime he will teach us both the steps."

Frances sighed. "You are fortunate in being married to one of the handsomest gentlemen of the *ton*, Bella," she said. "I thought there would be many more in town, but really the gentlemen here are not a great deal handsomer than those at home, are they?"

Arabella laughed. "And glad I am of it," she said. "I should positively quail if everyone was as splendid as his lordship."

"Sir John Charlton is very handsome," Frances said. "Did you know he is heir to the Earl of Haig, Bella? His uncle. And the earl is elderly. Sir John said he would call on me this afternoon. We do not have any plans for being from home, do we?"

"No," Arabella said with a frown. "Do you like Sir John, Frances? I danced with him too. He is very good-looking, indeed. But do you not think he knows it rather too well?"

"If he does, he has good reason to be somewhat

vain," her sister said. "He is so very fashionable, Bella. He quite puts most other gentlemen in the shade."

Including Theodore, Arabella thought rather sadly. If it were not for Theodore, she might not have been so eager to take upon herself the task of wedding Lord Astor. And she might now be comfortably at home with Mama and Jemima while Frances had all the responsibility of making his lordship comfortable. Not that Frances would have to make any effort to do so, of course. He would doubtless be blissfully happy with Frances as his bride.

The thought was thoroughly depressing. And surprisingly, the thought that she might be at home comfortably free of the necessity of being Lord Astor's wife brought with it no longing. Only a strange and quite unexpected gratitude to a providence that had kept from her family an essential truth that might have changed the whole course of her life.

Arabella did not pause to explore the feeling. "Will you write to Mama or to Jemima?" she asked. "We really should try to be finished before luncheon, Frances. I let several people last night know what we would be at home this afternoon. Perhaps we will have visitors."

But her hopes of letter-writing were dashed when a footman opened the door and the butler bowed himself into the room behind an enormous bouquet that had arrived for Frances from one of her dancing partners of the evening before.

Frances shrieked and Arabella proceeded to clean her pen.

The day after the ball, Lord Astor arrived home in the middle of the afternoon to find his drawing room almost crowded with visitors. He was not surprised to find his aunt there. She had quite adopted his wife and his sister-in-law and rarely allowed a day to pass without calling on them or inviting them to join her in some

diversion. It was to be expected too that several of
Frances' lady friends should call, most of them with
their mothers. And Sir John Charlton had been clearly
taken with Frances the night before and had under-
standably called this afternoon, bringing Farraday with
him.

What was perhaps somewhat more surprising was
that Hubbard was there, and the gangly youth who
could not dance. Lord Astor had not noticed the night
before that either had shown a marked preference for
Frances. And indeed, both seemed quite satisfied to be
in conversation with Arabella. He could see at a glance,
before she saw him, that she was talking to them with
great animation.

He bowed to a group of ladies seated with his aunt,
and resigned himself to a few minutes of conversation
with them. He had come home to take Arabella into the
park in his curricle. He would take a different carriage if
his sister-in-law did not have anything to do and needed
to be included in the invitation, but he had suspected
that someone would turn up to take her driving or
walking.

It was a beautiful afternoon, far too fine to be
indoors. He had originally planned to spend a few hours
with Ginny, but the thought of being confined for the
afternoon inside her cozy, perfumed boudoir did not
hold out its usual lure. He would visit her some other
day, when it was raining perhaps, or when Arabella was
otherwise engaged.

Lord Astor settled rather impatiently to outwait the
visitors. He caught his wife's eye after a couple of
minutes and smiled. She returned his smile, blushed,
and faltered in her conversation. He turned his attention
back to what Mrs. Soames was saying, quelling a twinge
of annoyance. What was it about him that Arabella
shied away from? He had never been unkind to her.
Why could she not talk to him except when she
appeared to forget who he was? She seemed always able

to talk to other people. Yet he was her husband. Did she find him uninteresting?

Arabella was busily assuring Mr. Browning that even if his tailor was not Weston, his coat looked remarkably dashing. After all, she said quite reasonably, if all gentlemen patronized only Weston, how would other tailors make a living? And sometimes one man could gain a reputation undeservedly. Other, unknown tailors might be quite as excellent as the famous man himself.

Mr. Browning looked somewhat reassured as Arabella smiled and nodded at him.

"I do not go to Weston myself," Mr. Hubbard said, "ever since he looked down his nose at me as if I were a worm when I offered to pay a bill on delivery of a waistcoat. A true gentleman will leave his bill unpaid for at least half a year, it seems, and then pay only in part."

"Well, how very ridiculous," Arabella said. "I do not blame you for refusing to encourage such nonsense, sir. So you see, Mr. Browning, you must not always fear that you are unfashionable. You must remember that Mr. Hubbard has a different tailor, and no one would say that he is unfashionable, would they?"

Mr. Browning looked even more cheered. Mr. Hubbard's cynical mouth quirked into a smile for a brief moment as he looked at Arabella's bright expression.

"May I take this seat, ma'am?" Lord Farraday asked, indicating an empty one beside Arabella. "I was walking all morning—on Bond Street again. I cannot think what keeps those ladies of mine so busy at the shops. After admiring a fan in one, they can walk the length of the street admiring a dozen others, and then decide to return for the first one, only to discover when they get there that it is not nearly as pretty as they had thought." He grinned.

"Please do sit down," Arabella said. "We simply must find out from you if you patronize Weston, my lord. If you do not, I believe we have won our point, for your coat looks remarkably fashionable.''

''It takes two footmen and his valet to pour him into it,'' Mr. Hubbard said languidly.

They all laughed, and Arabella caught her husband's eye again across the room.

The guests began to drift away eventually, and finally even Lady Berry took her leave, after promising to call with her carriage the next morning to take her two charges to the library to exchange their books.

Frances was starry-eyed. ''Sir John Charlton is to return later with his phaeton to take me driving in the park,'' she said. ''Which of my new bonnets should I wear, Bella? The blue, do you think? My lord, are you quite sure that the blue parasol I brought with me to town is quite fashionable enough for Hyde Park?''

Lord Astor turned to his wife with a smile when Frances' anxieties were finally allayed. ''Would you like to put on one of your new bonnets while I have the curricle brought around, Arabella?'' he asked.

She flushed. ''Oh, I am sorry, my lord,'' she said. ''I have just told Mr. Browning that I will drive with him.''

He inclined his head. ''I hope for your sake that Mr. Browning can drive rather better than he dances,'' he said.

''Oh, I am sure he can, my lord,'' Arabella said, her expression serious. ''He did not have the advantage of a dancing master, you see, because his grandfather raised him and would never send him away to school or allow him to associate with other children of his own age. But I am sure that he learned to ride and handle a conveyance.''

''Well,'' Lord Astor said, ''you had better go and get ready, then.''

''It is all right?'' she asked, looking anxiously up at him. ''Aunt Hermione has assured me that it is quite unexceptional for a married lady to be accompanied by a single gentleman in a public place. She even said that a lady will be considered positively rustic if she does not cultivate male acquaintances and that her husband will find her tiresome if she relies on him always to escort her everywhere. You are not angry, my lord?''

"Of course I am not angry, Arabella," he said. "Run along now. Perhaps I shall take you and your sister to the theater again tonight. There is to be a different play."

"Oh." Her face looked stricken. Her fingertips covered her mouth. "Mrs. Harris has invited Frances and me to accompany her and Adelaide—her daughter and Frances' friend, you know—to Mrs. Sheldon's literary salon. The conversation there is very superior, she says, though it sounds to me as if it might be tedious. I would far prefer the theater, my lord, but I cannot go back on my word now, can I?"

"Of course you cannot," Lord Astor said with a somewhat stiff bow. "I am pleased that you are so well-occupied, Arabella. If you are sure that you have plenty of diversions for the rest of today, I shall keep a dinner engagement that I was prepared to break."

"By all means, my lord," she said, brightening. "Please do not let me be the cause of your breaking your promise."

Less than an hour later, Lord Astor was on his way to his mistress's house, congratulating himself on having a part of the afternoon and all of the evening in which to relax and enjoy her company. And he would not even have to feel the guilt of wondering if Arabella was at home, bored and unoccupied. He did not drive through the park, although doing so would have taken him just as quickly and by a far more scenic route to his destination. Somehow he had forgotten that the sky was blue, the sun warm, and the trees and grass and flowers dressed out in all their spring freshness.

8

ARABELLA was seated at her escritoire in the morning room, trying yet again to write the letter to her mother that had not been written the day before. If only there were not so much to think about, she felt, the task would be very much easier. She had succeeded in describing the Marquess of Ravenscourt's ball, but there was so much more to write about. Poor Mama and Jemima had never had the chance to know what life was like in town—Papa had never been willing to make the journey even when he and Mama were younger.

But truth to tell, Arabella could not concentrate on bringing alive the splendors of the Season because she was beset by so many conflicting feelings that had no place in her letter at all. She was excited, depressed, contented, and unhappy all at the same time, and it was difficult to sort out her emotions and know what the exact state of her life was. In retrospect, life at Parkland seemed a time of incredible peace and placidity.

She had been happy in the last few days to find that after all she was being accepted by the *ton*. She had been somewhat afraid that she would be rejected as someone far too young and uninteresting to mingle on terms of equality with members of society. She had been convinced that people would consider her something of an impostor in her role as Lady Astor.

But it was not so. She was receiving numerous invitations, and several of them were for her alone and did not even include her husband. She knew that he had other interests. And Lady Berry had told her that husbands did not like to feel obliged to spend a great deal of their time with their wives. Lord Berry himself was living proof of that. And so she was pleased to find that she could live a life of her own and release her husband from any sense of duty that might keep him at her side. After feeling some guilt at having to reject two of his invitations the day before, it had been a relief to know that after all he had asked her only out of politeness. He had had a dinner invitation that he wished to keep.

A relief, yes. But also a little depressing. In the long-ago days of her youth she had thought of marriage as a companionship. She had pictured herself with a husband who never left her side and one with whom she could share a deep and personal friendship. That was long before her agreeing to marry Lord Astor, of course. Even so, it was depressing to know that marriage was nothing like that at all. At least the marriages she had seen in the past few weeks were not. And hers was not. Lord Astor was kind. He always made sure that she was fully occupied and properly clothed. He had bought her gifts. But for all that, there was no closeness between them. And how could there be when she was so inferior to him in every way? She continued to lose weight, but the loss of a few pounds would not transform her into a beauty.

Her problem, Arabella decided, trimming her pen and preparing to write to her mother about her drive in the park the afternoon before, was that she was not always willing to accept reality. And she was very perverse. She had always felt decidedly uncomfortable in the presence of his lordship because his splendor was a continual reminder of her own plainness. The present turn of events, then, should thoroughly satisfy her. It seemed they were about to lead their own fairly separate and busy lives. There was no reason whatsoever why the idea should depress her.

She had found poor Mr. Browning, with his dreadful lack of confidence in himself, very easy to talk with during the drive in the park, and she had not given one thought to her own lack of beauty while she was with him. So there was no reason why she should have

wished she was with her husband, torturing her mind
for ideas of what to say to him. And at the literary salon
the evening before, she had had a long and comfortable
conversation with Lord Farraday and avoided having to
listen to the languishing poet who tried so hard to look
as gloomy and romantic as Lord Byron was reputed
to be. Why should she have wished her husband was
there?

And he had not come to her the night before. He was
not at home when she and Frances returned—she had
asked the footman who admitted them. She had lain
awake for a long time expecting him, wondering if he
stayed away because he thought she was asleep,
wondering if perhaps he had not come home at all. She
had missed him. She had become accustomed to his
visits. She liked them.

She must finish her letter before Frances came downstairs, Arabella thought, bending determinedly over it
again. Once Frances came, there would be no more
writing. Her sister would be either too excited or too
unhappy about the news that was awaiting her. Either
way, there were bound to be tears.

His lordship had accompanied her again that morning
when she took George for a walk. When she had
suggested that she would take a maid if he preferred to
read his paper, he had assured her that he would enjoy
the exercise. She had let him put the lead on George and
take him along the street to the park. And indeed it did
seem as if her pet behaved himself better with his
lordship, as she had admitted to him when she knelt on
the path inside the gate and detached the leather strap so
that George could run free.

They had not talked a great deal, but she had enjoyed
their stroll nevertheless. He had chosen quite freely to
come. She must not feel guilty at taking him away from
his breakfast.

"Did you enjoy your evening, Arabella?" he had
asked.

"Oh, yes," she had said. "Everyone sat and talked, my lord. There was no music and no dancing. And no cards either. There was a poet there whose latest volume recently created a stir, though I cannot recall his name at present or the name of the book. Frances found his poems quite affecting, but I must confess that I did not hear them. I talked with Lord Farraday."

"Did you indeed?" he had said.

"Yes." She had been smiling, watching George snuffling around the trees that were becoming familiar to him. "He told me many stories about university and the scrapes you and he and Mr. Hubbard got into. I have never laughed so hard in my life. It is amazing you never got into deep trouble, my lord."

"I am glad you enjoyed yourself," Lord Astor had said. "Would you care to take my arm, Arabella?"

She had done so and been reminded of her very inferior stature. "Did you enjoy yourself?" she had asked.

"I beg your pardon?" He had looked blankly down at her. "Oh, at my dinner? Yes, thank you, Arabella, well enough."

They had said very little else. When they had arrived home, she had gone down to the kitchen herself to restore George to his new quarters rather than send him with a footman and hear him whine every step of the way. His lordship had handed her a letter when she returned to the breakfast room. He had been smiling. He knew how much she loved to receive news from home.

The letter had contained little beyond the ordinary, though she had devoured its contents with great eagerness. But there had been one thing, and when she had looked up flushed and eager, it was to discover that his lordship was sitting quietly watching her.

"What is it, Arabella?" he had asked, amusement in his voice. "Good news?"

"Theodore is coming," she had said. "Sir Theodore

Perrot, that is. He is coming to town, Mama writes. How splendid!"

"I met him," Lord Astor had said. "He is the fair-haired and rather broad one?"

"Yes," she had said, staring down at her letter, picturing Theodore coming to sweep Frances off her feet again. Dear, dependable Theodore, who would show Frances at a glance that he was twice the man Sir John Charlton was, or any of her other admirers. "Dear Theodore."

Lord Astor's eyebrows had risen. "And when may we expect his arrival?" he had asked.

"I think any day," Arabella had said, clutching the letter to her bosom and looking across at her husband, stars in her eyes. "We may invite him here for dinner the day he appears? And we will take him to the theater with us and introduce him to our acquaintances and make sure he is invited everywhere? Please, my lord."

He had lifted his cup of coffee and swallowed a mouthful before answering. "It will be as you wish, Arabella," he had said.

But her reaction had been calm in comparison with what Frances' would be, Arabella reflected now, realizing that she had written only a sentence since she had last bent her head over her paper. She blanked all thoughts, exciting and depressing, from her mind, dipped her pen in the inkwell, and wrote.

Frances' reaction to the news an hour later was not quite what Arabella had hoped.

"Theodore is coming?" she said blankly when Arabella ran forward, hugged her tight, and blurted out the news. "Here, Bella? But why now?"

"Perhaps to enjoy the Season, you goose," Arabella said. "Perhaps to see you."

"I do not see why he must come so soon," Frances said. "We have been here only two weeks, Bella. And Theodore and I are not betrothed."

"I thought you loved him," Arabella said bleakly.

Frances' eyes filled with tears. "And so I do," she

said. "But I have never had a chance to meet other gentlemen, Bella. Am I to have no chance to make a more eligible match? You have his lordship, and Melinda Sawyer says that all her friends consider you the most fortunate of ladies. Theodore is . . . well, he is just Theodore. I am fond of him. Oh, of course I am fond of him. But . . . Oh, I do not know what I think."

"Perhaps when you see him again you will be more sure of your feelings," Arabella said hopefully.

"Oh, I do look forward to seeing him," her sister said, drawing a handkerchief from her pocket. "Dear Theo. He is so faithful, Bella. How horrid and ungrateful of me to feel that I did not wish him to come."

She hid her face behind the lace handkerchief and sank into the nearest chair.

A note was delivered to the house on Upper Grosvenor Street two mornings later asking if Sir Theodore Perrot might do himself the honor of calling on Lord Astor before luncheon. Arabella, who was in the breakfast room with her husband at the time, exacted a promise from him that he would bring Theodore up to her sitting room before he left, and flew from the room in high good spirits.

Lord Astor awaited his guest in his downstairs office. While he waited, he tried to make sense of certain estate documents sent him by his bailiff at Parkland. He was determined to understand and become familiar with the workings of his property, perhaps even to spend part of the summer months there.

He had been puzzled and made a little uneasy by Arabella's enthusiastic reaction to the news that Perrot was on his way to London. He recalled the man as a friend of his wife's family, someone he had characterized as a quiet, solid, dependable citizen. Although there had been no open sign of affection, he had drawn the conclusion for some reason that there

was an attachment of sorts between the man and
Frances.

And it seemed a reasonable assumption. She was the
eldest daughter and the loveliest. He seemed to recall,
though he could not be sure of the fact, that Arabella
had told him at the time of their betrothal that her older
sister was to marry someone else. There seemed to be no
one else in the neighborhood with whom she was more
likely to have an understanding. It was a natural
assumption that if Perrot did have an attachment to
Frances, he would follow her to London and pay his
respects at the home where she was staying.

Arabella's reaction to her mother's letter was not in
any way inconsistent with that interpretation of facts.
She was delighted, naturally, for her sister's sake. And
she was delighted at the prospect of seeing a familiar
face.

Lord Astor did not even know why he felt any unease
at all. If Arabella felt any romantic attachment to
Perrot, she would have hidden her delight, would she
not? Or more likely she would not even have felt delight
but dismay at having to face such a real reminder of her
loss. And if the man felt any *tendre* for her, he would
surely not pursue her to town after her marriage and
present himself at her husband's home.

He was quite foolish even to think such thoughts,
Lord Astor had told himself more than once in the two
days since the letter had arrived. And it was equally
foolish to wonder what she had found to talk about for
a whole evening with Farraday. Or why she had looked
so glowing the day before when she had come home
from a ride with the lame Lincoln. Or why she had
agreed to drive in the park with the gangly youth a day
or so before that—he never could think of the boy's
name.

And yet she never seemed particularly to enjoy his
company.

And why should he care anyway? Lord Astor asked
himself in some puzzlement. Arabella was no beauty, no

great prize. He had married her purely for convenience. Indeed, he had not even chosen her himself. Their marriage had brought him neither close companionship nor great sensual bliss. It had brought nothing more than worries and responsibilities, in fact. He should be glad if she did attach herself to other men, provided that she was discreet and aroused no gossip or scandal, of course.

Yet, strangely, he had to admit, he wanted Arabella to like him. And he was not at all sure that she did. She never deliberately avoided him. She always spoke to him if he initiated a conversation; she always took his arm when invited to do so; she always accompanied him where he wished to take her, provided she had no previous engagement. But those facts proved only that she was an obedient wife. She had said from the start that she would be so.

She never shirked her duty in bed. She never feigned sleep, though occasionally he had gone late to her and approached her bed quietly, ready to leave if she were not awake. But always she opened her eyes and smiled up at him. And he could not understand his own enjoyment of those brief and dispassionate encounters with his wife. She offered herself to him only with a quiet and uncomplaining compliance with his will. He did not know how she felt about receiving him, except that on that one occasion when he had offered to leave if she were very tired, she had told him that she wished to make him comfortable.

He had begun to be a little unfair to her perhaps. He had begun to prolong his encounters with her so that he might feel her warm little body beneath his own for more minutes than was necessary. Yet she held herself open to him and made no protest and gave no sign that she knew what he was about.

It made no sense when he had Ginny with whom to do whatever the passions of his body urged him to do. And Ginny was beautiful and voluptuously formed.

Lord Astor pushed the unread documents to the side

of his desk and got restlessly to his feet at almost the
same moment as his butler knocked on the door and
opened it to announce the arrival of Sir Theodore
Perrot.

He was as Lord Astor remembered him: not any taller
than himself, but solid in build and upright in bearing;
his very fair hair already thinning, though he could not
be past his mid-twenties; his complexion florid; his eyes
steady and gray. He thanked the viscount for receiving
him, asked after the health of Lady Astor and Miss
Wilson, and requested permission to wait upon them
when convenient.

Lord Astor took him immediately to his wife's sitting
room, where he found both her and Frances sewing.
They both rose when he entered and ushered in his
visitor.

Arabella swept toward them, her hands extended in
greeting, her face lit up with a smile. "Theodore!" she
cried. She stopped when her hands were in his, the
length of her arms between them. Lord Astor had
thought that she was going to rush straight into his
arms. "How perfectly splendid to see you. It has been
an age. Where are you staying? Are you quite comfortable there? You must come to dinner tonight. You
will come? And here is Frances, and I have been
prattling and stopping you from speaking with her."

He squeezed her hands, his stiffness of manner
noticeably relaxing. "Hello, puss," he said with a
chuckle. "Do you still talk as much as ever? Hello,
Frances." He turned from Arabella and held out a hand
to her demure sister.

Frances curtsied but did not seem to notice his outstretched hand. "How do you do, Theodore?" she said.
"I trust you had a pleasant journey from home."

Arabella linked an arm through his and drew him
across the room to sit beside her on a love seat. "We
have been waiting with the greatest impatience," she
said, "have we not, Frances? We thought you would
never come after you had sent that note to his lordship

two days ago, and this morning has been interminable. You have not answered any of my questions yet. And I have a thousand more. Do you not think that Frances and I look very grand in our new frocks? They are quite up to the minute, I do assure you. Though, of course, I am the one to benefit more. Frances always looks perfect whatever she wears. I have had my hair shorn. Do you like it? Did you know that his lordship sent for George and Emily for me? George lives in the kitchen, and I swear he will get fat if Cook does not stop feeding him so many scraps. I scolded her for it just this morning.''

It was as he had guessed, Lord Astor thought as he stood silently close to the door, his hands clasped behind his back. Frances was very conscious of the new arrival, even though she had scarcely looked up at him and had spoken hardly a word. And Sir Theodore was looking at her quite as much as he looked at Arabella, despite the fact that he dealt with her prattle and answered her with the greatest good humor.

And Arabella was excited merely because she had grown up with this man as a neighbor and friend and was very familiar with him. She had no *tendre* for him.

Lord Astor's eyes came to rest on his wife's hand, which was patting the sleeve of Sir Theodore Perrot's coat. He looked up at her eager expression and her sparkling eyes, which were directed wholly at the visitor.

No, there was nothing flirtatious in her manner. But it was perfectly clear that she liked this man very well indeed and felt thoroughly easy in his presence.

He could not expect that she would be as easy and as friendly with him yet. They had been acquainted for only a month before their marriage, and they had been wed for less than three weeks. It would take time to win her friendship and trust. In time perhaps she would look at him as she was looking now at their guest, and talk to him like that without suddenly breaking off with blushing cheeks and downcast eyes.

But did it matter anyway? She was only Arabella. He

would not have afforded her a second glance if he had not been honor-bound to marry her. He strolled farther into his wife's sitting room.

"Arabella has not given you a chance to accept our invitation to dinner, Perrot," he said. "Will you come? I am hoping that the ladies will be free to go to the theater tonight. Perhaps you would care to join us too?"

"Oh, will you, Theodore?" Arabella asked, looking up into his face anxiously. "Do say yes. Frances, tell Theodore that he must say yes."

Arabella felt very proud that evening to be seated in her husband's box at the theater with her sister and two of the most handsome gentlemen of her acquaintance. Theodore and his lordship had conversed with each other with great ease at the dinner table, as if they had been friends all their lives, and Frances had looked her loveliest in green. Arabella had not contributed much to the conversation, but she had felt unusually relaxed.

And now she sat next to her husband, their shoulders almost touching, a warm feeling of pleasure and anticipation lifting her spirits.

"Have you seen the exquisite down below, Arabella?" he asked, leaning toward her so that her shoulder was against his arm.

"Which one?" she asked. "I do not like looking down there, my lord, for I find those gentlemen very rude. Several of them watch all the boxes through their quizzing glasses."

"But you simply must look at the one all in lavender," Lord Astor said. "Even his hair and his stockings, Arabella."

She looked down into the pit and saw immediately the gentleman referred to. "Oh, the poor gentleman!" she said. "His mother must not have loved him, my lord, that he has to draw attention to himself so."

Lord Astor threw back his head and roared with laughter. "Arabella," he said, "if we were watching a

murderer being hanged at Tyburn, you would probably
call him a poor man and find some excuse for his
behavior.''

"And so I should," she said. "People's troubles are
not a laughing matter, you know.''

He continued to laugh, though rather more gently.
He took her hand in his and laid it on his sleeve. "Ah,
the play is about to begin," he said.

Arabella was somewhat offended, assuming that he
was laughing at her childish notions. How very naive
and countrified her ideas must appear to him. She sat
quietly through the first act of the play, enjoying the
farce, but very aware of his sleeve and muscled arm
beneath her hand. He might laugh at her as much as he
wished, but she was not going to allow her evening to be
spoiled. For once she was feeling happy to be with her
husband, proud to be seen with him, contented to sit
quietly at his side, feeling his closeness.

In fact, Arabella was beginning to realize that she was
growing to like her husband and growing to believe that
at least he did not hate her or have any violent aversion
to her person. He could not admire her greatly, of
course, but he did not avoid her.

Her greatest wish was that he should grow to like her.
She would be happy if he liked her. She was not
positively ugly. Her short curls and the fashionable
clothes she now wore were becoming, and her face was
beginning to lose some of its childish roundness now
that she had shed a few pounds. And other people
accepted her as an equal. Surely if she could make an
effort to overcome her shyness and talk to her husband
more often, she could persuade him to like her.

"The play is very humorous, is it not, my lord?" she
asked, turning and smiling politely at her husband.
"And the acting is quite accomplished.''

"Mm," he said, patting her hand lightly and keeping
his eyes on the stage. He laughed at something one of
the actors said.

"I think it must be very difficult to act convincingly,''

Arabella said, "and to remember all of one's lines."

Lord Astor, Frances, Theodore, and indeed the entire audience with the exception of Arabella burst into loud laughter. Arabella bit her lip.

When the interval came, she was delighted at the arrival of Lord Farraday at their box, even though he brought with him Sir John Charlton. Theodore, with his solid, dependable strength, showed up to great advantage in contrast to the latter gentleman, she thought, and Frances must surely see it. Arabella was relieved when Lord Farraday began talking to Lord Astor. Her attempts at conversation with her husband had been somewhat labored.

Mr. Browning arrived to pay his respects, and she beamed and chattered happily with him for all of ten minutes.

She turned with flushed face and glowing eyes back to her husband at the end of the ten minutes. She was glad that friends she liked had come to talk with them. But how lovely it was to know that when they left, his lordship remained at her side for the rest of the evening. She was very glad he was her husband, for all her shyness with him.

Lord Astor sat with his eyes directed toward the stage ready for the second act. He did not look up as Arabella took her seat beside him or offer his arm to her.

9

ALONE in her own bedchamber later, Arabella was
singing quietly and wordlessly to herself. She was
feeling very happy. The play had been entertaining, they
had enjoyed good company, and Theodore had promised when they had conveyed him back to his hotel
that he would call on them the following afternoon so
that the four of them could drive out to the botanical
gardens at Kew.

And the day was not yet over. She still had her
husband's visit to look forward to. He would surely
come, as he was at home and knew she had only just
retired. She would have him for several minutes more,
all to herself, in the intimate act of marriage, which she
was growing to enjoy. Soon—but she would not spoil
the day by thinking of that embarrassment now—she
was going to have to find a way to tell him that he could
not visit her for five nights. Within the next few days
that was bound to happen unless she was increasing. But
it seemed that was unlikely to happen in the very first
month of her marriage. She must not expect it too soon,
and then she would not be disappointed to find that it
was not so.

In the meantime there was tonight to enjoy. Arabella
took off her dressing gown and climbed into bed. She
did not want his lordship to find her still up. She would
not know what to do if he did. She lay on her back, her
eyes on the door that led to her dressing room and his.

She smiled at him in her usual way when he came.
And she knew immediately that this day had one more
delight in store—yet something she had never considered a delight before. He sat down on the edge of her
bed as he did very rarely. Usually he took off his

dressing gown immediately and snuffed the candles.

"You enjoyed the evening, Arabella?" he asked.

"Oh, yes, my lord," she said. She smiled at him again. It was impossible to put into words for him the warm feeling about the heart that just thinking back over the evening gave her.

"You seem to have made several friends already," he said.

"Yes," she agreed. "People are very kind. Lord Farraday is a very dear person. I am glad you had him for a friend at university. And Mr. Browning likes me, I think, because I am younger even than he and am not pretty enough to tongue-tie him. I like him. He really has no need to be so shy."

"And Sir Theodore Perrot," he said. "He was a particular friend?"

"We grew up with him," she said, her expression eager. "He is seven years older than I, so to me he was always a big hero. A knight in shining armor."

He smiled rather stiffly down at her and said nothing for a while. "Do you wish you were still at home, Arabella?" he asked. "When the Season is over, would you like to spend the summer at Parkland?"

His meaning was unclear. She did not know if he intended to pack her off home with Frances while he remained in London or went elsewhere, or whether he intended to go with her. She swallowed rather painfully.

"If you wish it, my lord," she said. "I shall do whatever you say."

"Are you not homesick?" he asked.

"I miss Mama and Jemima," she said. "But my home is with you, my lord."

He laid the back of his fingers against her cheek. "I shall take you to them for the summer," he said. "I need to go there anyway, Arabella."

She smiled up at him, relieved. He was intending to be there too! He was not trying to be rid of her.

He took off his dressing gown and got into the bed beside her without snuffing the candles. Arabella wanted to remind him but did not like to do so. She was embarrassed. She closed her eyes tightly when he raised her nightgown and lifted himself on top of her. She positioned herself and drew in a breath in anticipation of his entry. She was thankful that the covers were decently over them.

She loved to feel him move in her. She relaxed and hoped that tonight it would last a long time, as it had on several occasions recently. But while her eyes were still shut fast, his rhythm slowed and he lifted himself on his elbows and forearms so that she knew he was looking down at her. It had happened before, but the candles had never been lit before. She opened· her eyes unwillingly.

He was looking down at her, his eyes heavy-lidded. They were a mere few inches from her own.

"Arabella," he said, his voice almost a whisper. "You are so very tiny. Do I hurt you with my weight?"

She shook her head. She could feel herself blushing. He was still stroking into her and withdrawing very slowly. His eyes had strayed to her mouth. Arabella ran her tongue nervously along her upper lip. And felt her breath catch in her throat when he lowered his head and kissed her with parted lips very gently and very warmly on the mouth.

"It is a hard fate to be married to a stranger and taken from your home and expected to serve him cheerfully, is it not?" he said softly, moving his head down so that he kissed her lightly on her cheek close to her ear. "I am sorry, Arabella."

"But I have not complained," she said, bewildered. "I try to do my duty, my lord."

" 'My lord,' " he repeated, raising his head to look into her eyes again. His mouth smiled, though his eyes did not change. "You do your duty very sweetly, Arabella. I am a fortunate man."

He laid his cheek against her hair and the rhythm of his body penetrated her own again in the final act of union. But Arabella no longer relaxed to enjoy it. She

lay bewildered and unhappy beneath her husband,
wondering what he had meant. He had let the candles
burn for the first time. He had kissed her for the first
time. He had talked to her for the first time while in her
bed. But there had been an edge of something to his
voice—bitterness, anger, sarcasm: she did not know
what—that had taken away from the totally unexpected
tenderness of his kiss. What was he trying to tell her?

He turned his face into her hair, sighed, and relaxed
his weight on her. Arabella lay still and anxious. She
watched him a minute later as he lifted himself away
from her, sat on the edge of the bed, and reached down
to the floor for his dressing gown.

He looked closely into her face for what seemed like a
long time. "Thank you, Arabella," he said at last.
"Perhaps soon I will get you with child and your duty
will be done for a year or more."

His smile looked somewhat twisted as he got to his
feet. "Good night," he said.

"Good night, my lord." Arabella's throat hurt, and
she realized that she was very close to tears. She was
bewildered. And hurt. What was the matter? What had
she done? She had never seen his lordship like this
before.

It was a long time before she slept, troubled, her
happy day in ruins, though she did not know quite in
what way or why.

Lord Astor's party made their planned visit to Kew
the following afternoon despite the fact that a brisk
wind and heavy clouds made the day chilly and gloomy.

Frances looked about her at the flowers and the
temples, all very lovely and very impressive when one
considered that they had been planned and built by the
royal family. She shivered inside her pelisse and lowered
her parasol before the wind could blow it inside out. She
had not taken Theodore's arm.

"You are not happy to see me, Fran," he said. He

spoke quietly. They were walking a little way ahead of Lord and Lady Astor.

"Not happy?" she said, darting him a conscious glance. "Of course I am happy to see you, Theodore."

"I thought you might be homesick," he said. "You were so upset the day of your sister's wedding that I thought you might be unhappy here. It is a relief to find that you are neither. I have always wanted to be here for the Season, you know. Now I will be able to relax and enjoy myself without worrying about you."

Frances darted him another look. "And you could not enjoy yourself if I had been unhappy?" she said.

"I hate to see you miserable, as you know," he said. "We have always been friends, have we not, Fran? I would have felt obliged to stay close to you all the time if you had been homesick. After all, your sister cannot do so, as she has a husband to attend to. But I am happy to know that you will not need me every moment."

"Are you?" Frances said. "I am very pleased to know that I will not be holding you back from your own enjoyment, I am sure, Theodore. I would never wish to be a burden to anyone."

"Oh, no, no," he said, "you are never a burden, Fran. You may call on me anytime you need me, you know. That is what friends are for."

"I will not trouble you, you may be sure," Frances said with a toss of the head.

"Well, as long as you know that you can if you must," Theodore said cheerfully. "I do believe that must be the famous pagoda ahead of us. It is rather splendid, is it not?"

"Quite magnificent, sir," Frances agreed.

"I say," he said, looking down at her in apparent surprise, "I have not said anything to offend you, have I?"

"Me, sir?" she asked, her eyes widening as she looked up at him. "Offended? What could possibly have offended me?"

"Quite so," he said. "Would you care to take my arm?"

Frances took it but walked as far from him as their linked arms would allow.

Arabella was also impressed by the pagoda, which was ten stories high and elaborately ornamented. But she had been far more pleased with the Temple of Bellona and several other temples because his lordship had told her that the present king had helped design some of them when he was a very young man. She had gazed at the first one, speechless with wonder.

"How very clever he was," she had breathed at last, clinging to her husband's arm.

He had smiled. "The buildings are not generally admired," he had said. "But they do have a certain charm, do they not?"

And when they finally glimpsed the Dutch Palace, where the king and queen sometimes lived, she was quite ecstatic.

"Oh," she said, "is his majesty there now? Am I gazing with my very own eyes at the palace where he is now? Is he well-tended, do you think? He is not treated cruelly?"

"I am sure he has the very best physicians attending him, Arabella," he said. "You must not worry. He has a devoted family, I believe. But he is said to be at Windsor, not here."

They talked all the time as they walked through the gardens. Arabella made a special effort, determined to overcome her shyness with her husband, eager to make him her friend. But she could not feel easy. Her attempts at conversation sounded forced and stilted to her own ears, and his responses were labored. And there was something between them—she had no idea what. They had never been close. Indeed, she had always felt uncomfortable with him. But this was different. There was something!

Lord Astor was attempting to make the afternoon a happy one for his wife. At the same time, he was wishing that he were a hundred miles away. Their marriage had been a mistake, he was beginning to realize. That was the plain truth stated quite baldly.

It had been a mistake for both of them. For him it had brought restlessness and uncertainty. His life had been a remarkably contented one before Arabella came into it. He had enjoyed spending his days engaged in manly pursuits with his male friends. And he had been thoroughly satisfied with his liaison with Ginny. That old life was still open to him, of course. He still had his friends and he still had Ginny.

But there was also Arabella. And why she should have upset the pattern of his life so much he could not understand. Really their marriage was much as he had expected and hoped. She was undemanding. She had made friends and was able to occupy her days quite easily without depending upon him. She was dutiful, obedient. Bedding her was not an unpleasant experience.

What was it, then, that made him spend more time with her than he needed to do? Why had he planned to take her to the theater the evening before, and why was he walking with her now at Kew? Why did he worry about her when he was away from her, even when he knew she was occupied? Why could he never quite forget about her, even when he was with Ginny? Why did he always feel guilty when enjoying—or not quite enjoying—his mistress? He was never able to go to Arabella's bed on the nights when he had been with Ginny. And he was always driven to buy her gifts the next day.

"Aunt Hermione is to take you and Frances up in her carriage this evening on her way to Mrs. Pottier's soiree?" he asked now.

"Yes, my lord." Arabella looked politely up at him. "Will you be coming too? You said you might."

"No," he said. "I have a dinner engagement, Arabella. I shall see you when you return."

"Yes," she said. And then she blurted, "My lord?" She was blushing quite hotly. Her eyes slid to his cravat.

"What is it, Arabella?" he asked.

"That will not be possible," she said in a rush, glancing nervously ahead to her sister and Theodore. "I will not be able to see you after the soiree. I mean, I will be able to see you, but . . . I cannot . . . That is . . ."

"I understand." He covered her hand gently with his own. "You are having your period, Arabella. It is the most natural occurrence in the world, you know. There is no need for such embarrassment. I see we are approaching the orangery. After we have walked through it, perhaps we should take tea and think of returning home. It is not a very pleasant afternoon for a prolonged stroll, is it? And perhaps you are not feeling quite the thing?"

"It has been a lovely outing, though," she said brightly, "has it not, my lord? I am so glad we came."

He patted her hand before standing aside so that she might precede him into the long, low building that was the orangery. "The gardens are certainly worth a visit," he said.

"The warmth feels very good, does it not, Bella?" Frances said, looking back over her shoulder.

Their marriage had been a mistake for Arabella too, Lord Astor thought. She was not happy. He had no complaint against her, of course. He could not ask for a more obedient and less troublesome bride. But he knew she was not happy.

And why should she be? She was eighteen years old, very naive and innocent, very new to the world. In many ways she was childlike. To her he must appear old. Seven-and-twenty would seem a very advanced age to an eighteen-year-old. And of course, she had not known him before their betrothal. Why was it that at the time his only anxiety had been lest his bride turn out to be ugly or uncouth? What must she have suffered? She had had no chance to enjoy life, no time to look about her at what life had to offer. She had had to prepare herself for a bridegroom she had never seen.

And she had expected his father. She had been willing

to marry a man in his late fifties. And he was sure that she had been willing. He knew her well enough, and Frances well enough, to imagine just how that situation had developed. One daughter must marry the new Lord Astor for the sake of the rest of the family. Frances was the obvious choice. She was the eldest and of marriageable age. But of course Frances would have shed many a tear over the prospect of marrying an elderly man. Arabella would have stepped in and offered to make the sacrifice herself. It was just like her. She had very little confidence in her own beauty and charm.

And she was unhappy when she deserved nothing but happiness. Perhaps it was his awareness of that fact that had made him worry about her and try to entertain her himself. He felt protective of her, tender almost. He had grown to like her far more than he had intended to or expected to.

But she did not like him. That was perhaps the hardest fact of his marriage to accept. She could not be easy with him or talk easily with him. At first he had thought she was merely showing the natural shyness of a new bride to the husband who performed such unaccustomed intimacies with her. But she had still not changed after three weeks. Unless he could call the evening before and this afternoon a change. She had been making a noticeable effort to talk to him, but her efforts were painful and only accentuated her basic dislike of him.

She had made friends since coming to London, several of them male. He had watched at first with satisfaction, then with amusement, and finally with something like annoyance as she chattered long and easily with Farraday and Hubbard, with Perrot and the gangly youth. And Lincoln. Why could she be so easy with them and not with him? Had he been unkind to her? Cruel?

And so he continued to try to ingratiate himself with her. Though whether he had been trying to do that the night before, he was not sure. He had known that light would embarrass her, as would his looking into her face and talking to her while he was being intimate with her. He had felt frustrated, angry, hurt—he was not quite sure how he had felt.

No, it was not a good marriage. It was bringing neither of them joy. Or contentment. Or even indifference. They were aware of each other and uncomfortable with each other. Unhappy with each other.

He would spend the evening with Ginny, he decided. He would tell himself quite firmly that Arabella was enjoying the soiree with one or more of her female friends and male companions, and he would soak up the sensual gratification that Ginny was so skilled at giving him.

Arabella was busily admiring the orange trees and other exotic plants with Frances and Perrot, he realized suddenly. He smiled down at his wife as she turned back to him and took his arm again.

"Shall I bring you back here one day when the weather is kinder, Arabella?" he asked.

"That would be very nice, my lord," she said politely. "Though it has been very pleasant even today. It was kind of you to bring us. Thank you."

• 10 •

FRANCES prepared for the Pottier soiree with particular care. She wore a deep midnight-blue gown that she had been saving for the next ball. She wished to appear at her best for Sir John Charlton and the group of some-what lesser admirers who showed interest in her wherever she went. More important, she wished to show Sir Theodore Perrot that she was indeed enjoying her stay in London and felt no homesickness whatsoever.

She was somewhat chagrined to find that Theodore was already there before them and in conversation with the Marquess and Marchioness of Ravenscourt and Lady Harriet Meeker. He looked quite as if he belonged in the drawing room. He did not look at all rustic, as she had rather expected him to look.

Frances smiled at Mr. Browning, who had approached them in order to talk with Arabella. She flirted her fan at him, and the young man looked some-what taken aback, and blushed.

"Oh, la," Frances said, "what a splendid drawing room. What story from mythology is depicted in the painting on the ceiling, do you suppose?" She smiled dazzlingly.

"The b-birth of Venus, I believe, ma'am," Mr. Browning said.

"Did you succeed in buying the pair of matched grays that you were going to bid on at Tattersall's this morning?" Arabella asked him. "You must tell me all about the auction, sir. I think it very provoking that ladies may not attend."

Frances felt Theodore looking their way. She smiled even more brightly at a clearly uncomfortable Mr. Browning, and fanned herself vigorously.

Theodore, viewing her from across the room, smiled and turned his attention back to what the marchioness was saying.

Frances was rescued at that moment by Sir John Charlton, who made his bows to both ladies and began to engage her in conversation.

"It was a great pity you were not able to drive with me in the park this afternoon, Miss Wilson," he said. "The company there was quite distinguished. Lady Morton was kind enough to remark that my new high-perch phaeton is quite the most fashionable conveyance in town."

"I really hated to miss the chance to drive with you, sir," Frances said. "I am longing to see your new phaeton."

"You would grace it with your beauty," Sir John said, removing a pearl-encrusted snuffbox from his waistcoat pocket and flicking the lid open with one elegant thumb. "You were at Kew this afternoon?"

"Yes," she said. "The gardens are quite splendid. Have you seen the pagoda, sir?"

"Once, as a boy," he said with a sigh. "A strange affectation of our royal family, is it not? But not in quite such bad taste as those other unspeakable edifices in the gardens. I suppose Sir Theodore Perrot was awed by their splendor? Visitors from the country generally are."

"Oh," Frances said. "Yes, Theodore liked the pagoda. Of course, it is somewhat out of place in an English setting. But an amusing curiosity, would you not say?"

He bowed and proceeded to inhale a pinch of snuff from the back of his hand. He withdrew a lace-edged handkerchief from his pocket.

"It is always amusing," he said, his task completed, "to pick out those people who are freshly arrived from the country each Season. They do tend to be rather noticeable. Of course, in some cases"—he bowed in Frances' direction—"one would assume a person had spent all her life in town under the influence of the most impeccable of fashion makers. You, for example, ma'am, must have a natural sense of style and elegance."

"I have always hated an unfashionable gown," Frances said with a blush.

"I am sure you have the very best of modistes," Sir John said. "I, of course, will patronize no other tailor than Weston. I would wager I could look around this room and point out to you all the gentlemen who do not."

"Oh, could you really?" Frances gazed in some admiration at the young man beside her.

A little later in the evening, Arabella was gratified to see that Frances was at the center of a group of young people. Guests at the soiree had tended to divide themselves into young and more mature. The young people were content to converse in the drawing room; the older people drifted toward the music room, where several talented performers were entertaining them. Frances was with some of her lady friends, though her group also included Sir John Charlton and two others of her regular admirers.

Frances had told Arabella when they had returned from Kew that she was not going to have Theodore hanging around her skirts all evening, even though Lady Berry had secured an invitation for him. And she seemed to have succeeded. Theodore was not part of the group. In fact, Arabella noted, looking around the room until she saw him, he was seated in one corner of the drawing room with Lady Harriet Meeker. They were talking to each other and smiling as if there were no one else in the room.

She did not know why she was surprised. Theodore was a good-looking and personable young man, after all. She had somehow expected to see him alone in a corner, brooding and dejected.

Really she had not been paying much attention to what went on around her. Since Mr. Browning had been borne off by a loud aunt, she had been deep in conversation with Mr. Lincoln and assuring him yet again that his limp alone was not likely to make Miss Pope completely scorn his suit. Of course, she had been careful to explain, perhaps Miss Pope would not encourage him either, but that would have nothing to do with his leg. It was foolish to be so conscious of a small handicap that one would not even try to become acquainted with someone one admired.

Arabella found it easy to sympathize with people who had little confidence in themselves. She knew exactly how they felt. Poor Mr. Lincoln had been languishing after the quite plain and ordinary Miss Pope since the start of the Season, yet could never summon the courage to talk to her or invite her out for a ride as he did with perfect ease with Arabella. And Mr. Browning was quite convinced that no one could take him seriously as a gentleman when he looked for all the world like a schoolboy. She had advised him to take up some manly sport like boxing—she had even offered to ask his lordship if he would befriend him and be his sparring partner on occasion. Mr. Browning had been horrified.

But she could not be impatient with either one of these two friends. She was like them in many ways. She was only just beginning to realize that her small stature, her plain looks, and her childish features did not therefore make her a person of no account. She had not found that she had made fewer friends than Frances or any of the other ladies around her. Ladies did not scorn her; gentlemen did not shun her. And it was true what his lordship had said on one occasion: there are no perfect people; we all have to make the most of our assets. Of course, there were some people who were very nearly perfect, like his lordship himself, for example, but really they were not many.

Her attempts to be more confident and more friendly with her husband had not prospered well in the last two days, but they would, she assured herself. He would see that she was no longer the timid, dull Arabella he had

married, and he would like her better. And he would see
soon that she looked more grown-up and feminine than
she had when he married her. He might not realize that
the reason was that she had lost weight, but he would
notice the result. She had had her maid take in the seams
of several of her favorite garments already.

There was this strange mood of his, of course. She
felt a dull ache of something low in her stomach when
she thought of it. But she would not think of it for this
evening, or brood on the fact that he had not come with
her after saying almost certainly two days before that he
would. The mood would pass. After all, she could not
even say that it was a bad mood. He had been kind to
her that afternoon at Kew. And he had spoken gently to
her in her bedchamber the night before and had kissed
her for the first time—oh, splendid moment! She had
wondered for weeks what his mouth would feel like
against her own. And now she knew that it felt quite as
good as she had imagined. But there was something,
something disturbing.

Arabella smiled brightly and crossed the room to join
Theodore, who was standing and bowing as Lady
Harriet moved away.

"Hello, puss," he said with a grin. "Are you
enjoying yourself?"

"Yes, I am," she said. "And you really ought not to
call me that now, you know, Theo. I am a married lady
and quite grown-up. I nearly died when you used that
name in his lordship's hearing."

"Did you?" he said. "I am sorry to have wounded
your dignity. I could never have imagined you with such
an air of consequence. So what is it to be? 'Arabella'?
'Bella'? Lady Astor'? 'My lady'? 'Ma'am'?"

She tapped him on the arm with her fan. " 'Bella' will
do nicely," she said. "Only his lordship is to call me
'Arabella.' Oh, and Lady Berry does too, of course."
She sat down in the place recently vacated by Lady
Harriet, and he joined her.

"I am pleased to see you cutting such a dash, Bella,"

he said. "And your mama will be pleased too. I think she does not quite believe your letters. She is convinced that you are putting the best face on a bad situation."

"Nonsense," she said. "And so I shall tell Mama myself. His lordship is going to take me home for the summer, you know. He has business there."

He smiled. "Frances is doing very well too," he said. "I knew she would, of course. I am glad that you and Lord Astor have given her the opportunity, puss."

"Don't you mind?" she asked hesitantly. "I thought it would make you angry or sad, Theo, to see her so very popular."

"Well, there you are wrong," he said. "I mean to marry Frances, Bella. And I mean it to be a love match and a happy marriage. How could we be happy when she has never tried her wings beyond Parkland? And how could she—or I—be sure she loved me if she had never had the chance to form an attachment to any other man?"

"But what if she does not wish to return to Parkland? And what if she grows to love another man?" Arabella watched him with rounded eyes.

"Then I have a choice," Theodore said. "I can crack her over the head with a club and drag her home by the hair or I can let her go. If she ever marries me, Bella—and I am confident that she will—she will do so because she freely wishes to do so. I would rather risk losing her than be married to a wife who thinks she might have done better for herself."

"I am not sure I could be as wise," Arabella said. "I don't think I could risk losing his lordship. But why did you come to London yourself, Theo, if you wanted Frances to be free?"

He shrugged. "I was restless and, frankly, I was afraid, puss," he said. "I had to give myself a reasonable excuse for coming, of course. Frances should see me as I look in this new world of hers. She should be able to make comparisons. She should be able to see, for example, that I am not quite as handsome as that milksop with her now, whose front teeth I would dearly like to plant in his throat.''

"Oh, Theo," Arabella said after a startled laugh, "you are ten times as handsome as Sir John Charlton, and Frances would have to be blind not to see it. And she had better see it because I refuse to have him for a brother-in-law. I want you."

"Well," he said, grinning, "if I miss Frances, there is always Jemima, you know. Did you know she climbed a tree last week and stayed up there for three hours until your mama was ready to call out the militia, thinking her lost? She was afraid to come down, it seems. She might still be up there if the vicar had not heard her screeches as he rode down the lane. Wicked little hoyden! I had better marry Frances. If I married Jemima, I would doubtless turn into a wife-beater."

"You had better not tell Frances that story," Arabella said, "or she will have a fit of the vapors and then soak ten handkerchiefs with her tears."

They giggled like a pair of childish conspirators.

"Do take me into the music room, Theo," Arabella said, "if you can bear to leave off your contemplation of Sir John's front teeth, that is. I am a respectable married lady, you know, and I should be able to say in all truth tomorrow that I listened to and appreciated the music."

"Come on, then, puss," he said, getting to his feet, "though I don't think you will deceive anyone into seeing you as a staid and respectable matron. I must see the singer, anyway. I have heard that she is a quite delectable female."

"You have no refinement of taste whatsoever, Theo," Arabella said, taking his arm and clucking her tongue. "It is a singer's voice that one is supposed to show interest in. Who is the lady, anyway?"

"A Miss Virginia Cox," he said. "And I shall listen to her voice too, Bella. I promise on my honor as a gentleman."

"Hm," Arabella said. "I remember you promised on

that that time when you swore you would not let me fall off those wobbly stepping-stones into the stream."

"And neither would I," he said, "if you had not bellowed out that you were going to fall and snatched your hand away from mine to saw at the air. Let us go see—and hear—Miss Cox, puss."

Lord Astor dined alone at White's. He was feeling thoroughly blue-deviled. He should have gone to Mrs. Pottier's soiree with Arabella, he thought. He had said he would. They had been married for less than three weeks, and he did not wish anyone to begin whispering that he had tired of his bride already. That would not be fair to her. And how could he expect her to grow easy with him and begin to like him if he did not spend his time with her?

Besides, he wanted to be with her. Coping with his sister-in-law's tedious conversation and his wife's self-conscious attempts to converse with him was preferable to sitting alone at White's. Where was everyone tonight? Had there been some mass conspiracy to eat elsewhere?

His thoughts irritated Lord Astor. Why should he not dine at his club? Why should he not plan an evening with his mistress, who was being paid handsomely to do less and less work? Why should he feel obliged to live in his wife's shadow? Other men did not. Indeed, he would become the laughingstock if he appeared everywhere she went. People would begin to think he was in love with her.

He was going to have to take himself firmly in hand. He treated Arabella with perfect kindness. He had clothed her for a Season in London and made sure she was properly entertained. He bought her gifts. He had taken her about quite as much as anyone could expect. He had been indulgent with her. He had scolded her only once, over the matter of going out unescorted, and he had done so with restraint. Many men would have beaten their wives for less. And he was doing his best to get her with child. Perhaps by the next month she would be increasing. She would surely be happy then. He really had no reason whatsoever to feel guilty about his marriage.

Lord Astor rose to his feet. He was going to visit Ginny without further delay. He was going to leave all thought of Arabella outside the door, and he was going to enjoy his mistress as he had enjoyed her for a full year before that damnable journey to Parkland. He would stay all night if he felt like doing so, and exhaust both himself and Ginny until there was no energy left for anything except blissful, dreamless sleep. He was not going to feel guilty. After all, he could not go to Arabella that night anyway, or for the four nights following. He would be depriving her of nothing.

He was disappointed half an hour later to discover that Ginny was from home, singing at one of her musical entertainments. He had not thought of the possibility. He hesitated as the butler stood politely in the small tiled hallway of Ginny's house. It might be hours before she came home.

But what were the alternatives? He could go home to an empty house or back to White's on the chance that some of his acquaintances would turn up. Or he could go to the soiree after all. And if he did, he thought, he would doubtless find Arabella surrounded by the gentlemen friends she seemed so comfortable with, and unable to grant him more than a self-conscious smile and flush.

No, he would wait. At least he could be sure of commanding Ginny's undivided attention when she did come home. And at least he could unleash all his frustrations on her unprotesting and doubtless eager body. Ginny would not mind an energetic lovemaking. She would prefer it so. And he did not think he would have the energy to be gentle tonight.

Lord Astor removed his hat and gloves, unbuttoned his greatcoat, and gave orders for brandy to be sent to the sitting room.

* * *

"Miss Cox is very beautiful, I must admit," Arabella whispered to Theodore as the singer's performance came to an end. "It does not seem fair that some women are allowed to grow so tall and elegant. And she has a lovely face."

"I thought you came to listen to her songs," he whispered back. "I must say she is everything I was led to expect in the breakfast parlor at Grillon's this morning. But she does not have nearly your air of breeding, Bella, if that is what is bothering you."

"I don't like the way everyone is turning to talk among themselves and quite ignoring her," Arabella said, "just as if she were a servant. Perhaps she has been hired for the occasion, but for all that, her voice is vastly superior to any I have heard among people of the *ton*. We are all being decidedly rude, Theo. I believe I shall go and commend her on her performance."

"I shall come with you if you must," Theodore said, his eyes twinkling. "That voice bears listening to at closer quarters."

Arabella clucked her tongue and rose to her feet to find Lord Farraday almost upon her and reaching for her elbow.

"Good evening, ma'am," he said. "I saw you earlier but have not had a moment to talk with you. They are serving supper immediately, I hear. May I lead you in?"

Arabella smiled at him. "I saw you too, my lord," she said, "but I was having a particularly important conversation with Mr. Lincoln, and when I was finished, you had disappeared. I daresay you have been listening to the music. Did you not think Miss Cox's voice quite superior?"

"Quite so," he said. "If we do not leave immediately, we will be at the back of the line and have to wait forever. May I have the pleasure?" He had a firm hold of her elbow. He was standing so close to her that she was almost forced to sit back down on her chair again.

"Have you met my friend and neighbor from home,

Sir—?'' she began, but Lady Berry interrupted her, catching at her sleeve and saying something that Arabella could not hear over the hubbub of conversation around them. "Excuse me a moment. I must see what Lady Berry wants. I shall be glad to go in to supper with you, my lord, after I have commended Miss Cox on her singing.''

She edged her way past the two men until she could hear Lady Berry, who had merely been trying to draw her attention to the fact that supper was being served and that they should hurry if they wanted the best choice of food.

When she turned back, Arabella found that a few people had moved between her and the two gentlemen, and everyone seemed bent on reaching the doorway and making his way to the supper room. She moved around behind some of them until she could worm her way between two large bodies, and reached up to tap Theodore on the shoulder. He was talking with Lord Farraday, both of them facing away from her and being jostled by guests eager for their supper.

"She has a kind heart," Theodore was saying. "She thinks Virginia Cox is being treated too much like a servant.''

"We have to get her away from here," Lord Farraday said urgently. "Ginny is Astor's mistress, for the love of God. There is no time for talk. Where is Lady Astor, anyway? I have lost her in the crowd.''

Arabella made sure that she remained lost for a few seconds longer. When the two men spotted her a little way to one side of them, she smiled gaily.

"One problem with being small," she said, "is that one is in danger of being trodden on. And no one would even notice me until the servants came in tomorrow to sweep up the night's debris. Are you going to take me to supper, my lord? Thank you.'' She laid a hand on Lord Farraday's sleeve. "And, Theodore, if you are not to be left all alone, I shall take your arm with my free one and be the envy of every lady present. At least with two such large gentlemen as bodyguards I may escape being squashed beneath someone's shoe.''

The two men exchanged a glance of relief over her head. She seemed to have forgotten her plan to commend the singer.

"By the way, I did meet Sir Theodore last evening at the theater,'' Lord Farraday said to Arabella. "Had you forgotten.''

"Oh, forgive me, please,'' Arabella said, laughing merrily. Her eyes were sparkling. Her cheeks glowed with heightened color.

"Geoffrey!'' Ginny swept into her sitting room, hands outstretched. She looked quite magnificent, Lord Astor thought as he rose to his feet, her daringly low-cut evening gown showing off her figure to advantage, her hair piled high and set with waving plumes. Her painted lips smiled at him. "What a delightful surprise. You have not been here at night since your marriage.''

He took her hands. "You look lovely, Ginny,'' he said. "Did you have great success tonight? Were you in good voice?''

"I believe so,'' she said. "The applause was more than just polite. I had one quite delightful pleasure.''

"Did you?'' he said, and waited politely.

"I shall tell you later,'' she said, reaching up to remove her plumes and pulling at the pins that held her hair up. "Are you hungry, Geoffrey? I shall not keep you waiting for long. And you may have the pleasure of watching me disrobe. I know you always enjoy that. Unless you would prefer to do it yourself, that is.'' She smiled and twirled before him as she ran her hands through her hair and shook it free about her shoulders. "I am ravenous, I would have you warned.''

He sat back on his chair and linked his hands behind his head. He watched her undress. She was quite voluptuously beautiful, her breasts generous and heavy, her hips and thighs shapely. Her fair hair hung, curled and disheveled, halfway to her waist. She was what he needed more than anything else that night. He rose to his feet and opened his arms to her as she came to him.

"Geoffrey," she said, her voice throaty with desire, "undress too. You cannot know how glad I am you came tonight."

He held her against him and felt desire for her grow in him. She was almost as tall as he. She felt very different from Arabella. Not that he had ever held Arabella against him. But he had lain on her. She was very tiny, but she was warmly and softly feminine. She always made him feel protective. He wanted to be gentle with Arabella. He could never forget the world around him and abandon himself to his own pleasure with her. He was always conscious of the still, submissive body beneath his own. He was always aware that it was the marriage act he performed with her.

He did not want to think of Arabella. It was Ginny he needed tonight. He found her mouth with his and proceeded to explore her with eager hands. He pressed her more closely against him as he recalled the soft warmth of Arabella's lips beneath his own the night before.

"Ah, Geoffrey." Ginny was stretched out on the bed beside him in the adjoining bedchamber much later, her head in the crook of his arm. "What a wonderful lover you are. I declare you will quite spoil me for all others."

"Mm," he said, gazing at the canopy over their heads.

"You are going to stay all night?" she asked. "I swear that by morning I will be too exhausted to get out of bed. Will you mind?" She looked across at him archly.

"Mm?" he said with a start. "What was that?"

"I asked if you would mind my being unable to get out of bed in the morning," she said. "Have I exhausted you so much already, Geoffrey, that you cannot think straight?"

"I was wondering if Ara . . . , if my w . . . It does not matter, Ginny. It is not important."

"If she is at home eagerly awaiting your attentions?"
Ginny said. "I think it unlikely. She was looking well-
pleased with herself when I saw her earlier, a gentleman
on each arm."

Lord Astor turned his head sharply. "You have seen
Arabella?" he asked.

She laughed. "That was the delightful pleasure I
mentioned earlier," she said. "Yes, I saw her, Geoffrey.
Someone pointed her out to me. And what a great
surprise she was. She is so small, a child merely. You
should be ashamed of robbing the cradle so. But she
seems quite firmly established with her *cicisbei*. You
must be well-satisfied."

"It was at the Pottier soiree you were singing?" he
said, dismayed. He had an arm over his eyes. "And you
saw Arabella. Good God!"

Ginny had turned over onto her side. "Are you ready
to be revived yet?" she asked, placing a hand lightly on
his chest. "You see how insatiable I am, Geoffrey? The
first course is no sooner over than I am ready for the
second. Shall I arouse your appetite too?"

Lord Astor had not moved. He had an image of
Ginny as she had appeared earlier, beautiful and flam-
boyant, in the same room with Arabella, tiny, eager,
and wide-eyed. And Arabella would have been watching
Ginny and listening. Applauding. Unaware that Ginny
was her husband's mistress. And Arabella with a gentleman on each arm. Farraday? Hubbard? Lincoln? The
gangly youth? Perrot? Someone new? And looking
well-pleased with herself. Yes, he knew the look. He
could well imagine it.

"I have to go home, Gin," he said, pushing her hand
away.

She pulled a face. "Oh, not so soon," she said. "You
said just a short while ago that you were going to stay
the night. Just once more, Geoffrey. You cannot be in
that much of a hurry."

He caught her hand, which had strayed to his chest
again, in a firm grip, leaned over her, and kissed her

hard and dispassionately on the lips. "Another time," he said. "I find I am not in the mood tonight after all. Thank you for the last hour. I needed it."

"You really do not demand a great deal for all you pay me," she said, pouting. "And I *am* complaining. Does your wife take so much of your energy, Geoffrey?"

He sat on the edge of the bed and reached down for his clothes. "Spite does not suit you, Gin," he said. "I will be back in a day or two to put you to work so that you may earn your keep. I had not realized you were quite so conscientious."

11

ARABELLA did not take George for his usual walk the
following morning. Neither did she go downstairs to
breakfast. She sent her maid down when she thought the
meal would be over, to ask if she might wait on Lord
Astor at his convenience. The answer came almost immediately. He was in his office and would be glad to see
her.

Arabella had not slept the night before. Indeed, she
had been up three separate times vomiting. She
frequently felt nauseated and otherwise out of sorts on
the first day of her month, but she had never been
actively sick before. Nevertheless, even though she still
felt wretched and at one remove from reality, she
dressed with care and brushed her curls neatly. She had
declined the services of her maid.

Lord Astor had settled to examine the books that he
had had sent from Parkland. But he was quite prepared
to set them aside for Arabella. He had been somewhat
concerned when she had not come down either for her
usual walk with George or for breakfast. It was possible
that she was not well. He knew that some women
suffered at that certain time of the month. He had
wanted to go up to her room to see if she was unwell,
but had been afraid of disturbing her sleep.

And he had remembered his feeling of the night
before when he had arrived home very late. A feeling of
guilt. Yes, quite undeniably and annoyingly, guilt. Even
if he could not possess her, he had thought, at least he
could have come home early and gone in to talk to her.
He could have assured himself that she was not in any
pain or discomfort. He could have sent down for
laudanum if she was.

He had shaken off his feelings with some annoyance the night before and resisted the urge to tiptoe into her bedchamber to see her, late as it was. It was a relief now to know that she was up and asking to speak with him.

He rose to his feet with a smile when a footman opened the door for her. But the smile faded. His guess had been right. She was pale almost to the point of being haggard. He moved hastily toward her.

"Arabella," he said, concern in his voice and on his face, "what is the matter? Are you sure you should be out of your bed?"

"I am quite well, thank you," she said. She was standing very upright, her eyes looking straight into his, her jaw set firmly. Something in her tone and in her face made him stop and look more inquiringly at her.

"What is it?" he asked.

"I want to know," she said. "I will not condemn you until you have had a chance to deny it. Is Miss Virginia Cox your mistress?"

He closed his eyes briefly and then looked at her again. "Who told you this, Arabella?" he asked.

"That does not matter," she said. "I want to know if it is true."

He said nothing for the moment, but stared back at her.

"It is true, is it not?" she said.

"I would rather not talk about this," he said.

"Indeed!" Arabella showed emotion for the first time. "But I insist that we do. She is your mistress, isn't she? Will you deny that you have been with her since our marriage? Can you tell me in all truth that you have not?"

"No, Arabella," he said after a pause, "I cannot tell you that."

"I did not believe it," she said very quietly. Her hands were clenched at her sides. "Until this moment I did not quite believe it could be so. How could you do such a thing? How could you go to another woman and do . . . and do those things to her? You married me.

You married me in church and swore before God . . .''

Lord Astor's face had turned chalky white. "Arabella," he said, "please don't distress yourself. It is really quite unimportant. You are my wife. It is you—''

"It is 'unimportant'!" she said, her eyes blazing into his. He looked away from her. "It means nothing to you, my lord, except base physical pleasure? Shall I tell you what it has meant to me? It meant pain on our wedding night, dreadful pain that lasted for several days. But I did not mind, because I was your wife and we had been made one, we were bound by a sacred tie. I have been careful in my duty to you, believing that only I could give you that. And I did not want you to be disappointed. And it is unimportant to you?''

"I did not mean you," he said. "Arabella, please, let me explain.''

"I have never said no to you," she said. "I have never shirked my duty. If it was not enough, if you wanted more from me, why did you not tell me or ask for what you wanted or come to me more often? I would not have denied you. I believe you know I would not. I have told you and I have tried to show during every moment since our marriage that I mean to be an obedient wife and that I wish to make you comfortable. You have sinned against me terribly to take a mistress.''

He turned away and walked to the window. He stood looking sightlessly out. "Yes, I have, Arabella," he said.

"I know I am not pretty and that I do not know much about the world," she said, "and I know you would have far preferred to marry Frances or some other attractive lady. I know that. But you did marry me. No one forced you to do it. You did it of your own free will. And so you took on a duty too. You owed it to me to be faithful. And I have always been willing to learn. If there was anything I could have done to make you more comfortable, I would have done it readily. But you have never asked, and you have never offered to teach me.''

"Arabella, don't do this to yourself," he said, his brow against a pane of the window. "None of this is your fault, believe me. You have been everything I could expect of a bride, and more. Perhaps if you would let me explain . . ."

"I don't want to hear you speak," she said, "and I don't want to see you or feel your touch. I don't want you near me anymore. I don't want you in my bed. I know I am your wife and that I must remain so. And as your wife I owe you obedience. You will not find me disobedient in future, my lord. If you choose to speak to me, I will listen. If you choose to touch me, I shall not flinch. And if you choose to come to my bed, I shall receive you dutifully. I shall bear your children if I must, and love them too because they are mine and cannot help being yours. But I want you to know one thing. Everything I do for you from this moment on will be done out of duty alone. I will do nothing willingly."

His hands gripped the windowsill. His eyes closed. "You will not find me making your life a misery, Arabella," he said.

"I thought you were perfect," she said. "I have felt awkward and tongue-tied and apologetic because I could not compete with your splendor. You have not deserved my admiration, my lord. I no longer respect or like you."

He took a deep breath and turned to face her. "It is sometimes a dangerous thing to put a living person on a pedestal," he said. "He has all the farther to fall. I am sorry, Arabella, but there is nothing I can say in my own defense, is there? I have a mistress, yes. She has been under my protection for longer than a year. I do not feel less for you as a result. But I have caused you pain and disillusionment, and I am sorry." He shrugged his shoulders. "You may leave to do whatever it is you have planned for this morning. I have work to do here before taking myself out of your sight for the rest of the day."

"I trusted you," she whispered before turning and

letting herself out of the room. "I was proud of you. I was trying to be your friend. This is worse . . . Oh, this is ten times worse than losing Papa."

Frances had tears in her eyes when she entered the morning room later to find Arabella with her sewing in her lap, though she had sewn only two stitches since picking it up half an hour before.

"Bella," she said, "I have been up half the night thinking. I am so dreadfully selfish. I have a dressing room filled with new and fashionable clothes, and scarce a day has gone by since we arrived in town when there have not been two or three entertainments at the least and many more invitations to choose among. And last night I lay down with the intention of persuading you to go shopping with me for a new parasol to replace my blue one, which I thought was dreadfully old-fashioned after all. And then it came to me."

Arabella bent her head over her sewing as Frances took her handkerchief from her pocket. "What came to you?" she asked.

"Mama and Jemima have had no treat at all," her sister said, her face tragic. "No new clothes and no visits to town and no entertainments. Nothing, Bella. How selfish I am! I have scarce spared them a thought, and I have written to them only when you have insisted. Dear Bella. You have such a good heart. I shall never forget the sacrifice you made for my sake."

"You forget," Arabella said quickly, "that Mama and Jemima are quite ecstatic to know that you have had such an opportunity, Frances. Mama derives her happiness from knowing that you are happy. And as for Jemima, her turn will come when she is older. I daresay his lordship will . . ." She paused and swallowed painfully. "I daresay he will see to it that she is brought out too when the time comes."

"He is so very kind," Frances said, smiling bravely, watery blue eyes sparkling over the top of her handkerchief. "And so are you, Bella. Will you come with me now to the shops so that I may buy gifts for Mama and Jemima? Mama would like a new pair of kid gloves. And for Jemima perhaps I will buy the parasol I would have liked for myself. Do you think that would be a selfless plan?"

Arabella smiled and folded up her work neatly. "I shall order the carriage," she said. "Don't forget to bring your book too, Frances. We might as well go to the library while we are close."

"Am I dragging you out against your will?" Frances asked, frowning and forgetting her tears and her handkerchief as Arabella looked up and rose to her feet. "You do not look well, Bella."

"I am all right," Arabella said. "Just a little tired, that is all."

"You do have this dreadful habit of rising at the crack of dawn," Frances said. "Perhaps that is it, Bella. You are not increasing, are you?" She flushed deeply.

"No," Arabella said firmly, "I am not."

They were walking along Bond Street later when they saw Lord Farraday on the pavement at the other side of the street. They raised their hands in greeting and prepared to move on, but he hurried across the road to meet them.

"Well met, Lady Astor, Miss Wilson," he said, raising his hat and making them a bow. "I was preparing to call on you this afternoon."

"We will be at home, my lord," Arabella said, "and will be pleased to receive you."

"Thank you," he said. "I had breakfast with your neighbor this morning. I told him that he must see Vauxhall Gardens, among other places, while he is in town. It gave me the idea to reserve one of the supper boxes there and organize a party for tomorrow night. There is to be music, it seems. And it is one of the nights for fireworks."

"How perfectly marvelous," Frances said. "I have heard it is a very romantic location, my lord."

"I hoped you ladies would be able to join the party,"

he said. "Sir Theodore will be there, of course, and will be glad to see familiar faces, I am sure. And Charlton will be coming, and Hubbard. Mrs. Pritchard—one of my sisters, you know—has agreed to come, as my brother-in-law is in Portugal at present. And Lady Harriet Meeker is to be invited. May I hope that you do not have a previous engagement for tomorrow night?"

"No, we have not," Arabella said. She looked at Frances. "We will be glad to make two of your party, my lord."

"Splendid!" he said. "Will Astor come, do you think, ma'am?"

"I think not," Arabella said. "He does have another engagement."

"A pity," he said. "I shall do myself the honor, then, of taking you up in my carriage tomorrow evening? My sister will be with me."

He raised his hat and continued on his way after Arabella had expressed her delight.

"Oh, Bella," Frances said, taking her sister's arm after tucking the package containing her mother's kid gloves into her reticule. "Vauxhall Gardens! It is all winding pathways and hanging lanterns, according to Lucinda Jennings, who has been there more than once. And handsome gentlemen roaming everywhere. I can scarce wait untl tomorrow night."

"We will have a lovely time," Arabella said brightly. "I have always wanted to see a display of fireworks. I am glad Theodore has been making some friends."

"Yes, so am I, I am sure," Frances said. "Though I do not greatly admire Lady Harriet Meeker, do you, Bella? However, she seems to be to Theodore's liking, and that is all that matters, I suppose."

"I believe he is merely friendly with her," Arabella said. "I would not worry that he is developing a *tendre* for her if I were you, Frances."

"Worry!" her sister said with a trilling little laugh. "I quite wish the best for Theodore. We have always been friends, as you know, Bella."

"I once thought you were more," Arabella said with a sigh.

"Well, that was very foolish of you," Frances said. "I had never even seen anyone else but Theodore and the others at home. Here there are far more eligible gentlemen. What do you think of Sir John Charlton?"

"That he is shallow and vain," Arabella said bluntly.

"Bella!" Frances looked reproachfully at her. "How dreadfully unkind you are. Is a gentleman shallow merely because he knows all there is to know about polite behavior and fashion? Is he vain merely because he is handsome and elegant? He has a very superior understanding, I believe. And I think he favors me. He is to be the Earl of Haig one day, you know."

"Yes, I believe he has told me so quite pointedly a half-dozen times," Arabella said.

"I see you are cross and out of sorts today, Bella," France said stiffly. "But I am glad you are taking it out on me. It would not do for you to speak thus to his lordship. He is like to be displeased with you. I think we will just avoid all sensible topics until you are in spirits again. Where is the best shop to look in for parasols, do you think?"

Arabella took her sister's arm and squeezed it. "Forgive me, Frances," she said. "You are quite right. I did not sleep well last night, as I told you earlier, and I am making you suffer as a result. Let us try this shop. This is where his lordship . . . This is where my fan was purchased."

"Bella!" Frances' eyes were filled with tears as she drew her sister to a halt outside the shop. "How can I ever reproach you for anything when you made such a great sacrifice for my sake? How very ungrateful I am. Dear, dear Bella! How fortunate it is that all has turned out well for you after all."

Lord Astor had ridden across Westminster Bridge and south away from London before he was fully aware that he was even on horseback. He drew back on the

reins and looked down in some bewilderment at the
sweat-beaded neck of his favorite stallion. When had he
gone home to saddle the horse? What had been his
intention when he did so? And where had he been going
with such speed and purpose?

He pulled off a glove, touched his nose gingerly, and
winced. It was still sore. No longer bleeding, though, he
thought, looking at his hand and finding no telltale red
streak. He should have known better than to challenge
Jackson himself to a sparring match that morning.
Normally he would have given the great pugilist a good
go for his money, but this morning he had not been in
any condition to concentrate. And Jackson himself,
standing over him and offering a hand to pull him to his
feet after planting him a facer that had had the blood
spurting all down his shirt front, had reminded him that
one of the first rules of boxing was that one must fight
with a cool head. One should never box in order to work
off one's anger or some other negative emotion.

Yes, he knew that. But why had he challenged the
great man anyway? He could not remember. Had it
been in the hope of pounding someone's face to pulp?
He would have challenged one of the weaklings or
novices if that had been his purpose, surely. He rather
thought he must have issued the challenge in the hope
that his own face would be reduced to blood and raw
meat. He had wanted physical punishment. But
Gentleman Jackson was just what his popular name
said. He would never continue to pummel an opponent
once he was down and clearly defeated.

So. Here he was with a sore nose that doubtless
resembled a beacon, riding a sweaty horse, bound he
knew not where. He might as well continue for a while,
he decided, though at a pace that would be kinder to his
mount, which had offended no one. After all, he had
nothing to return home for. Not now or ever again, it
seemed.

He could not have imagined Arabella behaving with
quite such cold dignity. His mind touched back to the

scene in his office that morning, and he found himself
spurring his horse on again. He had never in his life felt
such helpless guilt. That was what he was running from,
doubtless. And that was what he had been hoping to
have pounded out of him at Jackson's. Pointless efforts! He carried his guilt deep within, inescapable and
inaccessible from without.

He would not have hurt Arabella for worlds. He had
grown fond of her fresh innocence. He had taken her at
a very young age from her own home and had under-
taken to protect her with his name and his person. He
felt a great responsibility for her. But he had hurt her
quite dreadfully. She had looked wretchedly ill.
Obviously some fiend had told her the night before
about Ginny's connection to him, and she had been
tortured all night by the knowledge.

But there had been more than suffering in her face
that morning. If that had been all, he might have coped.
He might have taken her in his arms and soothed her
and promised her the earth as a recompense for having
hurt her. But she had been quite untouchable, cold and
controlled. Something had been killed in her overnight.
The remnants of her childhood, perhaps. Her faith in
him. Perhaps her faith in humanity.

Her great innocence was proving to be her worst
enemy, of course. If she just had a little more worldly
wisdom, she would realize that it was common practice
for a gentleman to keep a mistress. There was no
implied insult to one's wife in doing so. He was not less
respectful of Arabella, less fond of her because he kept
Ginny. But Arabella did not know that. She expected
the marriage service to be taken literally. She felt
slighted, rejected. This would be one more blow to her
very fragile self-confidence.

And he was responsible. Lord Astor pulled his horse
to the side of the road in order to allow a fast-
approaching vehicle to overtake him. A mail coach went
rattling past. It was time to turn back to London, he
decided, for his horse's sake if not for his own.

And what was he to do about the matter? he thought. Give up Ginny and beg Arabella's pardon? Was he prepared to allow his wife such power over his life? Was he going to allow himself to feel that he had committed some heinous crime? What had he done that was so very wrong, when all was said and done?

By the time he was in sight of London again, Lord Astor was feeling somewhat angry with himself for having allowed his wife to upset him so. Sooner or later she had to learn some of the harsher realities of life. Eventually she had to grow up. He could wish that she had not found out about Ginny. But the truth was that she had, although it was not his fault that she had done so. She must just learn to live with reality. Other wives did, yet appeared to have quite contented marriages.

He must speak to Arabella, he decided, without either harshness or apology, and explain to her what their marriage was to be like. There was no reason why they should not develop a friendship and an affection for each other. There was no reason why they should not have a satisfactory marriage. And there was certainly no reason for him to give up Ginny.

Arabella had admired him to such a degree that she had been nervous with him.

She had liked him.

She had trusted him.

She had been proud of him.

She did not wish to see him or speak with him. She did not wish him to touch her.

Damnation! Why had he had to be burdened with such a child for a bride?

She had looked haggard and gaunt that morning.

How would he be able to face her with the proper firmness of manner, without allowing her appearance to act as a reproach to him again?

How would he be able to assume a normal relationship with her? Had there been anything normal about their relationship anyway?

How would he be able to make love to her again at the

end of the week, knowing that his touch outraged and repulsed her?

Damnation!

Lord Astor dined at White's again that evening and accepted an invitation to move on to Brooks' later to play cards. By some miracle he won what a mere year before would have seemed a small fortune to him. Yet he would as soon have lost and been able to feel that his fortunes matched his mood. He drank to the point at which he had hoped to be roaring and blissfully drunk. Instead, his head was as clear and his mood ten times blacker than they had been when he had arrived hours earlier. He considered going to Ginny's but could feel no stirring of desire for her whatsoever. He slept somewhat less than he had the night before. He wondered if Arabella was awake and miserable.

Arabella dined at home with Frances, and the two of them joined Lady Berry at the opera in the evening, where Arabella sparkled with good humor and during the interval entertained both Mr. Lincoln and Mr. Hubbard with her bright chatter. In the middle of the first act she quietly removed her pearls when she realized she was wearing them, and dropped them into her reticule. She slept almost as soon as she lay down, being both physically and emotionally exhausted.

12

LORD Astor rose to his feet in some surprise when his wife entered the breakfast room the following morning. One glance at her face told him that her mood was as cold and set as it had been the previous day. She looked pale and surely thinner than she had when he first knew her.

"Did you miss your walk with George this morning, Arabella?" he asked. "The weather does look rather gray."

"It is chilly," she said, "but quite bracing. George had a good run. I took a maid with me, my lord. I was the height of respectability."

She came from the sideboard with the usual muffin and nodded to the butler to pour her coffee. Lord Astor looked at her, not knowing what he should say or whether he should say anything at all.

"Do not let me keep you from your paper," she said, cutting into her muffin.

He did not immediately resume his reading. "Did you enjoy the opera?" he asked.

"Yes, I thank you, my lord," she said.

"And do you have plans for today?" he asked.

"Frances and I are to call at Lady Berry's this afternoon," she said. "We are going to Vauxhall tonight."

"Vauxhall?" he said. "It is beautiful during the evening, Arabella. Also potentially dangerous. You will need to be careful."

"We are to be of Lord Farraday's party," she said. "Mr. Hubbard is to be there. Sir John Charlton. Theodore. Others. I shall be quite safe, thank you."

She had not once looked at him. Her voice was coldly polite. Lord Astor dropped his eyes to the paragraph he had been reading but found after two minutes that he no longer remembered even so much as the topic of the article. He closed the paper, folded it, and set it beside his empty cup.

"If you are not planning to be busy during the next hour, Arabella," he said, "I would like to talk with you in the library."

"After breakfast I always consult with the cook and the housekeeper," she said. "But my first duty is to you, of course, my lord. Are you leaving me now? Will you give me ten minutes?"

"At your convenience, Arabella," he said, rising to his feet, bowing to her, and walking from the room.

Arabella would not let her shoulders sag. The butler was still standing at the sideboard. And she would not leave half the muffin on her plate. She ate it in small mouthfuls, chewing tediously what felt like straw in her mouth. She would not show by even the smallest sign that she suffered. This day was to begin the pattern of all the rest of her days. She would approach it with dignity. She would not become a weepy, vaporish female.

There was still something very unreal about the whole situation. Soon she must wake up to find it all some dreadful nightmare. But she knew that there was no waking up to do. It was all true. She had married a man without any sense of honor or decency.

Whenever she allowed herself to think about the last three weeks—and just as much when she did not allow it—she felt nauseated again. And panic constantly threatened to grab her by the stomach. She had known all along that her husband could not care for her deeply, that she was not the type of lady to attract the very handsome Lord Astor. She had been beset by a strong sense of her own inferiority all through her acquaintance with him.

But she had never dreamed that he would be unfaithful to her. She must be very naive, she supposed. She knew that men kept mistresses. She knew there were such creatures as courtesans—she had seen some of them in the streets close to the theater and the opera house. But she had never thought that any of the fashionable gentlemen of her acquaintance would associate with such females. Perhaps some of the noisy, foppish young men who crowded the floor of the theater and ogled one with such impertinence might do so, but not the more respectable married men. And certainly not her husband.

She thought in great agony of the nights when he had come to her and she had been so scrupulous about giving herself completely to the man she had freely agreed to marry. Even when she had been afraid on the first two occasions. Even when she had been shy at the beginning. Mama had told her that men derived pleasure from the marriage act—it was not just for the creation of children. And she had wanted her husband to have pleasure even from her less-than-desirable person. She had wanted to be a good wife.

Yet he could have had no pleasure with her at all. All those nights in the past week and more when she had looked forward to his coming with some eagerness and had enjoyed his touch when he came, he had come only in order to create children in her. He would not have kept Miss Cox if he had had pleasure with his wife. He went to Miss Cox for pleasure. The beautiful, voluptuous Miss Cox. He did with Miss Cox the same things that had become so precious to her.

That terrible dull ache that was in her stomach, in her throat, in her nostrils threatened yet again to turn to panic. Arabella picked up her cup, held it with both hands in order to steady it, and sipped the strong, tepid coffee. He wanted to talk to her. Her husband had summoned her. She would obey.

"Thank you," she said, pushing back her chair even as the butler came to assist her. "You may clear away now."

She walked along the hallway to the library, nodded

to a footman, who rushed to open the door for her, and stepped inside.

Lord Astor closed a leather-bound volume with a snap and got to his feet.

"Come in, Arabella," he said, "and have a seat."

She perched stiffly on the edge of the chair across from the one he had just vacated. He did not sit down again.

"I see that your purpose has not cooled since yesterday," he said, pausing and looking down at her.

She was regarding the hands that were clasped in her lap. "No," she said. "I did not speak impulsively."

"We must talk this out," he said. "Otherwise our life together will become intolerable."

She looked up at him slowly, her eyes stony. She said nothing.

"Arabella," he said, "when I met you and married you, Ginny was my mistress. During the weeks when you have been growing to like me and become proud of me, as you put it yesterday, Ginny has been my mistress. I am not a different person suddenly because you have discovered the truth. I am not a monster."

"You are a liar," she said. "You lied to me on our wedding day, and—worse—you lied to God."

"I am sorry," he said. "You cannot know how sorry I am that you have discovered the truth. Not because I enjoy deceiving you. And not because I am ashamed. But because you have been hurt. But you need not be, Arabella. I respect you. I have grown fond of you. I hoped—and I still hope—that we can develop a friendship and an affection for each other."

"May I ask you something?" Arabella asked, looking steadily at him. "If you were to discover that I had been . . . had been . . . that I was Mr. Hubbard's mistress or Lord Farraday's or someone else's, would you be satisfied with my explanation that I still respected you, that I was still fond of you?"

"Don't be ridiculous, Arabella," he said impatiently. "That is an entirely different matter."

"Is it?" she said. "In what way?"

"You are a woman and will bear children," he said. "Besides, this is just the way our society works. Most ladies of any maturity accept the situation and would think it ill-bred to seem to know the truth."

"Ah," she said, "I see how it is, my lord. The blame must somehow be shifted to my shoulders. I am childish, of course. What can one expect of a bride of eighteen? And I am ill-bred. I have been brought up in the country and have never been exposed to the superior moral standards of London. Of course, if I were only more mature and better-bred, I would understand that there is nothing dishonest about promising fidelity to a bride when one employs a mistress."

Lord Astor put a hand to his brow and paced to the window. "We are getting nowhere, are we?" he said. "Let me be plain with you then, Arabella. I will not allow you to dictate the way I live. I am afraid you must learn to accept that. And if you do, you will not find me an inattentive or unaffectionate husband. If you find that you cannot accept reality, then I will allow you to return to Parkland Manor—until you are older, perhaps. What is your wish?"

"I am your wife," she said, "your property. Do with me what you wish, my lord."

He turned back to her in exasperation. "You will stay here with me, then," he said. "I shall stay away from you as much as I can while your hostility lasts. Ginny will doubtless be a more amiable companion. And you need not fear that you will be forced to do your duty—with a strong sense of martyrdom, of course. I have a bed to go to where I will be welcomed with no reluctance at all. I wish you good day, madam."

Arabella rose to her feet and sank into a deep curtsy. "Thank you, my lord," she said. "You will forgive me, perhaps, if I do not return the greeting."

* * *

Frances must be feeling some disappointment, Arabella thought as they were entering the main arched gateway to Vauxhall Gardens that evening. It was true that they had had all the excitement of driving across the new iron Regent's Bridge, and certainly they had arrived faster than they had expected. But Frances had had her mind set on approaching the pleasure gardens by river. Arabella thought that she probably had had a romantic image of herself being handed into a boat by Sir John Charlton and comforted by his strong arm during a choppy crossing.

But Sir John would have been nowhere in sight even if the bridge had not been in place and they had been compelled to take a boat. Lord Farraday had taken them up in his carriage with his sister. They were to meet the rest of the party at Vauxhall.

One could not be disappointed with Vauxhall Gardens, though, even if one approached by the less romantic route, Arabella discovered. She stepped through the main gateway with Frances on her arm, Lord Farraday and Mrs. Pritchard close behind, and discovered that they had stepped into an enchanted world.

"Ooh, Bella!" Frances pulled on her arm and gazed about her in wonder. "It is magical. Look at all the lanterns."

The night was perfect. The clouds that had obscured the sun all day had moved off to leave a clear, moonlit, star-studded sky. There was scarcely a breeze. But there was enough to move the top branches of the trees that were everywhere around them and to set the myriad lanterns to swaying. Patches of light and shade chased themselves along the many pathways and over the trunks of trees.

"It is like a fairy tale," Arabella said. "Cinderella and her glass slipper."

Mrs. Pritchard stopped behind them. "I always love to see and hear the reactions of people who have not been here before," she said. "And tonight you are fortunate. Everything is perfect. How did you know it was going to be quite such a night, Clive, when you planned this party?"

He grinned. "When I said my prayers last night," he told her, "I explained that for my sister nothing but the best was good enough, or I would never hear the end of it."

"Oh, foolish!" she said. "Let us take Lady Astor and Miss Wilson to your box before the music begins. We are rather late. Your other guests will doubtless be waiting."

Arabella proceeded with her sister along the path that led straight from the gate. She deliberately shook off the mood of deep depression that had been with her all day. She was going to enjoy herself, she decided. She was eighteen years old and she was a member of a party at Vauxhall. There was going to be music to listen to and supper to eat among congenial company. There were paths to walk along and lanterns to light her way. And later there were to be fireworks. It was to be the sort of evening she could only have dreamed of a year before. She was going to make the most of it.

The rest of the party was there before them: Theodore, Sir John, Mr. Hubbard, Lady Harriet, and her elder sister with her husband. They occupied one of the lower boxes, Arabella saw, close to the orchestra. She smiled gaily at everyone and acknowledged the bows of the gentlemen. Had Theodore brought Lady Harriet? she wondered. He sat next to her. How clever of him if he had done so. Frances, she saw at a glance, was settling herself at the opposite side of the box, next to Sir John Charlton.

"Ah, my dear Lady Astor," Mr. Hubbard said, indicating a chair close to his, "you are just in time for the music. Handel, if you like the man's music. Or if you do not, I suppose. I was rather hoping for dancing, myself, but it seems we are not to be that fortunate tonight. The proprietors are catering to superior tastes."

"I am just as pleased," Arabella said, taking the proffered seat and smiling at him. "These are lovely surroundings in which to listen to music. Which of Mr. Handel's works is to be played?"

"The Water Music," he said. "Good music to drink by, ma'am." He laughed at his own joke, lifted his glass, and bowed to her. "Farraday, wine for the ladies."

Arabella looked more closely at the bright eyes of her companion. Was Mr. Hubbard foxed? How scandalous. She had never actually seen a gentleman in his cups before. She hoped Mr. Hubbard would not disgrace them all by trying to stand up and sing to the crowd. She remembered Papa's stories of one of their neighbors who had a tendency to burst into song in public places when he had been drinking, though one scarce knew the sound of even his speaking voice when he was sober.

"The music is about to begin," Lord Farraday said to the box at large. "Would anyone care to eat now, or shall we wait until afterward?"

"We have come straight from the dinner table," Lady Harriet's sister said. "I pray you not to concern yourself about us, my lord."

Everyone seemed to be in agreement, though Mr. Hubbard renewed his suggestion that wine be ordered for the ladies. Arabella settled herself to listen to the music, having just been enthralled to hear from Mr. Hubbard that Mr. Handel had written the music to be played for the king as he was rowed down the River Thames. He could not recall which king, whether the present poor King George or his father. But Arabella was determined to believe that it was his present majesty whose mind had been soothed by the music.

Dining at White's for the third night in a row was not an enjoyable experience, Lord Astor found, though he supposed he must have done it quite frequently in the past before his marriage. It seemed so long ago! He did not lack for company or for suggestions on how he might spend his evening. But he could not face another night of cards, the theater held out no allure for him, and he had no wish to attend Mrs. Bailey's salon. He still could not face going to Ginny's. The trouble was, he did not feel like going home either. He sat on, not making any decision at all.

Arabella was at Vauxhall Gardens. He was glad that the weather had changed for the better since the late afternoon. She would enjoy herself there. With Farraday. He was a decent-enough sort. He would look after her. Hubbard too, had she said? Hubbard had been a steady-enough fellow before his wife had run off with a wealthy wine merchant the year before and caused a huge scandal. He had taken to the bottle rather heavily at that time and still had frequent laspes. He would never harm Arabella, but would he be protection enough for her in a place like Vauxhall if she happened to be separated from Farraday?

That neighbor of theirs, Perrot, was to be there too, of course. As solid and dependable as a rock, if his judgment did not fail him. Though, of course, he was more likely to have his attention wrapped up in Frances than in Arabella. And Frances was just as likely to be fluttering those long eyelashes of hers at Charlton.

He must not forget his responsibility to Frances, Lord Astor thought. It was true that she was older than Arabella, but even so, she was not yet of age and she was quite as innocent in the ways of the world as his wife. He was not at all sure that he trusted Charlton. He had not heard anything bad about him, but his impression was that the man was vain and selfish. And Farraday was not fond of him. It seemed they were neighbors. There was no telling what might occur if Charlton happened to get Miss Wilson off on her own in Vauxhall.

Was he mad? He had allowed his wife and his sister-in-law to go off to one of the most notorious pleasure spots in London without even talking to Farraday, who had invited them. He should never have allowed them to go without his protection.

And indeed, it was not too late, he thought, rising from his table and interrupting a conversation that was holding the rapt attention of the four other listeners. Arabella would not like it, and he would probably end up merely with the irritation of watching her sparkle among her male admirers, but go he must. He must make sure that both his charges were safe.

"I have to meet Lady Astor at Vauxhall," he murmured to his table companions by way of excuse.

"How long has it been, Astor?" one of his friends asked with a grin. "A month? Six weeks? She has you firmly in leading strings, eh?"

"What does a leg shackle feel like, Astor?" another acquaintance asked.

"It must be love," a third said with a sigh, his hand over his heart.

Lord Astor joined in the general laughter.

When he reached Vauxhall Gardens, he could not immediately locate the right box. He had arrived after the main entertainment of the evening was over, he realized, and before most people settled down for supper. Crowds were milling around in the open semicircular area before the boxes. Others were doubtless taking the air by strolling along the numerous paths that led off in different directions. Eventually he spotted a box that was empty of all except the slouching figure of his drunken friend.

"Hubbard!" he said, entering the box and taking one of the empty seats. "All alone?"

"Abandoned," his friend agreed cheerfully. "I would have stayed sober if there had been dancing, old boy, but what else was there to do during that interminable fiddling and trumpet-blowing except drink? Now I have boneless legs. Sorry about it, too. I couldn't oblige your wife by walking with her. Fetching little thing, Astor."

"Where did she go?" Lord Astor asked.

Mr. Hubbard gestured along the main path leading away from the gates. "That way," he said. "Five minutes ago. Probably closer to ten."

"The whole party is walking together?" Lord Astor asked.

"Oh, Lord, no," Mr. Hubbard said. "Let me see. First Farraday and his sister went to pay their respects to a second cousin or something remote like that. They all disappeared along that path." He pointed. "Then that large silent character—friend of Lady Astor's—went for a stroll that way with Lady Harriet. Her sister and what's-his-name, her husband, trailed along to make it all respectable, I suppose. No one else wanted to join them. Lady Astor insisted on staying to stop me drinking more and making myself ill or foolish, she said. Seemed to be under the impression that I was about to start warbling or something. Then Miss Wilson and Charlton found it imperative to set off in the same direction as the other four."

"And Arabella went with them?" Lord Astor asked after a pause had indicated that no further information was forthcoming.

"Oh, Lord, no," Mr. Hubbard said with a yawn. "She was busy chattering my head off so that I would not think about tipping back more drink. Sweet little thing, Astor. All heart."

"Where did she go then?" Lord Astor was frowning and beginning to feel a twinge of alarm.

"Fellow came by," he said. "Tall, thin, gangly. Spots."

"Er, Browning?" his friend suggested.

"Right first time," Mr. Hubbard said. "Browning. That's it. Told her he had just seen her sister. 'With Lady Harriet?' says Lady Astor. 'No,' he says, 'with Sir John Charlton.' And then he moved on."

"Yes?" Lord Astor prompted.

"Oh. Your wife got all excited about chaperones and dark alleys and whatnot," Mr. Hubbard said. "Wanted me to go with her to find them. I couldn't, Astor. Sorry, old chap. I suppose I should have. She shouldn't be running around here alone, should she? No harm, though. She will be with her sister by now and ripping up at her, no doubt." He chuckled. "She is younger than Miss Wilson, isn't she? Acting like a mother hen, she was. Where are you going, old fellow? Have a drink."

Lord Astor did not even hear him. It was worse than he had thought possible. Arabella had gone wandering off on her own. And where would he look if she had not kept to the main path? Surely she would not have wandered onto one of the darker side paths alone?

Damn Farraday for inviting her and then not looking properly to her safety. And damn Hubbard for getting drunk in the presence of ladies.

He felt a surge of relief a couple of minutes later to see a group of familiar figures approaching him on the main path. Frances was in the lead, arm-in-arm with Lady Harriet.

"My lord!" she called. "What a pleasant surprise. Bella will be delighted. Is not all this truly enchanting?"

"Where is Arabella?" he asked as he drew closer to the group.

"Oh, she stayed back at the box with Mr. Hubbard," she said. "We will have to tease her about her laziness, my lord."

"But she followed you," he said. "Is she not with you?"

"Bella came after us alone?" Theodore asked, pushing his way past the two ladies. "And Hubbard allowed it? Wherever can she be?"

"I am going to find her," Lord Astor said. "She must have turned down one of the other paths." And he hurried past the group without even hearing Theodore's worried declaration that he would search back closer to the boxes.

Lord Astor knew the impossibility of his task even as he hurried on, his head swiveling from left to right to peer down paths that curved away out of sight into the darkness. She could be along any one of them. She could be ahead of him or behind him or to either side of him. And if he turned off the main path he stood almost no chance at all of finding her. He felt his heart begin to pound against his chest.

It was a sheer miracle, he decided much later, that he happened to be peering down one dark path when she came running along another one behind him. She was calling his name before he turned. She had hurled herself into his arms almost before he had opened them to receive her.

13

"OH, my lord!" Arabella cried, her arms flying up around Lord Astor's neck, her face burying itself against his chest. "It *is* you. Oh, thank God! I have been so very frightened."

His arms came tightly around her and held her close. "Arabella!" he said. "You are quite safe. I have you now."

"I was so frightened," she said, trying to burrow still closer.

Lord Astor looked hastily to either side of them along the path. There was a lull in the crowd of revelers for the moment, but there was a group approaching. He drew his wife off the main path onto the quieter one down which he had been looking when she came running up behind him. He drew her into the shade of a tree so that they would not be observed from the main thoroughfare.

"You are safe now, Arabella," he murmured soothingly. He opened back his cloak, drew her against him again, and wrapped it around her. She put her arms around his waist and laid a cheek against his chest. She was trembling uncontrollably. "No one is going to harm you. I have you."

She pressed herself against him, silent for a while. Her teeth were chattering. Lord Astor cupped the back of her head with one hand and held it against him.

"I was very foolish," she said. "You will be very cross with me, my lord. I was looking for Frances, you see. She had gone off with Sir John without a chaperone, and I thought they would soon catch up to Lady Harriet and Theodore. But I found out I was wrong and they were still alone together. I thought I had better go along to find them. Mr. Hubbard was unable to accompany me because his legs would not support him. I fear he is grieving for Mrs. Hubbard again. I passed two gentlemen—except that they were not gentlemen at all—and they teased me and said things that made me blush. I was so embarrassed that I did not know where to look. And Frances and Sir John had gone farther than I thought."

She drew breath at last and lifted her head away from his chest to look up into his shadowed face. Her own was eager and mobile. "I could see another group of gentlemen approaching," she said, "and I did not know what to do. I could have died of mortification. I dared not turn back because of those other two, but I could not face having to walk past this new group. So I ducked off the path onto that smaller one, and I went a little way along it so that they would not see me when they passed. That was very foolish, was it not?"

"But understandable," he said soothingly. "I should never have let you come alone, Arabella."

"When I stopped to listen to make sure they had passed," she said, her hands on his neckcloth, playing with its intricate folds, "I thought I heard something in the trees beside me. A crackling. I thought it must be a wild animal or a desperate murderer, though I am sure now that it was nothing at all. I started to hurry away from there, but I kept going farther along the path instead of coming back. It was very dark. I suddenly realized what I was doing and stopped, and then I could not move one way or the other. I have never been so terrified in my life." She buried her face against his neckcloth. She was still trembling.

"What happened?" he asked, his voice tense. "Did anyone hurt you, Arabella?"

"I finally told myself that I had to go back," she said. "I told myself that I would be safe once I reached the main path, and that once I was close I could scream if necessary. So I just took a breath and ran. I thought my heart was going to burst with beating so hard. And I

wanted you more than anything in the world. And then
suddenly there you were. I could scarce believe it. I
thought you would turn and it would be some stranger.
I am so very thankful it was you." She looked earnestly
up into his face again.

"I am glad too," he said, his fingers smoothing back
the soft curls at either side of her face. "You are safe
now, Arabella." He lowered his head and kissed her
gently and lingeringly on the lips.

She looked a little dazed when he lifted his head.
"But where is Frances?" she asked. "And what are you
doing here?"

"Your sister is quite respectably chaperoned," he
said. "She was walking with a group of six a few
minutes ago. They were on their way back to Farraday's
box. I came to see that you were safe, Arabella. For
your sake I am sorry I was not much sooner."

She was looking up at him, her face illuminated by
the light from a lantern shining on it from the main
path. He watched her expression change from bewilderment to awareness. He relaxed his hold on her as she
took a half-step backward. His cloak fell back into
place around him. Her eyes slipped to his neckcloth.

"I thank you, my lord," she said, "for coming to my
assistance. I was really being very foolish. There was
nothing to be afraid of."

"You must never walk alone in a public place,
Arabella," he said. "I have told you that before."

He wished he could recall the words as soon as he had
spoken them.

"Then my fear was a just punishment for my dis-
obedience," she said. "I shall try to remember in
future, my lord."

She was going away from him even though she had
not moved. And he was reluctant to let her go. He
reached out and laid a hand against her cheek. "I
should have been here with you," he said. "I should not
have passed on my responsibility to Farraday. I must
look after you more carefully in future. And you were

quite right to be concerned about your sister's reputation, Arabella.''

She held her neck rigid, though she did not draw back from his touch.

"Come," he said, "I will take you back to the others. You will be ready for your supper. Take my arm, Arabella, and stay close."

She did as she was bidden, though she walked at his side without speaking or looking up at him. It felt as if she had withdrawn a hundred miles.

She had wanted him more than anything in the world, she had said a few minutes before, when she was still so dazed and frightened that she had forgotten that she had no feeling left for him but contempt. She had clung to him and talked to him as fast as her mouth would form the words. And she had responded to his kiss.

She was cold again now, unyielding and unforgiving. But she was hurt inside. And she needed someone to lean on, someone to look after her. He could not just shrug off his responsibility by telling both himself and her that she must accustom herself to the way he chose to live his life.

Lord Astor had the uncomfortable feeling that his life was going to have to change whether he wished it or not.

Frances smiled when she saw Arabella approach Lord Farraday's box. "There you are, Bella," she said unnecessarily. "His lordship found you. You had us all worried. Theodore has been searching all the paths close to here. Wherever did you go?"

"I merely stepped off the main pathway for a minute," Arabella said. "You must have walked past before I turned back."

"I declare I was so deep in conversation with Lady Harriet," Frances said, turning to smile brightly at the young lady beside her, "that I did not see you. I was not looking for you, of course."

Frances' emotions were being pulled two ways, and she had no leisure in which to analyze them. She had come to Vauxhall Gardens determined to ignore Theodore, to show him that there were numerous important personages—particularly gentlemen—with whom she could consort. It had been disconcerting to find him already in Lord Farraday's box, quite comfortably established with Lady Harriet Meeker and her sister and brother-in-law. Apparently he had dined with them. And though he had bowed to her and greeted her with perfect civility, he had made no move to sit by her or engage her in conversation.

She had somewhat forgotten her chagrin when Sir John Charlton chose to be attentive. And she had felt a stirring of excitement when he showed no desire to accompany Theodore's group on their walk, but waited until they were out of sight, gave Mr. Hubbard an assessing glance, and then suggested that after all they join the walkers. She had fully expected him to declare himself.

"What a pleasant night it is," he had said, strolling along the path and making no attempt to hurry in pursuit of the other group. "You must be very impressed with the gardens, Miss Wilson."

"Indeed I am, sir," she had assured him. "I never saw anything so enchanting in my whole life."

"Yes," he had said, "people who have spent all their lives in the country generally feel as you do. When one has traveled, of course, one sees such pleasure spots more in perspective. Vienna, Rome, Naples, Paris: they all have their own charm, you know."

"Oh, I am sure they must," she had said, looking admiringly at him.

"I am thinking of traveling again," he said, "now that all the tiresome wars seem to be at an end."

"You are?" Frances had held her breath in anticipation.

"I have some friends who have been begging me to accompany them," he had said. "I can probably grant them a year or so of my life."

"Oh," Frances had said, her heart plummeting. "I

am sure it would be well worth your while, sir."

"Of course," he had said, looking sidelong at her along his nose, "there are some things in England one must be reluctant to leave behind. Perhaps I should say some persons."

"Oh." Frances had flushed and lowered her eyes so that her dark lashes fanned her cheeks.

"Perhaps I will seek out Parkland Manor as soon as I return, and find one of those persons," he had said, reaching across and covering one of her hands as it rested on his arm.

"Oh!" she had said. "Would you? Would you really wish to, sir?"

"Would I wish never to set eyes on the loveliest lady in London again?" he had said. "I suddenly find this thoroughfare quite annoyingly crowded, Miss Wilson. Shall we try one of these more peaceful side paths?"

But Frances had drawn back in some alarm. "I think we should not, sir," she had said. "I have no chaperone."

"Am I not chaperon enough?" he had asked. "Do you not trust me?"

"Of course I trust you," she had said. "But Lord Astor would be angry if I went off alone with you."

He had not argued the point. They had walked on, and soon met the other four. And once again she had been irritated to see Theodore with Lady Harriet on his arm. Not that she resented his being interested in other ladies, of course. But not Lady Harriet. She was not even pretty! She had taken Lady Harriet's arm herself and led the way back with her.

And now she did not know quite how to feel. Theodore had stepped out of the box to talk with Lord Astor and Lord Farraday, while Sir John sat close to her. What would have happened if she had stepped off the path with Sir John? Would he have kissed her? Proposed to her? Had she lost her chance with him by being missish and refusing to go?

Theodore caught her eye and smiled for the first time

that evening. Or was he smiling at Lady Harriet next to her?

Arabella sat in Lord Farraday's box eating a bread roll and the thin slices of ham for which Vauxhall Gardens was so renowned. She might as well have been eating paper, she thought as she swallowed one mouthful. She was listening to Mr. Hubbard, who had begun by apologizing profusely for his boneless legs, and who had then proceeded to tell her with rather slurred speech about his marriage.

"I never was a wealthy man," he said. "Not poor, mind. And Sonia always seemed contented enough until we met that damned Bibby at Brighton. The man is a Croesus."

Arabella bit her lip and continued to look at him in polite sympathy.

"She took our son when she left," he continued. "Did you know that, Lady Astor? Did you know my wife had left me? It wasn't fair to take the boy, though, was it? My only son, you know."

"I am very sorry," Arabella said. The words seemed inadequate, but deep sympathy shone from her eyes.

"I don't know where they are," he said. "I could find out, I suppose. Hire Bow Street Runners or something. I could get my son back perhaps. Do you think I should, ma'am? Or is it better for a child to be with his mother even if she is a slut and the man she is with a damned cit?"

"Perhaps your son and your wife will both come back," Arabella said, reaching out and patting his sleeve. "Perhaps Mrs. Hubbard will realize what she has given up."

He laughed and reached out for his glass, realized it was empty, and set it back down with exaggerated care. "Wouldn't take her back," he said. "Out of the question. Unthinkable. No man would do such a thing and keep his self-respect."

"I suppose not," Arabella said.

.Mr. Hubbard lurched suddenly to his feet. "Fresh air," he said. "Must go for a walk. Wish I could feel my legs."

Arabella looked around her as he stepped from the box. She had almost forgotten her own troubles for a few minutes. Sometimes it did one good to realize that others suffered even more than one did oneself. She felt desperately sorry for Mr. Hubbard. From her few conversations with him, she guessed that before his wife had deserted him, he had been a gentle and good-humored man. Now he was bitter and cynical and unforgiving.

Sir John Charlton was talking with Mrs. Pritchard and Lady Harriet's sister and brother-in-law quite close beside her, while Theodore stood outside the box with Lord Farraday and her husband. Her sister was deep in conversation with Lady Harriet. Frances seemed quite unconcerned with either Sir John or Theodore. It seemed strange to see her seemingly quite unaware of the handsome gentlemen surrounding her.

Arabella focused her gaze on her husband as he stood talking, half-turned away from her. She was mortified to remember just how eagerly she had hurled herself into his arms and felt safe and happy. She had hugged him and poured out her tale of fright into his ears as if he were her best friend in all the world. And she had allowed him to hold her and soothe her.

She had let him kiss her!

It was humiliating too to recall how she had stood in terror on the dark side path, unable for a whole minute to persuade herself to move, wanting and wanting him, almost crying for him. Not for Lord Farraday or Theodore, either of whom was more likely to be close enough to rescue her. Not even for her mother, on whom she had relied all her life for protection. But for her faithless husband, who did not want her at all, who would not dream of calling on her to satisfy any of his needs.

It really was quite demeaning to be a helpless female,

Arabella decided. She did not like the feeling at all. She wanted to teach herself courage and independence. It was amazing how in less than one month she had come to rely so heavily on his lordship. It must not continue. She must harden her heart against him. If she continued to need him, she would end up forgiving him before she knew what she was about and accepting his interpretation of what marriage was all about. And she must never do that. What he had done was unforgivable, and his way of life was unacceptable.

She must hold firm. She had felt downright ill all of the previous day, imagining that he had gone to his mistress and was consoling himself in her arms for their quarrel. And all of this day she had felt no better. He had made it so very clear that morning that he had no intention of changing his ways and that he did not feel shame at what she had discovered. Of course, it all really did not matter to her at all. It was no concern of hers any longer how he spent his time or with whom. She had divorced herself from him emotionally even if she could not do so in fact.

But it still hurt, for all her determined efforts not to care, to look at him now, to see his handsome person, so familiar after three weeks of marriage, and to think of him holding another woman as he had held her a short while before, murmuring soothing words into her hair. Kissing her. Doing those things with his mistress that she, Arabella, had come to enjoy.

Lord Astor came to sit next to his wife before the fireworks display began. He set his chair a little behind hers so that his presence would not inhibit her pleasure and so that he might watch her delight without feeling obliged to make conversation with her.

And Arabella truly was entranced. She did not think she had seen anything quite so enchanting in her life. She sat rapt in her seat, leaning forward, totally unaware of her surroundings, as light and sound flashed and roared around her. If only Mama and Jemima could be there to see it too! Frances, Lady Harriet, and her sister were applauding and exclaiming with delight, but Arabella did not hear them.

She felt as disappointed as a small child when the treat was over and the night around her fell relatively quiet and dark again. And she was disoriented. She did not know where she was for a moment. She felt an instant's panic that she was alone again. There was no one on either side of her. She leaned back in her seat and turned with a little cry of alarm.

"I am here, Arabella."

And truly she was comforted by the low, steady voice and the warm hand rubbing against the back of her neck. She stared into her husband's eyes and felt all the despair of being married to a man she could not—and must not—forgive.

"I never saw anything so splendid in all my life," she said brightly to the occupants of the box. "I do thank you for inviting us, my lord." She smiled at Lord Farraday.

"I think you have me to thank, Bella," Theodore said with a grin. "Lord Farraday wished to make sure that I saw as much as possible of London while I am here."

"Then thank you, Theodore," she said, smiling gaily back at him.

Lord Astor was shaken. During the brief seconds when Arabella's eyes had looked into his, they had been raw with pain. And he knew, without the comfort of the defenses he had put up earlier that day and the day before, that he had put that pain there and that it would remain there as long as he continued with his chosen way of life. The rawness would disappear with time. Perhaps even the pain. But something would die with them.

It lay within his power to kill the gentleness and brightness in Arabella as surely as he had already killed her innocence.

He did not want that responsibility. He did not want the introspection and the soul-searching his marriage was bringing him.

She had felt very small and precious in his arms earlier. He had wanted to fold her into himself, to protect her against all the evil of the world. He had wanted to kiss away all her fears, swear that he would not allow anything to harm her for the rest of her life.

Yet he was the evil in her life. How could he protect her when he was her worst enemy?

He wished he had known a month before what he now knew about marriage. He would have turned all his fortune over to Arabella's family and taken himself off to the farthest corner of the earth sooner than be tempted to enter the respectable state of matrimony.

Lord Astor handed his hat and cane to Ginny's butler the following afternoon and showed himself into the sitting room while the servant went to inform her of his arrival. He must get his life back to normal, he had decided that morning. Arabella would grow up and learn to accept what could not be changed. She was out visiting with her sister and his aunt that afternoon.

"Geoffrey!" Ginny always made a theatrical entrance. She came through the door now, both hands extended. She looked as beautiful as ever. Her very distinctive perfume reached him before she did. "How lovely to see you again. I was just thinking about you and longing for you."

He took her hands and jerked her roughly into his arms. "Have you?" he said, his mouth already seeking hers. "I will have to find out just how much, Ginny."

"Ah," she said, wriggling in his arms in a way that she knew from experience heightened his desire to fever pitch, "I love you when you are hungry, Geoffrey. Will you come straight to my bedchamber?"

She was as beautiful, as voluptuous, as skillfully enticing as she had ever been. She lay naked on her bed, touching him, caressing him, crooning to him, moving her body against his, offering herself with an abandon that went beyond the desire to earn her generous salary. She used every skill and trick that experience had taught

her would render him mindless with the need to drive
out his passion in her.

Lord Astor sat up on the side of the bed and put his
head in his hands. "Not today, Ginny," he said at last.
"It is not your fault. I am just not in the mood."

"Are you ill?" she asked, her own voice still heavy
with desire. She sat up behind him and put her arms
around his naked shoulders and chest. "What is it,
Geoffrey? Come and lie down beside me and I will make
you feel better." She began to nuzzle his earlobe.

He shook her off none too gently. "Not today, I said,
Ginny," he repeated, getting to his feet and reaching for
his clothes.

"I don't understand," she said. "I have never failed
to arouse you before. There is no one else, is there?"

"I have told you," he said, "that it is not your fault.
It is me. I think perhaps you would be happier with
another protector. I know of several men who would
kill for you, Gin. Let me give you the house and arrange
for a settlement on you. It will be best." He pushed his
shirt inside his pantaloons and buttoned them up.

"What!" She was out of the bed and standing before
him, unselfconsciously naked. "You are turning me off,
Geoffrey? For failing to arouse you? It is her, is it not?
What power does she have over you and those other
men who hang about her? I wish I knew her secret. She
is not beautiful. She does not have a good figure. She is
a mere dab of a thing. Yet you give me up for her, when
you could have us both? She will never satisfy you, you
know."

"She is my wife," he said, tying his cravat with
impatient fingers.

She laughed. "And since when has that relationship
ever guaranteed a man satisfaction?" she said. "You do
not have a *tendre* for her, do you, Geoffrey? You are
not in love with her?"

He pulled on his Hessian boots. "She is my wife," he
said.

Ginny threw back her head and laughed. "Lord Astor

is in love with his child bride,'' she said. ''How famous! And the child has discovered that men may be enticed and is beginning to enjoy the feeling of power. And Lord Astor is jealous. How delicious! I shall make you the laughingstock, Geoffrey.''

He drew on his coat. ''I shall send my man of business to settle with you, Ginny,'' he said.

''Is he handsome, Geoffrey?'' she asked. ''And is he is love with Lady Astor also? Has she rendered him impotent too?''

Lord Astor closed the door of her bedchamber behind him.

14

ARABELLA arrived home from her walk with George two mornings later to find Lord Astor still in the breakfast room. She would have retreated if she could. She found being in his company difficult at the best of times. It was almost insupportable when there was no one else present. However, he rose to his feet, smiling, when he saw her, and held out a package to her.

"This will please you, Arabella," he said.

At first she thought it was a letter from home, but when she took the envelope and drew out the cards, she knew immediately what they were.

"Vouchers for Almack's!" she said. "Aunt Hermione really has been busy on our behalf. Frances will be very excited. I should go and tell her immediately."

"Is it not a few hours too early to waken Sleeping Beauty?" he asked. "Sit down and have your breakfast, Arabella."

"The next ball at Almack's is only two evenings away," Arabella said, nodding to the butler to put a muffin on her plate and taking her place reluctantly at the breakfast table.

Lord Astor indicated to the servant that he could leave. "I shall accompany you myself," he said. "Your first visit to Almack's is too grand an occasion for you to go alone or with only my aunt for company. Will you wear your blue silk, Arabella?"

"If you wish it, my lord," she said primly.

"Yes, I do wish it," he said. "I have noticed in the last few days that you are looking thin and almost ill. It is not my imagination, is it?"

"I am quite well, I thank you, my lord," Arabella

said. "I do believe I am slimmer than I was a month ago."

"Slimmer?" he said. "I would say 'thinner.' Am I responsible, Arabella? Is this what unhappiness and disillusionment are doing to you?"

"You need take no blame, my lord," she said, looking coolly up into his face. "I have been deliberately losing weight so that I might look less childish. I wish to look more like a woman. I can do nothing about my height, but I can control my weight."

"That is strange," he said, leaning back in his chair and looking thoughtfully at her. "Yes, when I first knew you, Arabella, I thought you younger than your years. But not since we have been married. You had a pretty figure. Very feminine. And certainly not fat. Nowhere near, in fact. I liked you better as you were. I take it that you do like ices and butter and apple tart?"

Arabella concentrated her attention on her muffin.

"Will you put the weight back on again?" he asked. "I was about to add 'for me.' But that would be no inducement, would it? And even a request you will interpret as a command and obey because you are determined to be a dutiful wife. Will you accept my advice, then, Arabella, as a gentleman who appreciates the female form? You looked prettier as you were."

"I am not pretty," she said, hearing with some dismay the petulance in her voice.

" 'Pretty' is a very relative term," he said. "To me you are very lovely, Arabella—even as you are. I will leave you now, as I can see that my presence makes you uncomfortable. And now that you have learned the steps of the waltz, will you reserve the first one for me at Almack's on Wednesday?"

"If you wish it, my lord," she said as he rose to his feet.

He smiled fleetingly. "Yes, I do wish it," he said.

He paused behind her chair, hesitated, and laid a hand lightly on her shoulder. "Arabella," he said,

"Ginny is no longer in my life. Neither is any other woman. Only you. Perhaps you can make of me a model husband after all."

She neither moved nor replied. He continued on his way from the room.

Frances was indeed excited by the news that at last they would be able to attend the weekly ball at Almack's. Her particular friend, Lucinda Jennings, would be there too, she said. Theodore would not. Only that fact clouded her mood somewhat. Not that she would miss his presence, of course, she explained to Arabella, when there were so many other gentlemen eager to dance with her. But it was sad to think that he had come all the way to town to enjoy the Season, yet was not to be in attendance at the most fashionable assembly of all.

Sir John Charlton would be there, of course. He had asked her to reserve the opening set and a waltz for him, she told Arabella when they were both in her dressing room an hour before they were to leave for the ball. Frances was still not sure that she had made the right decision in choosing her pink satin gown.

"Though it is still new," she said, more to her reflection in the mirror than to her sister. "At least no one will have seen it before. But is pink the wrong color for me, Bella? Is it too pale when I am blond? Both Lady Berry and his lordship approved the color, but I am not sure. What do you think?"

"I think it is quite perfect," Arabella said. "If it were a paler shade, perhaps you would be right, Frances. But it is such a rich color. And your hair is not dull, you know, as blond sometimes is. Yours gleams."

"Perhaps you are right," Frances said. "Do I have too many ringlets bunched at the sides of my head, do you think? Lady Berry said that the style is very fashionable, and indeed I have noticed that it is so. What do you think, Bella?"

"I think," Arabella said, "that if I do not return to

my own room soon, I shall be forced to leave for Almack's in this dressing gown. There is no arriving there late, you know. The doors close at eleven o'clock.''

"I do hope Sir John arrives on time," Frances said. "How dreadful it would be, Bella, to have no partner for the opening set."

Arabella was frowning as she hurried back to her own room. Frances had told her what Sir John had said to her at Vauxhall. And whereas Frances seemed quite convinced that the man had a *tendre* for her and was about to offer for her, Arabella was far more sure that he was involved merely in dalliance. Frances had not told her how he had tried to lure her from the main path, but Arabella had been able to put her own interpretation on the fact that he had left the box when the others were already far ahead and when Mr. Hubbard was too foxed to join them.

She shook off the thought as she allowed her maid to button up her blue silk dress. She wore it because she had been directed to do so, but she had to admit that she liked it. It was the least plain of all her dresses, the hem being caught up into delicate scallops, which were embroidered with tiny dark blue flowers. The sleeves had matching but even smaller decorations.

She had had to have the seams taken in slightly. And was it true, she wondered, as she sat at her dressing table for her hair to be coaxed into soft curls, that she had looked better before she had started to lose weight? She had had a pretty figure, his lordship had said. But then, he had also said that she was very lovely to him, and that was clearly a bouncer. He was trying to coax her out of her anger with him, and he was doing it in a very unsubtle way. She was not going to believe him.

Besides, even if she did believe him, even if he had meant what he said, did it matter? Was Lord Astor's good opinion of any importance to her now? She bent her head for her maid to clasp her pearls at her neck. These too she wore as a concession to duty. She had not worn them since removing them at the opera nearly a week before.

Arabella stood up at almost the same moment as a light knock on the door that adjoined her husband's dressing room preceded his entry into hers. Her eyes widened in surprise. He had not entered her rooms for a week. She turned to dismiss her maid.

"Ah, yes," he said when they were alone, "I knew you would look lovely in that gown, Arabella. That particular shade of pale blue complements your dark hair."

"Thank you, my lord," she said, fixing her eyes on his neckcloth and finding herself momentarily distracted by the intricacy of its design. Henry had outdone himself for the occasion.

"The pearls are not quite right, though," he said, strolling toward her and examining them thoughtfully.

He reached his hands around to the back of her neck. It seemed an age before he finally had the pearls unclasped and held them in one hand. Arabella was very aware of the scent of his cologne. His neckcloth and the lace that half-covered his hands were a dazzling white. A diamond among the folds of the neckcloth gleamed in the candlelight.

"I do not have anything else suitable, my lord," she mumbled.

"Do you not?" he said. "I will have to see what I can do about that. Turn around."

She obeyed and looked down to examine her fingers, which were twining themselves into intricate formations against her gown.

"Ah, just the thing," Lord Astor said, and her eyes caught the flash of jewels as his hands came over her head, placed something cold and heavy around her neck, and again grappled with a clasp at the back.

"What do you think?" he asked, taking her by the shoulders when he had finished and turning her back to the mirror.

They were sapphires, in an exquisitely delicate setting. Her hand went up to touch them. She did not say a word.

"There is a bracelet to match," he said. "Draw on your gloves, Arabella, and I shall clasp it around your wrist."

She obeyed, watching in silence as he completed the task.

"Let me look at you," he said then, taking her by the shoulders and holding her at arm's length. "Ah, yes. Lady Astor. Now you look quite grand enough to make your appearance at Almack's."

"Why?" she asked his neckcloth.

He was silent for a moment. "Because I wanted to," he said. "Perhaps because I have not liked the tension in which we have lived for the past week. Truce, Arabella?"

Arabella swallowed painfully. She reached up one hand and touched his waistcoat lightly. But she withdrew it again as if she had scalded herself. "You wish to bribe me into condoning your way of life?" she said quickly. "Is this how married ladies acquire their many jewels? Has this been the reason for your other gifts to me too? My pearls? My saddle? I will not be bought, my lord. My integrity is not so lightly for sale."

He stepped back from her. "What more can I do, Arabella?" he asked somewhat impatiently. "I have given up my mistress. I have decided to remain faithful to you after all. I have tried to treat you kindly. I have spent much of today choosing a gift for you. What more do you want? My soul? Is that it?"

"Perhaps some shame and sorrow," she said. "Some realization that what you have done is wrong."

"I am afraid you will have to wait a lifetime if you wish to see me at your feet in sackcloth and ashes," he said. "I am sorry I have hurt you, Arabella. I truly am. I have grown fond of you. Beyond that I cannot go. There is nothing so unusual or so terrible, you know, about a married man also having a mistress. You should be thankful that I have at least given up mine just to keep the peace between us."

Arabella looked up into his eyes. "Thank you for the sapphires, my lord," she said. "They are very lovely. I think Frances will be waiting for us."

He bowed stiffly. "This is the cloak you are taking?" he asked, picking up the dark blue velvet one that was hanging over the back of a chair. "Allow me to help you on with it."

"Do you like your sapphires, ma'am?" Lord Farraday was dancing the opening set with Arabella. "I must say they look quite splendid."

"Yes, thank you," she said. "His lordship has just given them to me, you know, because this is a special occasion, he said. It is my first appearance at Almack's."

He grinned. "I rather think Astor may find a bill from my bootmaker on his desk one morning," he said. "For resoling. I swear I walked to every jeweler in town with your husband today, and to some of them twice. Only the best would do for Lady Astor, it seems. I must confess he has made a good choice, though."

"Yes," she said. "They are more impressive than my pearls. They are what I was going to wear, you see."

"Did Astor tell you about my house party?" he asked.

Arabella shook her head and looked inquiringly at him.

"It was supposed to be a garden party," he said. "But my country home is a three-hour drive from town, and no one in his right mind is going to enjoy making the journey both ways merely to stand on my lawn for a few hours and drink my wine. My mother solved the problem while my mind was still grappling with it. Convert it into a house party of two or three days, she suggested. Nothing longer because this is the height of the Season and there would be too much to miss in town."

"What a lovely idea," Arabella said. "I assume we are to be invited, my lord?"

"I couldn't possibly have it without my closest friends in attendance," he said. "Astor and Hubbard and I have remained close even six years after finishing university."

"Mr. Hubbard is to be there too?" Arabella said. "I am glad."

"It is good of you to say so, ma'am," Lord Farraday said. "I was rather dismayed to see that you were exposed to one of his difficult moods at Vauxhall. He had no business getting foxed with ladies present, as I told him the next day."

"I did not mind," Arabella said. "I understand his need to drink, and that helps me excuse him."

"Poor Hubbard," he said. "He was always the most cheerful and sunny-natured of the three of us until his misfortune. But that is not a suitable topic of conversation. Your sister looks pleased with herself. You must be happy for her, ma'am. She has taken very well this Season."

"Oh, I knew she would," Arabella said, glancing across to where Frances was dancing with Sir John Charlton. "She has always been the beauty of the family."

"Perhaps so," Lord Farraday said gallantly, "but she was not granted all the beauty in your family, ma'am."

Arabella grinned at him. "Flattery will gain you my undying devotion, my lord," she said. Her grin changed to a warm smile suddenly. "And there is Mr. Hubbard. He must have slipped through the doors when they were already being closed."

Lord Astor, dancing with one of Frances' friends, observed both the grin at Farraday and the smile at Hubbard with irritation. Arabella had refused the olive

branch he had offered earlier and almost ignored the
gift he had chosen with such care. Yet she had nothing
but bright smiles and conversation for his friends. And
doubtless she would be dancing with the gangly youth
before the evening was out. He was standing alone at
one end of the room watching her, his arms folded
across his thin chest.

She did want his soul, he thought. He had been quite
right. She was just the sort of woman who would not be
satisfied until she had all of him. And for all her
diminutive size and childlike manner, she had a certain
subtle power that he was only just becoming aware of.
Without any apparent effort, she was succeeding in her
aim. He could feel her power, and it was going to take
all the vestiges of his willpower to resist giving in to her
entirely.

His way of life had already changed drastically in the
month since his marriage. Only a month! It seemed like
at least a year. He had come to devote a great deal of his
time and attention to Arabella. He had given up Ginny
and had not even begun to look about him for her
successor. What was more, he knew that he was unlikely
to do so. Somehow, without any deliberate decision on
his part, he had been converted into a faithful husband.

And now, as if all that were not enough, his conscience was being plagued, and he was having a battle
royal to defeat it. But he would be damned before he
would grovel before his own conscience—let alone
before Arabella—and confess that he had been wrong,
morally wrong, to keep Ginny and to visit her bed after
his marriage. He had given up Ginny because he no
longer had pleasure with her and because he did not like
to see his wife hurt. It was a personal decision he had
made, not a moral choice.

But the pressure was on him. He could feel it every
time he looked at Arabella, and every time he thought
about her, for that matter. He had to fight against the
feeling that he had wronged her terribly. He was sorry
that she had been hurt—he had admitted that and told

her so from the start. But he was not sorry for what he had done. He could not be. If he admitted that he was, then he was also admitting the total sanctity of marriage. He would be bound to Arabella by far stronger ties than he had ever contemplated or was willing to contemplate.

He could not be so bound. The thought was more than a little frightening.

"One can tell that you have had the best of dancing masters," Sir John Charlton said to Frances after they had been waltzing for a few minutes. "You perform the steps of the waltz with elegance as well as competence."

"But we never did have a dancing master at all," Frances said.

"Indeed?" Sir John looked down at her along the length of his nose. "You amaze me, Miss Wilson. You must have a natural sense of rhythm."

"Oh, we did learn all the steps of the various dances," she said. "Mama taught us some, and Theodore taught us others. Sir Theodore Perrot, that is. He was in his grace of Wellington's army, you know, and attended many assembles in Spain and Belgium."

"Ah, yes," he said. "One of our noble heroes. And he has doubtless been using the glory of his military past ever since to ingratiate himself with such a lovely lady and one of such superior manners."

"I don't know about that, sir," Frances said, a trifle disconcerted. "Theodore has always been our friend since childhood. I was almost sick to death with anxiety all the time he was gone, especially when news came of the Battle of Waterloo. That is, sir, my family was very worried. We are all very fond of him. Bella is too. You may ask her."

"Quite so," he said, looking around the ballroom, an expression of some boredom on his face. "Almack's is quite a tedious place to be, is it not?"

"I am surprised at its fame after seeing it," Frances said. "There is nothing so very special about the assembly rooms. But nevertheless, sir, I am sensible of the honor of being here.''

"Quite so," he said. "Will you be attending Farraday's house party next week?''

"I know nothing about it," she said.

"You will probably be invited," he said, "Astor being such a great friend of his. And Lady Astor too, I might add. It will doubtless be tedious. Farraday has the most amiable of good natures, but he does not always cultivate elegance, I fear. I shall be positively reluctant to accept my invitation if you are not to be there.''

"Oh." Frances blushed deeply and could think of nothing else to say.

"It would give me the chance to show you my own home," Sir John said. "It is only four miles away from Farraday's, you know. We are neighbors, you see. That is the connection between us. You might have thought it rather odd that we are sometimes seen together, since we are vastly different in, ah, manners, shall we say?''

"I would love to see your home," Frances said.

"It has a certain elegance," he said, "as you will see for yourself. Of course, when I become the Earl of Haig, I shall also inherit the mansion which my new position will demand.''

"Of course," Frances said.

"We will ride over to my home when we are at Farraday's," Sir John said. "Alone, if possible. I believe it is time you and I had a chance to get to know each other a little better, is it not, Miss Wilson?''

"Yes," Frances said, blushing again. "I mean, I will probably need to take a maid or a groom, sir.''

"Oh, quite," he said. "You showed some shyness at Vauxhall, if you remember. And that is to be commended. A reserve of manner is a necessary element of elegance in a young lady. However, prudishness is not a mark of an experienced lady of the *ton*. And I am sure you have been in town long enough to realize that country manners are not always town manners.''

"I . . . er . . . yes," Frances said, "I have been in town for a month, sir. One learns a great deal in that time."

He looked down at her with narrowed eyes. He never smiled, Frances thought, and a thrill of something like excitement crept down her spine.

"I shall look forward to Farraday's house party after all, then," he said. "I shall be leaving for my travels abroad in July. I would wish to know you quite well by that time, Miss Wilson, so that I might look forward the more eagerly to returning home. Or should I say, to returning to Parkland Manor?"

"Oh." Frances flushed yet again.

Arabella was dancing the second waltz with Mr. Hubbard. They danced in silence for a few minutes until he looked down at her and coughed in some embarrassment.

"I owe you an apology, Lady Astor," he said.

"Whatever for?" she asked, looking up at him wide-eyed.

"I understand I was somewhat, ah, foxed at Vauxhall," he said. "In fact, I know I was. I was not so far gone that I cannot remember. That was quite unforgivable in your presence, ma'am."

"No, of course it was not," she said. "You did not say or do anything offensive. And I like to think that at that particular time you needed someone to listen to you. I was happy to be the listener. Please do not apologize."

He smiled. "You are more forgiving than your husband," he said. "He ripped up at me the next morning about letting you run about the Gardens unaccompanied. But no more than he was ripping up at himself for allowing you to go without him in the first place. It does my heart good, you know, to see two friends of mine happy together. It helps restore my faith in marriage."

Arabella bit her lip and continued to look up at him. She felt an alarming urge to confide in him and pour out all her woes.

"But you do not need all this sober talk about marriages when you are celebrating your first visit to Almack's," he said. "Are you going to be at Farraday's house party?"

"Yes, I believe we are," Arabella said. "And I have just had a ridiculous idea. Do you think he will let me take George with me? He is desperately in need of more exercise than he can get in the park. Oh." She giggled suddenly. "George is my dog, sir."

He laughed. "Knowing Farraday," he said, "I am sure he would be delighted if you brought your whole kennels. Why don't you ask him?"

"I think I will," she said, and they danced in companionable silence for several minutes.

"Did I tell you?" Mr. Hubbard asked suddenly, his voice tense. "No, of course I did not. My wife and my son are back in Brighton, you know. Someone saw them there and told me so a couple of days ago."

Arabella looked up at him, some of her own pain in her look of sympathy.

"I am sorry," she said. "I mean . . ."

"I know what you mean," he said. "I am sorry. I should not keep referring to the subject. You are almost too kind a lady, ma'am."

15

THE weather during that spring had not been kind to
those who enjoyed the outdoors either for the fresh air
and exercise or for the opportunity it gave to show off
new bonnets and new conveyances. But on the morning
one week later when Lord Astor's traveling carriage set
off for Lord Farraday's country home, the sun shone
down from a cloudless sky, and the breeze was just
strong enough to prevent the heat from being
oppressive.

Arabella was gazing out through the window, her
whole attention focused on the trees and fields that
stretched away on either side of the road.

"How lovely it all is," she said. "It is amazing that
one can spend most of one's life longing to go to town,
only to find when one does so that one is closed in by
buildings and roadways and pavements. It is going to be
marvelous to have two days in which to breathe in
country air. George is going to be ecstatic."

"I imagine Henry will be so too when we reach our
destination," Lord Astor said. "I don't believe he
objects to traveling in the coach behind us with your
maid and all the baggage, Arabella, but he looked quite
indignant when I informed him that he would also be
sharing the carriage with George."

"Oh, dear," she said, "I hate it when Henry is cross
with me. He has a way of looking at one that would
make one swear that he is a royal duke at the very
least."

She found herself laughing with her husband before
she recollected herself and turned to stare resolutely out
through the window again.

Frances was looking dreamy. "I could almost

imagine that around the next corner we would come across Parkland," she said. "Do you not wish it were, so, Bella? We could see Mama and Jemima again. Do you think Jemima will have changed? Do you think she has grown more?"

"We have been away for less than five weeks," Arabella said. "Of course she will not have changed in that time, Frances. It is just that so much has happened that it seems we have been away forever. Oh, you are not about to cry, are you? Look at all the lovely scenery you will miss if you do."

"How foolish I have been," Frances said, two tears spilling over from her brimming eyes, "thinking that I would not have lived until I had been to town and attended all the *ton* events and met all the fashionable ladies and gentlemen who live there or spend the Season there. And all the time I had Mama and Jemima and you, Bella. And Parkland. And Theodore."

Arabella moved across from her seat beside her husband to sit besides Frances. "Don't take on so," she said, putting an arm around her shoulders. "Parkland and Mama and Jemima are still there, you know. And Theodore. And it is never a bad thing to have new experiences and to broaden one's knowledge of life."

"But Theodore is going to offer for Lady Harriet, I am sure of it," Frances said. Two very blue eyes appeared above her lace handkerchief. "And how dreadfully ungrateful you and his lordship will think me after you have brought me to London for the Season."

"Not at all," Lord Astor said. "A healthy dose of homesickness never did anyone any harm. I have promised to take Arabella home for the summer, Frances. A few more weeks and we will be on our way."

"You are very kind, my lord," Frances said.

"It was very kind of Lord Farraday to invite us to stay for a few nights, was it not?" Arabella said cheerfully, patting her sister on the back.

She was not so grateful two hours later after they had been greeted by their host and his mother and had been put into the housekeeper's care. That was when she discovered that she and her husband were to share a bed-chamber.

He looked at her apologetically when they were alone. "I am sorry about this, Arabella," he said. "Of course, we might have expected it when there are several house-guests staying here."

"Yes," she said, wandering to the window in some embarrassment.

"You need not fear," he said. "Doubtless I shall stay up almost all night with Farraday and Hubbard. We usually do a great deal of talking when we get together."

"Yes," she said. "Though you need not sit up on my account. I am your wife, you know."

Her voice sounded so martyred that Lord Astor found himself smiling. He strolled over to stand beside her at the window. It looked out across a long and sloping lawn to the north of the house and beyond it to dense trees.

"I have lived so much of my life in town," he said, "that I sometimes forget that the countryside can offer beauty and space. And peace. I have a home in Norfolk, you know—smaller than both this and Parkland, but it is set in attractive surroundings. I think you would like it, Arabella. Perhaps I will take you there toward the end of the summer."

She said nothing.

"Perhaps we can make a new start on our marriage," he said. "Pretend that the last month did not happen. We can be alone together in Norfolk, Arabella. We can get to know each other. Become friends. Shall we try?"

She was silent for a while. She continued to stare from the window.

"I don't think it is possible," she said. "The past month did happen, and no amount of pretending can make either of us forget. It is too late to start again. Everything has been spoiled. However, I am your wife, and I will continue to do my duty. You may take me where you will. But I can never be your friend, my lord, or you mine.''

Lord Astor stood silently beside her, tapping one fingernail against the windowsill for several moments. Then he moved abruptly and turned away from her.

"You will want to change your dress for the garden party,'' he said. "I shall see you downstairs later, Arabella.''

"Yes,'' she said. She still stared through the window.

Frances found Theodore talking with Lord Farraday and Lord Astor out on the terrace when she came downstairs. She raised the yellow parasol that complemented her pale blue muslin gown like the sun in the sky and strolled toward them. All three gentlemen turned to bow to her. Theodore separated himself from the group and came to offer her his arm.

"You look very lovely, Fran,'' he said. "As usual. Would you care to stroll about the lawn for a while? Not many people are down yet.''

"Thank you, Theodore,'' she said, taking his arm, giving her parasol a twirl, and gazing carelessly about her.

"How does this compare with town?'' he asked, indicating the immaculately kept lawn and the flowerbeds beyond it with his free arm. "Do you ever feel homesick?''

"Oh, la,'' she said with a laugh, "I never have a spare moment in which to think about home, sir. We have a great number of invitations to choose among each day, you know.''

"I am quite sure you do,'' Theodore said. "Two such lovely ladies must be much in demand. Bella has been turned into quite a little beauty with her curls and her new gowns. Is it Astor who has had the good taste to forbid all the frills and furbelows that used to make her look like a slightly overgrown child?''

"You must not be unkind about Bella, sir,'' Frances

said stiffly. "She is the sweetest, kindest sister anyone ever had."

"I believe you," he said. "She is also lacking in natural good taste, I would say. You are not about to start weeping, are you, Fran? It is quite unnecessary, you know. I admire Bella's character quite enough to wish to make her my sister too."

"You always did lack sensibility," Frances said, tears sparkling on her long lashes. "It must come from having been a soldier for several years."

"It is a good thing, too," he said. "It would not do if we were both watering pots, now, would it, Fran? One of us has to retain some common sense."

"Well of course I would not expect you to cry all the time," Frances said, drawing a handkerchief from her pocket and dabbing at her eyes. "That would be most unmanly. But you might at least show some sympathy. You have always made fun of my tender sensibilities."

"That is not true," he said. "I distinctly remember taking you into my arms to comfort you not a year ago when you were crying over a dead bird we had found by a hedgerow. I even kissed the top of your head, Fran, and had my face soundly smacked for all my sympathy."

"Oh," she said, tossing her head and twirling her parasol angrily. "I do not know why I ever try to hold a sensible conversation with you, Theodore."

"No," he agreed. "You show great fortitude. Tell me, does Sir John Charlton show you greater sympathy?"

"He appreciates me," Frances said.

"Oh, I have no doubt he does," Theodore said. "Don't marry him, though, Fran. You would be unhappy. You need someone less in love with himself and more dependable. Me, for example."

"Sir John is not in love with himself," Frances said crossly. "Are you making me an offer, Theodore?"

"By no means," he said. "If I offered for you now, I

would probably be sent away with a box on the ears. I
have been a soldier, you know. Let us stroll back toward
the house. I see there are more people on the terrace
than there were. Ah, there is Lady Harriet Meeker. She
said she was coming. I must go and pay my respects.
Bella is out too. You will doubtless wish to join her.''

"You are probably all impatience for the chance to
make her an offer,'' Frances said spitefully, giving her
parasol such a spin that the breeze noticeably increased
about her head.

"Bella?'' he said. "She is already married, Fran.''

"You know I mean Lady Harriet,'' she said.

"Lady Harriet?'' He slowed his pace and looked
down at her indignant face in apparent surprise.
"Impossible, Fran. She is betrothed. Did you not
know? To an earl who prefers the wilds of Yorkshire to
London. She talks about almost no one else. When she
is with me, anyway. Besides, I doubt if I would offer for
her in any event. I just happen to have other plans.''

"Oh,'' Frances said faintly, but the expected
declaration did not come. Theodore strolled in amiable
silence at her side until they reached the terrace, where
they went their separate ways.

"Your dog has been settled in the kennels,'' Lord
Farraday told Arabella when she joined him and Mr.
Hubbard on the terrace. "Apparently my poor groom
was near deafened by the enthusiastic welcome he
received from my own dogs. He will be exercised this
evening. If you wish to take him for a longer walk
yourself, of course, feel free to do so at any time,
ma'am.''

"I am very grateful,'' Arabella said. "I hope you did
not think it dreadfully forward of me to ask if I might
bring him. If you do, you must blame Mr. Hubbard just
as much as me. He thought that it might be all right to
ask you.''

Mr. Hubbard grinned. "Farraday is always so overrun here with dogs and cats and female relations that he will not notice one extra dog," he said.

"Come out onto the lawn and meet one of those female relations," Lord Farraday said. "You have not met my mother, have you, Lady Astor?"

"I shall come too," Mr. Hubbard said, "to pay my respects."

Arabella took an arm of each gentleman and was led out into the sunshine. However, a few guests were still arriving and demanded the attention of their host and his mother. She was soon left alone with Mr. Hubbard.

"I have something I wish to show you," he said after they had chatted for a while and strolled across the lawn. "It is in my room. Will you wait while I fetch it?"

"Yes, certainly," she said. "I shall stay here and smell the roses."

Mr. Hubbard disappeared in the direction of the house.

"Are you all alone, Arabella?" Lord Astor asked, coming up behind her after a couple of minutes. "Would you like some lemonade or something to eat? Shall I take you across to the tables?"

"No, thank you," she said. "I am neither thirsty nor hungry. And I am waiting for Mr. Hubbard."

"Indeed?" he said, his eyebrows raised. "Your other friend is here too. Lincoln. Have you seen him?"

"Yes." Arabella smiled. "He is with Miss Pope. I am so glad."

"Is there something special about Miss Pope?" he asked.

"Mr. Lincoln seems to think so," she said. "He did not have the courage to approach her at the start of the Season. On account of his leg, you know. I tried to persuade him that a handicap like that is of no significance whatsoever."

"So you have been matchmaking," he said with a smile. "You have a kind heart, Arabella, do you not? Have you found anyone yet for your gangly youth?"

"I believe you refer to Mr. Browning," she said stiffly. "He does not have a *tendre* for any lady, my lord. He needs to gain confidence first as a man. He looks so young, you see. I can sympathize with that. I did suggest that he try boxing. I said that you would perhaps be his sparring partner on occasion. But he was far too shy to consider the suggestion."

Lord Astor looked down at her, a smile lurking in his eyes. "That sounds like a good suggestion," he said. "I must have a talk with . . . Browning, is it? I will not embarrass him. I will make it seem that the suggestion comes from me."

"Thank you," Arabella said, looking fleetingly up into his face.

"Here comes Hubbard," he said.

The three of them stood talking about trivialities for a few minutes until Lord Astor, raising one eyebrow and looking from his wife to his friend, excused himself and strolled away to join another group of acquaintances.

"I could have shown Astor too," Mr. Hubbard said, "but he would have thought me foolish and sentimental, doubtless. And perhaps you will too, ma'am. I cannot think why I burden you with my concerns. I never feel the urge to do so with any other female."

"I am flattered," Arabella said. "And, of course, my curiosity is thoroughly piqued."

"Shall we walk right into the rose garden?" he asked. "I can see a seat in there."

He drew a package from his pocket when they were seated side by side on a wooden bench. He uncovered it carefully and handed it to Arabella.

"Oh," she said. "It is your son, isn't it? What a very lovely child! Is it a good likeness?"

"It was painted just a month before they left," he said. "Yes, it was very like, though he looks quite the angel here. He was always into mischief."

Arabella could feel an ache in the back of her throat. "How you must miss him!" she said.

"I did not tell you quite the truth, you know," he said abruptly. "I told you someone had reported seeing them in Brighton. That is not so. It was Sonia herself. She wrote to me."

Arabella looked up at him. He had a strange, twisted smile on his face as he took the miniature from her hands and wrapped it carefully again.

"She is unhappy," he said. "She wants to come back. Can you imagine? After all the scandal, she thinks I will take her back again. No, she does not think it. But she asks it, anyway."

"What are you going to do?" Arabella asked.

"It would not be right to forgive her, would it?" he asked. "Some things are unforgivable. What she has done is unforgivable."

"Yes," Arabella said sadly. "But your son?"

"She wants to send him back to me, whatever I decide," he said. "She wants him to have a chance of a decent life. But I cannot take him from his mother. It would kill her. She loves him dearly, you see."

They sat side by side for a few minutes. He turned to her finally and smiled before getting to his feet. "This is a garden party," he said. "My pardon, ma'am. I merely wished to show you my paternal pride in my son. I did not intend to make both you and myself gloomy. Shall we go in search of refreshments? This heat must have made you thirsty."

Arabella took his arm and allowed herself to be led across the lawn to where tables set with white linen cloths were loaded with drinks and delicacies of all kinds.

"There is Lady Berry," she said, raising one hand and waving to her husband's aunt. "I should go and speak to her, sir."

He bowed and released her arm.

"Thank you for showing me the picture," she said before leaving his side. "I know it must be one of your most precious treasures."

* * *

Lord Astor was leaning against the stone balustrade at the edge of the terrace later that evening, looking out across the moonlit lawn. The air felt delightfully cool after the heat of the drawing room, where all the guests had just finished playing a spirited game of charades. His team, captained by Lady Harriet Meeker, had been soundly beaten by Frances' team, despite the fact that they had had Farraday, a natural actor, on their side. Frances had had Sir Theodore Perrot.

He was aware of Frances now, walking quietly along the terrace behind him with Sir John Charlton. Several other guests had also discovered the coolness of the outdoors. He wondered about Charlton. He had been remarkably attentive to Frances in the last month. Was he about to offer for her? Somehow Astor doubted it. The man seemed to be puffed up with his own consequence. It seemed unlikely that when choosing a bride he would choose someone of relative social insignificance, like Frances. She was remarkably lovely, of course, but she had no title or large dowry to bring along with her.

Would the girl be disappointed at the end of the Season? Would Arabella have to cope with her tears and laments all through the three-day journey back to Parkland? If she had any sense, Frances would grab Perrot and hang on to him for life. He was clearly besotted with her, for all his apparent interest in Lady Harriet. Besides, wasn't Lady Harriet promised to someone? He seemed to have heard that Ravenscourt had brought her to London for her come-out but intended to take her back to Yorkshire again for her betrothal.

Lord Astor sniffed the air. He longed to take a walk across the lawn to the rose garden. But not alone. He wanted Arabella with him. She probably would come too if he asked her. No, not probably. She would construe his merest request as a command, and the moonlight and the smell of the roses would be ruined by the distance she would set between them.

He had left her in the drawing room in the midst of an animated conversation with Lincoln and Miss Pope, Hubbard, his aunt, Farraday's mother, and one or two others. She would have stopped talking and laughing if he had joined them. As she had that afternoon when he had stood outside the rose garden with her and Hubbard. He had left them there eventually almost with the feeling that he was interrupting a lovers' tryst. And when he had turned later, they had disappeared into the rose garden.

He knew it had not been a lovers' tryst. Hubbard was still pining for his Sonia, and Arabella was strictly loyal to her marriage. But he still felt sick with . . . What? Was he jealous of Hubbard and Farraday and Lincoln and the gangly youth—Browning?

Why would he be jealous? What was it he wanted from Arabella exactly? The smiles and the easy friendship that she bestowed on other men around him? If she treated him as she did them, would he be satisfied?

Lord Astor tested the thought in his mind as he shifted his weight and rested his elbows on the balustrade. He wanted to make love to Arabella. No, he wanted to make love *with* her. He wanted her to love him.

He wanted her to love him? Did he? Why? Surely it could make no difference to him whether she loved him or not, unless he loved her.

He did not love her. That was an absurd idea. She was merely Arabella, the little, only slightly attractive daughter of his predecessor, the addition to his life who had caused him endless upheaval. The woman who wanted his soul.

Of course he did not love her. He wanted to bed her because he had been two weeks without a woman. It was as simple as that. A simple biological urge.

It was almost bedtime. And they were to share a room. They were to share a bed for the first time since their marriage. And he must not touch her. He could not touch her for as long as her hostility lasted. It would seem like rape, even though she was his own wife.

Lord Astor pushed himself away from the balustrade and made his way back inside the house again. He would see if Hubbard or Farraday fancied a game of billiards after most of the guests had retired for the night.

"It is so much like home to stand here and breathe in the smell of clean country air and roses," Frances was saying to Sir John Charlton. They had walked to the end of the terrace and had stepped onto the lawn that led to the stable block west of the house.

"We could walk closer to the roses," he said. "I shall pluck one for your hair. There is always the danger of pricking one's finger, of course, and shocking one's manicurist, but I am sure we can manage."

"The rose garden is too far away in the darkness," Frances said. "We had better walk back to the house, sir."

"A month in town has not educated you in the ways of the world, has it?" he said. "What a prude you are, Miss Wilson. Come, you must prove to me that you are not quite the country mouse."

He slid an arm around her waist and pulled her against him. A startled Frances was being kissed before she could even begin to defend herself. She stood still in utter shock and revulsion. His mouth was open over hers, and softly moist.

"We will drive over to my home tomorrow," he said when he finally lifted his head. "I see that you are learning after all."

"I really think I should not," Frances said. "I do not know what I have done to give you the impression that you might take liberties like this, sir."

"Are you crying?" Sir John asked, peering at her in some surprise. "You are a tender creature, are you not? Here, take my handkerchief. I had no idea my embrace would be so overpowering to a lady of such tender sensibilities. I will have to remember to be more gentle the next time, until you are accustomed to my attentions. Come, I will take you back to the drawing room. The rose garden will have to wait for another night."

"Thank you, sir," Frances said as he took her arm and led her back onto the terrace.

16

ARABELLA sent her maid away as soon as she was in her nightgown and had had her curls brushed out for the night. She paced restlessly to the window and back to the bed. Would he come soon? Or would he stay up for most of the night as he had half-promised, talking to Lord Farraday and Mr. Hubbard?

The four-poster bed with its domed canopy and heavy velvet hangings suddenly looked very narrow. She and her husband were to share that bed, sleep together side by side. They had not been together as man and wife for more than two weeks. They had never spent a night together.

It seemed to Arabella impossible to climb into that bed and address herself to sleep. She would not be able even to close her eyes. She would be as stiff as a board.

She did eventually climb in on the side farthest from the window and then wondered if she should move over to the other side. Which side would he prefer? She stayed where she was, as close to the edge as possible, clinging to the side with both hands.

She closed her eyes and then opened them wide again. The candles were still burning. Should she leave them so or should she snuff them? She jumped out of bed, snuffed the candles hastily, and almost ran back to the bed. It seemed to be far safer to be hidden beneath the covers than to be caught standing in the middle of the room.

Arabella tried to coax her mind into thinking of pleasant things: the conversations she had had at the garden party during the afternoon; the friendly exchanges she had had with her neighbors at the dinner table; the hilarity of the charades, in which she had acquitted herself not at all well; the good fellowship afterward. She tried not to think of the depression that was waiting to oppress her.

Her husband had tried to patch up their quarrel earlier that afternoon. He had suggested that they start all over again, put the first month of their marriage behind them, try to become friends. He wanted to take her to his home in Norfolk so that they could be alone together.

And she had rejected him. She had pointed out that the past was forever with them, that there was no way now to make something pleasant of their marriage.

And she was right, was she not? Even if he was sorry for what he had done—and he had never said that he was—how could she ever trust him again? If he had needed a mistress when he first married her, would the need not return? After all, she had no great attractions either of person or of character with which to hold his interest.

How could she forget? How could she become his friend? A friend was someone one trusted.

She was right. It was too late for them.

But she did not want to be right. She wanted to trust him and admire him as she had at the start of their marriage. She wanted to be able to depend upon him as a wife should upon her husband. She wanted to obey him from inclination and not merely because her marriage vows dictated that she must.

She wanted . . . She did not know what she wanted, but she knew that if she did not think of something else very quickly and concentrate her whole mind on it, she would cry.

She would not cry. If she did, her nose would get stuffed up and she would have to breathe through her mouth. And she would snore when she slept. If she slept! How very humiliating that would be.

Much later, Lord Astor lay awake, his head turned to one side, watching his wife. She was curled up on her side of the bed, facing away from him, so close to the edge that he wondered that she had not fallen off. She was sleeping. He had his hands clasped behind his head. He had resisted the temptation to touch her. It was a strong temptation. She looked like a child, positioned as she was. But he knew that she felt very much like a woman. And he had not had her for more than two weeks.

She turned suddenly, making a great to-do about the matter, wriggling into a comfortable position, burrowing her nose into the pillow, pulling the blankets up to her chin. Her curls brushed against his arm. Lord Astor smiled.

And then he knew that she had awoken. There was an unnatural stillness about her body. She opened her eyes and looked at him without moving. She stared at him for a long time. The faint light from the window was behind him. He realized that she could not see that his eyes were open.

"Hello, sleepyhead," he said.

She still did not move. "I was sleeping," she said. She sounded surprised.

"Did you think you would not?" he said. "Because I would be coming?"

"Yes," she said.

"Arabella!" he said softly. He took his hands away from behind his head and turned onto his side, facing her. "I am not quite a monster, you know. I am a man, the same one you trusted just a few weeks ago. The only difference is that at that time I was unfaithful to you and now I am not." He touched her cheek lightly with his fingertips.

She lifted her hand and unexpectedly caught at his. She pressed it against her cheek and then turned her head so that her lips were against his palm.

"Arabella." He kissed her temple, her cheek, and—when she turned her head—her lips. "Let me make love to you. Don't freeze me out. Don't just be dutiful. Love me. Please. Love me, Arabella."

He feathered kisses on her lips and cheeks until she took his face in her hands and offered her mouth to him. She whimpered when he kissed her more deeply. He pushed an arm beneath her pillow and brought her warm, tiny body against his. He teased her lips with tongue and teeth until she opened her mouth and allowed him entrance. She grew hot in his arms.

Arabella had lost herself. She had been sleepy and quite without defenses. Now there was no possible way of fighting. Indeed, there was not even any thought of putting an end to what had begun. Her husband's arms were about her, she was pressed to the heat of him, his mouth was over hers, his tongue creating erotic aches and arousing a desire that totally precluded thought. She wanted him, all of him. Then. There could be no holding back, no waiting.

"Yes, oh, yes," she gasped when his mouth left hers and began to blaze a hot trail along her throat. She twined her fingers in his hair. "Yes. Love me. Oh, please, love me."

Then she was helping him unbutton the front of her nightgown. Hindering him, rather, in her impatience, her hands plucking at his. And then she gasped as strong hands lifted the fabric right away from her shoulders and down her arms and returned to touch her breasts, to explore them lightly, to touch her nipples, to tease them, to arouse them so that she cried out with the pain of her longing.

"Arabella." She was on her back, her husband leaning over her, kissing her eyes, her mouth, her throat, her breasts. "My love. Oh, so beautiful. So very beautiful."

She cried out to him again as he took one nipple into his mouth and touched the tip with his tongue.

They were both naked suddenly. She reveled in the feel of powerful muscles beneath her fingers and palms as she ran her hands over his chest and shoulders, down his arms. And she ached and ached with painful desire as his hand aroused her and readied her for his entry.

"Make love to me," she pleaded against his mouth. "Make love to me. Oh, please, please."

But when he pushed inside her, there was none of the relaxed enjoyment that she had learned to expect from their earlier beddings. There was no detached and pleasurable analysis of what he was doing to her. There was only the need to feel him drive even deeper and more powerfully toward that unbearable ache of her longing.

He could feel her coming. He had his weight on his arms so that he would not crush the small body beneath his own. But he had her against him, taut with a passion that he had not suspected her capable of, on the brink of release.

Every move of his had been calculated from the moment he had felt her turn hot in his arms. Everything was for Arabella, so that she would know the power of his love, so that she would be satisfied, so that he might see her happy in his arms afterward. Gratification of his own desire became nothing. Only Arabella mattered. He would not care if he took nothing at all. He was making love, something he had never done before. He was giving her everything he had to give. He was giving himself.

And yet—strange reward of a love only now recognized by the heart, still not by the mind—as he felt her come, he knew that he was coming to meet her. He knew that they were to experience the rarest of all blessings of physical love: they were to unite at the moment of a shared climax.

Lord Astor held his wife's hands against the bed on either side of her head as it happened, his fingers twined in hers. His face was buried amongst her curls.

"Geoffrey?" she whispered, her voice surprised. And then she gripped his hands, cried out against his shoulder, and shuddered into release. He sighed, relaxed his weight on her, and went with her into the land beyond passion, beyond feeling, almost beyond consciousness.

* * *

Arabella awoke the following morning with the feeling that it was late, much later than she had intended to get up. She had planned to rise early so that she might take George for a walk before anyone else was about. But she had overslept.

She turned her head suddenly as memory overtook her. But she was alone. She must have been very deeply asleep indeed to have missed her husband's getting up and dressing. Arabella blushed despite the emptiness of the room as she stretched and felt her nakedness beneath the covers.

How could she have! She had given in to utter wantonness, ignored the dictates of reason and morality, and allowed her physical needs to lead her on. How could she now convince either her husband or herself that she was bound to him only by the ties of law and the church and duty? And what defenses would she have against her own misery when the novelty of having her had worn off and he turned to a more practiced courtesan again?

She could not even blame him. She had started the whole thing the night before. It was true that he had spoken to her and touched her, but she was the one who had pressed his hand against her cheek and kissed it. And she had eagerly followed him every step of the way in what had ensued. She could even recall begging him to love her.

She could have pleaded sleepiness if that had been all. He had touched her before she was properly awake, and by the time she was, she was so physically aroused that there had been no resisting what had happened. But that could not be pleaded for the second time. She had been awake, staring at him, studying his strong and handsome profile in the gray of early dawn, touching his chest, long before he opened his eyes and smiled sleepily at her. And she was the one who had snuggled closer and raised her face for his kiss.

She had not been unaware that time of what she was

doing and with whom. She had let him arouse her, lift her on top of him, and bring her knees up under his arms. And she had put her hands on his shoulders as he moved with powerful strokes in her, and gazed into his eyes until the end, when she had lowered her forehead to his chest and taken into herself all that he had to give, and gave in return all that was herself.

She had known that he was Geoffrey, her faithless husband, and she had not cared. Not, at least, until several minutes after it was finished and he had rolled over with her and set her down on the bed and kissed her deeply on the mouth. Then, the passion gone, she had wanted to cry, knowing how vulnerable she had made herself, knowing that now she had given him the power to hurt and hurt her. She had allowed herself to love him, she had opened all of herself to him, and given all she had to give. Not just her body, but her very self. And now she would never be able to wrap herself around with the assurance that she did not care, that she could make a meaningful life for herself independent of her husband.

She had turned over onto her side, facing away from him, and concentrated every effort of body and mind on not sobbing aloud. Her body had been rigid with tension when he had moved over behind her and smoothed back the curls from the side of her face with a gentle hand.

"Are we friends now, Arabella?" he had asked. "Am I forgiven?"

She had been quite incapable of answering.

"What is the matter?" he had asked, running his hand down her side and feeling how tense she was. "Are you crying?"

She had bitten both lips and willed the sob that was trying to escape her back down her throat.

"This has made no difference, has it?" he had said at last. "I am still the erring husband who must grovel at your feet. And even then I will not be forgiven, will I,

Arabella? You will never trust me. I will never be allowed to forget."

He had rolled away from her and she could feel him lying awake behind her even as she lay, fighting to control her tears, knowing that she might as well get up then and go out for George before the grooms were up even. She would certainly never sleep.

But she had slept. And deeply so. And lay now bitterly regretting her lack of moral control the night before. And filled with wonder at the ecstasies of physical passion. And utterly confused.

Arabella threw back the bedcovers, flushed yet again at her nakedness and all it had meant the night before, and pulled on her nightgown before ringing for her maid.

Lord Astor was out riding with Lord Farraday and several of the other gentlemen from the house. They were inspecting a newly drained portion of the estate that had been seeded for the first time that spring.

"Where is Hubbard?" Lord Astor asked his friend when they had a moment together.

"He is taking himself off back to London," Lord Farraday said. "I can't think why, when he made the journey all the way out here with every intention of staying until tomorrow. Strange fellow, Hubbard. I suppose one can understand it when one remembers what he has gone through in the last year."

"Yes," Lord Astor agreed. "Arabella seems remarkably friendly with him. She has a weakness for lame ducks. I hope she did not say anything yesterday to upset Hubbard."

"I can't think she would," Lord Farraday said. "Sweet little thing, Astor. How is it you were so fortunate? She don't have a sister, I suppose? Apart from the beauty, I mean."

Lord Astor grinned. "There is Jemima," he said. "Fifteen years old and straight as a beanpole, Farraday.

Something of a hoyden, by all accounts. And she has reddish hair. One would shudder to imagine what your children would be like. Shall I secure you an introduction?''

"No," his friend said with a mock sigh. "I had in mind someone more like Lady Astor. She wouldn't bully a fellow, would she? And always cheerful. She must be good to come home to. Mama is constantly coming up with likely prospects, managing females all of them. They would have me in leading strings before we left the church."

Lord Astor laughed.

"There goes Charlton now," Lord Farraday said, squinting his eyes and looking off to the roadway in the distance. "He must be going home. Whoever is that with him?"

Lord Astor shaded his eyes. "She is female, anyway," he said. "I would lay a wager it is Arabella's sister. And no maid or groom in sight. What a brainless girl that is, Farraday. She has no business being alone with him."

"I say," Lord Farraday said. "If he is taking her to his home, Astor, one or other of us should get along after them as fast as possible. Not a savory character is Charlton. Fancies himself. And is not above seducing young ladies he has no business seducing. It has happened before. Miss Wilson don't strike me as a female of very strong character, if you will excuse my saying so."

"Devil take it!" Lord Astor said. "I am on my way, Farraday. I can take care of this myself."

And he cantered off, trying not to draw the attention of the other gentlemen. He could not follow directly after the distant phaeton, as there was still some marshy ground to be skirted beyond the reclaimed fields.

He really should not have been so careless about his charge of Frances, Lord Astor thought, not for the first time. The girl had taken very well with the *ton* and never

lacked for friends and admirers. The connection with
Charlton had seemed quite proper, even eligible. But it
had been going on long enough that he should have
found the opportunity to ask the man his intentions.

He had not known what he now knew, of course. He
wished that Farraday had seen fit to warn him before
now. But it was plain to common sense that Charlton
was a vain and shallow man, very unlikely to have
serious intentions toward someone like Frances. Clearly
her beauty was the lure.

And now he was taking her, unaccompanied, to his
own home. What on earth had induced the girl to go
along with him? She must have windmills in her head.
Did she not realize that she was probably being taken
there to be seduced, perhaps even raped? He did not
have any high opinion of Frances' character, but he did
believe her virtuous. She would not willingly give in to
seduction. Her only hope seemed to be that she would
drown Charlton with her tears.

What a blessing that Farraday had spotted them,
Lord Astor thought. How would he ever comfort
Arabella if her sister was ruined? Not that Arabella
would be the principal sufferer, of course, but it would
be her suffering that would be his chief concern.

He wanted Arabella to be happy. He had only very
recently realized that that had become his life's goal.
She deserved happiness if only because other people's
contentment always seemed more important to her than
her own. He was convinced that she had offered to be
the one to marry him—or his father, as she had
thought—just so that the rest of her family could be
secure and free to pursue their own happiness. And he
had seen that several of her friendships were with people
for whom she felt sympathy and whom she tried to help.

She deserved some happiness herself. He had known
it with his heart the night before when he had found
himself making love to her with no thought to his own
satisfaction. That he had been far more deeply satisfied

than he had with any woman before her had been an irony of the whole situation. He had wanted Arabella to know the full joy of physical love.

And that morning he had known it with his head. He had woken to find her curled up beside him, her cheek on one hand, the other cheek flushed, her top lip curving upward, her white teeth just showing beneath, and he had looked at her for a long time.

She had become very dear to him almost without his realizing the fact. She had been his wife for longer than a month, but he had been slow to acknowledge the fact that the relationship had changed his life. And far slower to admit that she was becoming the wife of his heart. He had fought and fought against the truth because it had always seemed to him that love was a trap, a prison that took away a man's freedom to enjoy life.

But he had acknowledged it at last. Arabella had become far more precious to him than anything he had ever considered important to his life. And freedom to enjoy his life could mean something to him now only if he were free to make Arabella happy. And not just physically. He wanted to fill her whole life with love and joy, not just her bed. Unfortunately, he had no experience whatsoever in making another person happy. His life had been a very selfish one.

He was going to have to apologize to Arabella, grovel, get down on his knees at her feet if necessary. Would she forgive him? he wondered. And was he really sorry at last? Was he sorry for the cause as well as for the consequences?

Lord Astor's horse reached the roadway at last and he turned its head in the direction the phaeton had been taking a few minutes before. He could no longer see it, but he could not be far behind. Charlton would not have a chance to proceed too far in his seduction scheme before he came up with them.

Arabella must be saved from suffering. He must

impress upon Frances that her sister was not even to know about this episode.

Frances had been up unusually early, having been awakened by the brisk morning air blowing through a window that Bella's maid had neglected to close the night before. She had been surprised to find that neither her sister nor any of her particular friends were yet in the breakfast room. Indeed, only a very few people were there, several of the gentlemen apparently having gone out riding.

Frances stepped out onto the lawn after breakfast in order to while away the time until someone else came downstairs. She breathed in the morning air in some enjoyment and wondered why she did not get up early more often.

"Ah, Miss Wilson. You are an early riser, I see."

When Frances looked back, it was to see Sir John Charlton striding toward her.

"Good morning, sir," she said. "I thought all the gentlemen had gone out riding together."

"I have been home already," he said, "to fetch my phaeton for your convenience. I am delighted to know that I do not have to wait until almost noon for you to rise."

Frances could see the phaeton on the driveway behind him. A groom was holding the horses' heads.

"I do not believe it would be proper for me to accompany you now, sir," she said.

He looked startled. "Did I give the impression we would be alone, Miss Wilson?" he asked. "How very remiss of me. Lady Astor will be there too, and Mr. Hubbard. They have ridden on ahead."

Frances frowned. "I didn't think Bella was even up yet," she said. "But of course. She is always up early. But why did she not wait for us?"

"I believe she wished to exercise that dog of hers," Sir John said.

"George?" Frances said. "Yes, of course."

"I believe we should be on our way," he said, glancing back at the house. "Your sister might think it somewhat improper to be left alone with Mr. Hubbard."

"Yes," Frances said, and took his proffered arm after only a moment's hesitation.

It was only after they had been traveling in the phaeton for several minutes that Frances turned to her companion with a frown on her face. "But you did not expect me to be up until noon," she said. "Bella would have been alone with Mr. Hubbard an awfully long time by then."

He turned a haughty look on her. He never did smile, Frances recalled. "Will you not enjoy the beauty of the morning, Miss Wilson?" he said. "You do not need to worry your head with complicated thoughts."

17

DESPITE the earlier than usual rising of Frances and the later than usual rising of Arabella, Arabella was still up, breakfasted, and outside before her sister came downstairs. She made her way as soon as she could to the kennels in order to take George for his belated walk. She had to pass the stables on her way there, and as she did so, she almost literally ran into Mr. Hubbard.

"Ah, well met, Lady Astor," he said. "Wish me well. I am on my way to Brighton."

"To Brighton?" she said.

"I have told Farraday that I am returning home on business," he said. "But I am glad of the chance to confide the truth to someone. I am going to bring Sonia home, and my son. Do you think me quite mad?"

Arabella stared at him for a moment. "No," she said at last. "I think perhaps you are very sane, sir. You are unhappy without them, are you not? With them you will have a chance of happiness at least."

"I knew you would understand," he said. "I did a great deal of thinking after I had talked to you yesterday afternoon. And really, being unforgiving and protecting myself from further hurt makes no sense at all. All I am doing is protecting and preserving my own misery. I have to forgive Sonia. Only so can I perhaps heal myself. Do I make any sense?"

She nodded. "Your life is going to be very difficult," she said. "There will be great scandal. And your marriage can never be as it was, can it? But, yes, you are right. I know you are right, and I wish you well, sir. Believe me I do. Perhaps I may call on Mrs. Hubbard when she is home?"

He smiled and took her hand. "If you do, you will

probably be the only lady of reputation who will for a long time to come," he said. "Yes, I am not expecting an easy reconciliation. I am not looking for a happy-ever-after ending. But my marriage is worth hard work and risk. Sonia is worth it, and our son. And I am worth the risk."

He raised her hand to his lips.

"I wish you a safe journey, sir," Arabella said.

"Thank you," he said. "You are a fine lady, ma'am."

Arabella watched him stride into the cobbled yard of the stable block, and continued on her way to the kennels. George was soon barking ecstatically and making eager rushes at her ankles in protest against the words she stopped to exchange with a groom.

She spent a whole hour exercising both her dog and herself. She walked while she was in sight of the house, but when it was left behind, when she found herself in open pastureland, then she caught up her skirts and ran, laughing and dodging as George sensed a game afoot and tried his best to bowl her off her feet.

She felt lighthearted suddenly. The day was clear and warm, the landscape green and open, and there was no place for misery or despair. Life could never be so bad that there was no hope. She was married and she and her husband were still together. The night before, they had made love as she had never dreamed it could be, and he had been warm and tender. He had given up his mistress and wanted to make a new start with her. He wanted them to be friends.

And she loved him. Achingly and eagerly so.

Surely there was no cause for despair in those facts. It was true that he might tire of her again and take another mistress. It was true that he had proved to be faithless. And it was true that he had never expressed real sorrow for his wrongdoing. But then, life was uncertain. No one could ever see into the future to know what would happen. Perhaps one of them would die within a year. Perhaps the world would end within a year.

Life was a risk.

If Mr. Hubbard could take back his wife after what she had done, and be willing to face up to all the undoubted hardships that a reconciliation would mean, then surely she could give her marriage another chance. If he could forgive his Sonia, then surely she could forgive her husband.

Perhaps she should go and find him then, Arabella decided, and tell him that after all she would go gladly with him to Norfolk in the autumn and that she would give their marriage a chance there. Perhaps she would take the risk of accepting him even without his acknowledgment of his own guilt.

Perhaps they could begin that very day, and not wait until they were alone together. They could start to be friends immediately. There was no reason to wait. And perhaps they could love again that night and know that there was some affection between them as well as physical attraction.

It was difficult to adjust her pace as she drew closer to the house. It was hard to walk sedately when she wanted to run and run until she could hurl herself into her husband's arms. But perhaps he would not even be at the house. He had gone out with Lord Farraday and a few more of the gentlemen even before she had gone downstairs for breakfast.

As she drew closer to the house from one direction, Arabella could see a phaeton in the driveway on the other side of the house and Sir John Charlton handing Frances into it. At least, it looked like those two.

Arabella frowned. Where could Frances be going at that time of the morning? And why was there no one with her except Sir John? She quickened her step, abandoning George to a groom's care without her usual hug.

She ran headlong into Theodore as she went up the marble steps to the main door and through it into the tiled hallway.

"Where are you off to in such a hurry, puss?" he

asked with a grin, gripping her by the arms to steady her.

"Do you know where Frances was going?" she asked. "She just got into a phaeton with Sir John and drove off somewhere."

He frowned. "Just the two of them?" he asked.

She nodded. "Oh, it is too bad of her, Theo," she said. "She really ought not to be doing anything so improper. I must find his lordship and get him to ride after her with me. I dare not go alone or he will be dreadfully cross."

"I should think so too," Theodore said. "Go and change into some riding clothes quickly, Bella, while I try to find out where they were headed. I shall see if there are two horses left in the stables that can be saddled up for us. You will have to have me for an escort. Astor has not returned yet."

Ten minutes later they were on their way to Sir John Charlton's country home, hoping that the groom who had held his horses' heads for a few minutes was correct in his assumption that that was his destination.

Frances was feeling dreadfully afraid by the time the phaeton drew to a halt outside a square red-brick house. There was no sign of either Arabella or Mr. Hubbard or of anyone else for that matter, except a groom who appeared from around the far side of the house and came to steady the horses while Sir John vaulted to the ground and turned to lift her down. Suddenly he seemed like a total stranger, and a rather menacing one at that.

"Where is Bella?" she asked as he set her on her feet and kept his hands at her waist for rather longer than was necessary.

"Perhaps inside the house," he said, "or more probably still on the way here. She was exercising that dog of hers, if you will remember. Come inside, Miss Wilson. You will be ready for some refreshments."

"Oh, no," she said, "not until Bella comes, sir. Will you show me the flowers? They look quite splendid.

Mama prides herself on the flower gardens at Parkland, you know.''

"Indeed?'' he said. "Perhaps another time. We will step inside out of the cool breeze.''

"Will you call your housekeeper?'' Frances asked nervously as he took her by the elbow and led her over the threshold. "Perhaps she will stay with me until Bella comes.''

"I am quite sure she will not,'' he said firmly. "I do not encourage servants to linger in rooms which I am occupying, Miss Wilson. Come now, step inside the salon here. You will hear your sister the moment she arrives.''

"Will you send for tea?'' Frances crossed the room to stare out of the window. "I am rather thirsty, sir.''

"Are you?''

She jumped and felt her heart begin to thump. She had not heard him come up behind her. He set his hands on her shoulders, caressing them with his palms.

"Yes, I am,'' she said quickly. "I do believe I forgot to have tea with my breakfast. It was very careless of me, but the weather was so glorious that I was in a hurry to go outdoors.''

They both saw Lord Astor riding up to the house at the same moment. Sir John muttered an oath and released his hold on her. Frances sighed with relief and felt her knees turn weak.

"I shall ring for tea immediately, then,'' Sir John said with a bow, crossing the room to the bell pull. "Perhaps Lord Astor will have some too. Or perhaps something stronger. I shall have to wait to ask him.''

When Lord Astor was shown into the salon, it was to find an unsmiling but genial host and Frances standing at the window looking out at the garden. She turned when he was announced.

"Ah, Astor,'' Sir John said. "What a pleasant surprise. Miss Wilson has joined me for tea, as you can see. May I offer you some, or perhaps something more palatable?''

"I was out riding with Farraday and saw you drive past," Lord Astor said with a smile. "The chance of seeing your home seemed too good an opportunity to miss, Charlton. Good morning, Frances."

"Good morning, my lord," she said, her eyes looking a suspiciously bright shade of blue.

"I am delighted you decided to follow us," Sir John said with a bow. "Perhaps after refreshments I can show you and Miss Wilson something of the house and garden. My servants keep both immaculate even though I am rarely here."

"Your maid is in the kitchen, Frances?" Lord Astor asked, strolling across the room to look out through the window next to the one against which she stood.

"N-no, my lord," she said, "I did not bring a maid. Bella is on her way here with Mr. Hubbard. I expected that she would be here already, but she is exercising George."

"Indeed?" Lord Astor said. "How fortunate, then, that I arrived when I did."

"Y-yes," she said.

Lord Astor's eyebrows rose. "But here she comes now," he said. "With Perrot, it seems, not Hubbard. And George is nowhere in sight."

Frances turned to look through the window. Sir John stayed where he was at the other side of the room, his hands clasped behind his back.

"Frances," Lord Astor said, "perhaps you would care to join your sister and Sir Theodore Perrot outside. The weather is far too glorious to be wasted indoors, is it not?"

"Yes, my lord," Frances said. She wasted no time in obeying his direction.

Lord Astor turned to face his silent host. "I will want an explanation of this, Charlton," he said. "I somehow have the feeling that my wife's arrival is quite coincidental and quite unexpected by you."

Sir John raised one eyebrow. "Your sister-in-law is no child, Astor," he said.

"No, exactly," Lord Astor agreed. "She is a woman, Charlton, and in my care. I cannot believe that you were unaware of how she would be compromised by a visit here with you alone."

Sir John shrugged. "So what do you intend to do about it?" he asked. "Challenge me? That would be a trifle old-fashioned and more than a trifle illegal, would it not?"

"But very much in my mind nonetheless," Lord Astor said.

"It seems I have no choice but to offer for her, then," his host said carelessly. "I believe we have a certain understanding anyway. To whom must I address myself, Astor? To you, or to her mother?"

Lord Astor's eyes narrowed. "You have an understanding with Miss Wilson?" he said. "She has agreed to be your wife? I will have to talk with her about this. If you tell the truth, I shall expect a visit from you one morning within the next week. If you do not, you may expect a call from me. Good day, sir."

Frances was crying. Lord Astor saw that as soon as he strode from the house. Arabella was beside her, patting her on the back, offering a handkerchief. Theodore was hovering close by, clearly reluctant to offer closer comfort in that relatively public setting. The three horses were grazing on the lawn, probably a forbidden activity, Lord Astor decided. Both Arabella and Theodore turned toward him.

"All is well," he said. "I arrived not long after them. Frances is quite unharmed. She is frightened, that is all."

"Where is he?" Theodore asked, stepping toward the house.

"Cooling his heels, I would imagine," Lord Astor said. "I have had a brief talk with him. The matter will be cleared up back in town."

"The scoundrel will not escape as lightly as that," Theodore said. "He is going to be dealt with now." He strode off in the direction of the house.

"He will be dealt with," Lord Astor called after him, but his words were drowned in Frances' shriek.

"No, Theo!" she cried. "He will kill you. Come back. Oh, Bella, bring him back. He will be killed."

She swooned as Theodore disappeared through the door without even stopping to knock first.

"Oh, dear," Arabella said, kneeling on the cobbles beside the inert form of her sister and flapping her handkerchief over her face, "she has fainted. She has never before done that before. Oh, poor Frances."

Lord Astor moved around to the other side of his sister-in-law, slid one arm beneath her shoulders, and brought her up to a sitting position.

"Keep fanning her," he said. "She will revive in a moment. I could almost find it within myself to say that she deserves this, but that would be unkind. What makes her so foolish, Arabella, when you are so sensible?"

"Well," she said, flapping the handkerchief vigorously and peering anxiously into her sister's face, "Frances is the beauty, you see. She has never needed common sense. But sometimes I do wish she had a little more fortitude. How pale she looks!"

"She is beginning to stir," he said. "I hope Perrot is not carving up the furniture in there."

"My lord!" Arabella looked up at him suddenly, her fanning movements slowing. "What did you mean when you said that he would be dealt with? You are not going to fight a duel, are you?"

"I don't think it will come to that," he said.

Her face showed instant alarm. "Oh, you are!" she cried. "You are going to fight him with pistols and he is going to kill you. I won't let it happen. Oh, I won't. He is not worth all the trouble. I will shoot him myself."

Lord Astor grinned unexpectedly.

"Oh," Frances said faintly. "Is Theo dead?"

"I think not," Lord Astor said, "unless this is his ghost coming from the house."

Sir Theodore Perrot strode over to the group and

stood looking down at them. "I don't believe Sir John Charlton will be troubling you any longer, Fran," he said. "And I doubt if he will be able to give you satisfaction for a week or two to come, Astor."

"Oh!" Frances shrieked, her head falling back over Lord Astor's arm. "You have killed him, Theo, and they will hang you."

"Not quite that either," he said. "You have not been swooning, have you, Fran? And crying? There seem to be handkerchiefs lying around all over the place. Come on, my girl, up with you. Time to get back to Farraday's, or we will miss luncheon."

He took Frances' hands in his and pulled her unceremoniously to her feet.

"Oh," she said, "you always did lack sensibility, Theo. You would not care if you had been killed and I had been left on the stones here to grieve alone, would you?"

"Not at all," he said. "I would have been too dead to care."

"Oh!" she shrieked, looking up at him. "Your cheek, Theo. And your lip!"

"Nothing that will not heal," he said. "You will have to share my horse, Fran. Will that wound your sensibilities?"

"Perhaps it would be better if Frances rode the horse Arabella came on," Lord Astor said. "Arabella can come up with me."

"We must find some salve for your bruises when we get back to Lord Farraday's, Theo," Arabella said. "I truly am sorry to see you hurt, you know. But I am happy that Sir John Charlton must look a great worse. I really am."

"Thank you, puss," Theodore said. "I assure you he does. Now, Fran, set your foot on my hands and I shall help you into the saddle."

"You two may ride on ahead," Lord Astor said. "I am going to try to find a shorter way back with Arabella across the fields. She is as light as a feather, but our combined loads will be rather hard on this poor horse.''

Frances, having quite recovered from the vapors and having even put her handkerchief away in a pocket, rode away after Theodore along the roadway back to Lord Farraday's estate.

''Do you feel quite well enough to ride, Theodore?'' Frances asked. ''If you were to fall from your horse, I would not kow what to do to revive you. And Lord Astor is not following us.''

''I don't think I am about to take a tumble on account of a bruised cheek and a cut lip,'' Theodore said. ''In fact, I am quite happy to suffer them, Fran, knowing that that scoundrel has been more or less fairly dealt with.''

''It really was quite splendidly brave of you to go into that house and confront him,'' Frances said. ''I could have died, Theo. What would I have done if he had killed you?''

''Fallen comfortably back into the vapors for a time, I imagine,'' he said. ''I don't know what you would have done afterward. You tell me, Fran.''

''I would have worn black for the rest of my life,'' she declared passionately. ''I would never have left it off, Theo. I would never have forgotten how brave you were and how you sacrificed your life for my honor. And I would never have let anyone else forget it, either.''

''You need your eyes for the road, Fran,'' he said. ''This is not the time for tears. Would you really have grieved for me, though? What about all your grand admirers in town?''

''Oh, mere dandies, all,'' she said, bravely sniffing back her tears. ''I have not met a real man since I went there, Theo. Except his lordship, and he is married to Bella.''

''And I am a real man?'' he asked.

''Well, of course you are, Theo,'' she said. ''I have never been in any doubt about that. Not since I was twelve years old and you rescued me from the bull.''

"Which was in a quite different field from you and held back by a perfectly stout fence," he said.

"Yes, but he was angry, Theo," she said. "And you know that Papa himself said that when bulls are angry they can run through a fence just as if it were not there."

"I think I had better take you home and marry you, Fran," he said.

"Oh, will you, Theo?" she said. "Please?"

"This summer," he said. "I'll talk to Astor later today. What were you doing with that scoundrel, anyway?"

"He lured me away," she said. "He kidnapped me. He told me that Bella had gone on ahead of us with Mr. Hubbard and that I would be needed to chaperone her."

"You really do need looking after," he said. "Bella would not do anything that cork-brained. I say, Fran, if I were to get down off this horse and lift you down from yours, would you let me kiss you? I badly want to, but I won't risk it without asking because last time you smacked my face and it is feeling sore enough without that."

"Oh, I would not strike you, Theo," Frances said. "How could you think I would, when you have just been so courageous and when we are betrothed? Oh, do be careful. I am quite heavy, you know, and I would not wish you to hurt yourself further. Oh, Theo!"

She was down off the horse almost before the last words were out of her mouth, and being very thoroughly kissed in a most shockingly public part of the roadway.

"Don't cry, Fran," he murmured after a long while, kissing the tears from her eyelashes. "It was not that bad, was it?"

"Oh, Theo," she said, definitely not obeying the first command of her newly betrothed, "I was just thinking of Bella and what a great sacrifice she made, marrying his lordship so that I would be free to wed you. Dear,

dear, Bella! I am so happy for her that all has turned out well. I could not feel so good about loving you if she were unhappy. Truly I couldn't. But I do love you so, Theo. And how very foolish I have been.''

"No, you have not," he said. "I knew that you loved me, Fran. But I wished you to know it too. And now you do, you see. Give me another kiss quickly before someone comes along this road and has an apoplexy.''

Frances obeyed her intended husband's second command.

Arabella was perched awkwardly on the horse's back in front of her husband. She had no choice but to lean sideways against his chest. But she did not feel any great reluctance to do so. After a few moments she rested her head against his shoulder. They rode in silence for several minutes, across a pasture, past a marsh, through some trees.

The horse slowed its step—almost of its own volition, it seemed. And Arabella raised her head without ever planning to do so. Lord Astor kissed her slowly, lingeringly, allowing the horse to pick its own slow way through the trees.

The horse had stopped walking altogether by the time he lifted his head and sat looking down at Arabella as she snuggled her head against his shoulder again.

"Arabella," he said, "words are so very inadequate. I have done you a terrible wrong. And the worst of it is that I did not even admit it to myself until very recently. I thought it my right to retain my freedom even after vowing to both you and God that I would keep myself only for you. I thought it my right to wrong you and to feel angry with you for feeling hurt. I have treated you as a possession, not as a person at all. If I get down from this horse and beg your pardon on my knees, will you ever be able to forgive me?''

"Yes," she said, turning her face in to his neck. "You are already forgiven. And you need not get down."

"But I have hurt you," he said. "You will never be able to trust me again, Arabella. Our marriage will always be marred by the memory of its beginning. You will never be able to forget."

"I don't think I want to," Arabella said. "I have realized something about life, my lord. Everything that happens has a purpose, I think. It is how we grow, perhaps. We cannot grow on just the pleasant things. I think I know both you and myself better for what I have suffered in the last weeks. And I cannot think that is a bad thing."

"But does our marriage have a chance?" he asked. "Can we start again, Arabella, as I suggested yesterday? Can we become friends?"

"I think so," she said. "I think our marriage perhaps has a better chance now than it had a month ago. At that time I thought you perfect and I was terrified of you. It is hard to love someone who is not quite human. But now I know that you are human, and I do not feel inadequate any longer. I feel free to love you and be your friend."

He rested his cheek against the top of her head. "I did not think you would forgive me," he said. "I do not deserve forgiveness, Arabella. Will you ever be able to trust me again?"

"Yes," she said. She withdrew her head from his shoulder and looked earnestly up into his face. "Trust is not blindly believing in someone. It is knowing and loving that person and expecting what one knows is best in that person. Yes, I trust you, my lord. You told me the truth when I asked. You did not lie to me. I want to do what you suggested. I mean about going to Norfolk, just the two of us together, and getting to know each other and becoming friends. Oh, may we? Please?"

He hugged her to him suddenly. "Arabella," he said, his voice not quite steady, "what have I ever done to deserve you? I love you so very much."

"I think I am going to scream very soon," Arabella

said quite calmly. "Your saddle is digging so hard into my hip, my lord, that the pain is becoming unbearable."

One moment later he was on the ground and lifting her down so that she slid along the full length of him. She twined her arms around his neck and looked eagerly into his face.

"Do you really love me?" she asked. "It is quite all right if you do not. I know I am not pretty or very elegant and I will undoubtedly become plump again since you commanded me to start eating. And I know you married me in order to do a kindness to my family. If we can be friends, I will be happy. If I can just make you comfortable, I will be happy. You do not have to feel that you must love me."

"Arabella," he said. Her face was framed by his hands. "Will you remember last night? Were my actions then those of a friend merely? Or of a man who was looking for comfort from his wife? Look into my eyes. Are they the eyes of your friend only?"

She looked and shook her head slowly.

"My actions were those of a lover," he said. "I loved you last night. And I will tell you in all truth that I have not loved another woman as I loved you then. And these eyes are the eyes of a lover. I love you, unworthy as I am to do so."

"Oh," she said, "I think I am going to cry, my lord."

"Don't," he said, bringing her forehead against his and continuing to hold her face. "I gave my handkerchief to Frances. Kiss me instead. But after you have called me what you called me last night. Will you, Arabella?"

"Geoffrey?" she whispered.

"Yes," he said. "Say it again, love, please."

"Geoffrey," she said out loud. She flushed.

He smiled and brought his lips to hers. "Will you call me that from now on?" he asked.

"Yes, Geoffrey," she said.

"We now have a very serious choice to make," he

said. "We can either climb back onto that horse and ride back to Farraday's for luncheon, or we can stay off that horse and not ride back to Farraday's for luncheon and for whatever activity he has planned for immediately after. Which will it be, Arabella?"

She looked around her at the shady trees, the grass underfoot, and the horse grazing a few feet away. She looked up at her husband and flushed again.

"I am not very hungry, my lord," she said.

Lord Astor wrapped his arms around his wife and drew her full against him. "What a dreadful thing to say to your own husband, Arabella," he said, "when you have just declared that you wish to make me comfortable. I will just have to create a hunger in you, it seems."

"Oh," she said, "I thought we were speaking of food. How foolish of me! Yes. I have just realized that I am quite ravenous, my lord—Geoffrey."